Ordinary World

— THE SEQUEL TO FAKING IT —

ELISA LORELLO

South Fayette
Township Library
412-257-8660

PUBLISHED BY

Published by AmazonEncore
P.O. Box 400818
Las Vegas, NV 89140

ISBN-13: 9781935597360
ISBN-10: 1935597361

Ordinary World

For Tracy,

in loving memory of Lisa and Rahma

ACKNOWLEDGMENTS

I don't even know where or how to begin to express my gratitude for all the support I've received. Without it, *Ordinary World* could not have come this far. So many people deserve to be mentioned by name in these acknowledgements, but I only have so much space. I'm going to do the best I can.

First, many thanks to Terry Goodman and everyone at AmazonEncore for their enthusiasm and support. Thanks to them, *Ordinary World* is going to new and exciting places.

Thanks to everyone at Quail Ridge Books and Music in Raleigh, North Carolina, for their support of local authors, myself especially.

I am indebted to my "travel guides": Elisa DiLeo, Tracy Branco Medeiros, and Gavin Hymes. Without them, Andi would have been completely lost. Thank you also to my translators (and cousins), Andrew and Daniel Mottola.

Aaron Sorkin continues to be a major inspiration and influence on my writing, and his insight and advice have been indispensable, not to mention a thrill. Likewise, the new friends I've made as the result of the now extinct "Aaron Sorkin and the Facebook movie" discussion forum have kept me smiling, and I bask in their awesomeness on a regular basis. Special thanks to Elspeth Antonelli, Heather Grace Stewart, and all those from the forum who bought my books. To Larry H. Leitner: Thank you especially for telling me that I "got it." That meant so much to me.

To all the Undeletables (and you know who you are): I offer you cake and my gratitude for keeping it fun.

Thank you to my cousin, Ron Mottola, who enthusiastically spread the word about *Faking It* without a penny of compensation, and those who followed his lead (in alphabetical order): Marc Cerrone, Katherine Hagopian, Kathy Jackson, Ellen McCabe, Vicki Nadal, and Mia VonBeeden. Many of them were also some of the first readers of *Ordinary World*, including my dear friend and writing partner in crime, Sarah Girrell.

Thank you to all who supported me on the blog tour, especially Stacey Cochran and the Raleigh Write2Publish group; Jodi Webb and WOW; Jerry Blitefield, the English Department, and the students at UMass-Dartmouth's *Temper*; and Crystal Medeiros and her family, who gave me a place to stay during my visit to Massachusetts.

To Susan Miller-Cochran, the entire First Year Writing Program faculty, and the English Department at North Carolina State University: I am honored to be among such outstanding colleagues and friends on a daily basis. To my students: You probably don't know how much you teach me. Thank you all. To Tina Shasteen: Thanks to you and your family for your sacrifice and service.

A special thanks to my Facebook friends and *Faking It* Fans, Twitter followers, Kindle kin, "I'll Have What She's Having" blog readers, and every reader who has bought and/or passed on my book to someone else, as well as taken the time to write and post a review or a personal note of appreciation to me—your support means so much to me!

To my parents, Michael and Eda; my siblings: Michael, Bobby, Ritchie, Steve, Mary, and especially Paul, my twin brother, and their spouses/significant others; my grandmother, Mary Mottola; my nieces and nephews, aunts, uncles, and cousins: I love you dearly. To Kelly Lennon Sutphin, my best friend since birth: I can't wait for the birthday trip, even if it happens when we're forty-one!

Special thanks to all those authors who make me better at what I do (Richard Russo, Jennifer Weiner, David Sedaris, and Nora Ephron, to name a few), and to every independent author who dares to dive in head first—go for it!

Finally, my deepest gratitude to the band Duran Duran, especially its original five members: John Taylor, Simon LeBon, Nick Rhodes, Roger Taylor, and Andy Taylor. For the last twenty-seven years and counting, Duran Duran's music has been my primary source of comfort during times of sorrow, joy, and celebration, and companionship for everything in between. Their song "Ordinary World" was the inspiration for this novel, and I don't know how I would've survived the most turbulent times of my life without them. I love them as much as I love my own brothers.

If I have left any person out of these acknowledgements, please accept my sincere apology and know that your name is etched on my heart.

Namaste.

Elisa Lorello
October 2010

CHAPTER
ONE
October

I DON'T REMEMBER SLEEPING, MUCH LESS waking up.

There I was—eyes open, looking at the pillow beside me, untouched, the absence of warmth so obvious it practically choked me while numbing me to any tactile sensation.

My mother was downstairs, making tea and toast, which she already knew I wouldn't eat. I did everything in a zombie-like fashion: shower, blow-dry my hair, apply makeup. I was running low on body lotion. Sam usually bought it for me. His favorite. Freesia Breeze.

I stood inside the walk-in closet. My skirts and slacks and jeans and dresses hung opposite Sam's suits and jeans and button-down shirts, all neatly aligned on wooden hangers. I pulled out my black velvet, thrift-store blazer, a pair of dark blue jeans, and tan suede boots. Mom knocked and entered without waiting for an answer or an invitation.

"What on earth are you wearing?" she asked after taking in an eyeful.

"What's wrong with this? The blazer is black. It's Sam's favorite."

"You can't wear that, Andi. You simply can't. You've got a closet of more appropriate clothes."

I had neither the time nor the energy to tell her that I only wore the pantsuits when there was a function with the university chancellor or when the department was recruiting candidates for hiring—or that Sam thought I should be walking into court when I was wearing a pantsuit. I scanned the rack. *What else does Sam like?* I spied a black cocktail dress and pulled it out, remembering the first time I'd worn it.

"Now that's a pantsuit," he'd said.

"How is that possible?"

"'Cause it makes me pant when you wear it."

Standing in front of the full-length mirror, I stared at my reflection but didn't recognize who stared back. Long, bottled auburn hair falling in wide ringlets, its real gray appearing at the roots. Lifeless ashen eyes, once the color of emeralds. Round, faded pink lips. Just standing there, staring at me. *Who the hell are you?*

Mom disapproved again.

"Don't you think that's a little too dressy?"

"Sam likes it."

"Andi, I understand—"

"No, you don't. I'm wearing this."

She closed her mouth and left the room.

A half hour later at the kitchen table, Mom stirred her coffee while I pushed away the plate of toast.

"Are you sure you're up for giving the eulogy?" she asked.

"Again with this?"

"I just don't see how—"

"We're not discussing this, Mom. I'm doing it."

I don't remember how we got to the church or who drove me there; it just sort of magically appeared. I don't remember walking inside or seeing anyone in particular. Just a sea of black, like a big tarpaulin spread out over the pews. *How depressing,* I thought. I don't remember anything the priest said. I didn't feel my brother Joey holding my left hand or my brother Tony holding my right. But, at some point, I stood up. Rather, my brothers stood up and pulled me along. One of them escorted me to the lectern. In one hand I clenched a piece of paper folded in quarters, crinkled and damp with perspiration. I looked out at the black tarps on each side of the church. *Oh, I know where we are,* I said to myself. *We got married in this church.* I saw my best friend Maggie on the left, dabbing her eyes with a handkerchief. Was the left side for friends of the bride or the groom? I always forgot.

As I unfolded the paper, it then occurred to me that I was inappropriately dressed. When I looked down at the paper and scanned the words scrawled in my longhand, a more horrid realization came to me: this was crappy writing.

My mouth dry, I licked my lips and tried to clear my throat, but nothing happened. So I opened my mouth and let the sounds come out. I read, and spoke:

Anyone who knows me knows that my love life was a train wreck from day one. In fact, I don't think I ever really understood

3

love until I met Sam. We met at a writing conference six years ago in New York. Then we long-distance dated via e-mails and phone calls. Looking back, I'm glad that's the way it happened because I'm not sure I would've really given him a chance otherwise. I didn't trust my instincts—hell, when it came to men and love, I didn't even have instincts. But I fell in love with him over the course of that correspondence, and fortunately I was offered a teaching position here, so I took it and left New York and the rest is history.

I looked up from the paper and added, "But you know all of this, don't you."

I continued:

Sam's my best friend in the world. I can think of no one else I'd rather be spending my Saturdays with. No one makes a better pancake. No one imitates Jimmy Stewart as badly as he does, and no one can make me laugh quite the way he does.

"Did," I corrected.

His students absolutely loved him. He often had grad students over to the house, and both they and his undergrads would give him collectibles—the study is filled with these bobble-head dolls. But the real reason they love him so much is because he's real to them. His humanity comes out on every page that he writes with them, that he reads in their own writing, that he shares. And man, his writing was so good. Sometimes I wanted to cover my own with a sheet...

"...like now, for instance."

I heard a couple of laughs, albeit nervous ones.
"No, really," I said. "This is bad."
I continued.

*He loved being imperfect, being human. He really has—
had—this curiosity for life and took pleasure in simple things.
Books. Trees. A cup of coffee. A photograph. He couldn't carry
a tune to save his life, but loved those who could.*

I looked at Joey and Tony; they were smiling wistfully.
I looked down at the paper and realized I was at the end.
Where was the rest of it?
"Well, that's all I've written. I don't know what else to
say, except thank you all for coming."
I left the lectern and returned to my place between
Joey and Tony. Aside from the whirring noise echoing
through the heating ducts, the church was dead silent. I
suppose dead silence was an appropriate metaphor.
*How could I write such crap? How could I show up so un-
prepared? God, Sam, how could I have let you down?*

The house was full of people to whom I was oblivious. I
stood at the window upstairs in Sam's study, surrounded
by his stupid bobble-head dolls, looking out at our bench
swing among the autumn maples in the backyard—they
were more bare than usual at this time of year. I pressed
my face against the glass, leaving an oval of steam on it.
When's he coming back? I wondered. *He's coming soon. I know
it. He'll walk through that door any minute, bottle of sparkling*

cider in hand. It was all a mishap, he'll say. And he'll tell me a spectacular story, grossly exaggerated, voices and all, about how one little innocent trip to the store somehow wound him up in Cuba.

I shuddered and folded my arms to grip my shoulders in a self-sustaining hug, wearing Sam's hooded Edmund College sweatshirt over the cocktail dress; it was the one I always stole from him.

I T WAS THE FIRST COLUMBUS DAY WEEKEND
that we'd not gone away. Instead, we had walked the familiar streets of Amherst and Northampton and picnicked
at our usual spot by the lake at Northampton University,
where I was recently tenured. We were celebrating our fifth
wedding anniversary. That very night, Sam had planned
and cooked everything on the menu—grilled salmon
with herbs and garlic, roasted red potatoes with rosemary
and thyme, arugula salad, and strawberry cheesecake for
dessert. He set the table with the good china and silver-
ware—the stuff we hadn't used since we got married—and
lit the candlesticks, only to realize that he'd forgotten to
buy the sparkling cider. I told him that we didn't need it.
Water in wine glasses sufficed, or maybe some flat ginger
ale that sat abandoned in the back of the fridge. But no.
He insisted, stubborn rat-bastard that he is. Was.

"Shit, man!" he said, half laughing. He put on his
leather aviator jacket.

"You're going to get it *now*?" I asked. "It's almost nine
o'clock. We're already eating so late."

"There's something romantic about it, don't you think?
Besides, this has to be perfect, sweetheart. Five years. I

want you completely blissed out so you can be ready for your present."

"Geez, Sammy. Don't lay on the pressure. I just got you socks."

His blue eyes twinkled the way sunshine dapples on a lake. After he grabbed his keys by the door, he then turned and rushed me like a linebacker, pinning me against the wall and kissing me, running his hand along my thigh and up under my skirt.

"Not yet, stud muffin," I said. We both laughed. Our mutual disdain for the term had actually transformed it into one of our favorites. I wrapped my leg around him, reconsidering. "Ya know we could just skip dinner altogether…give it to the cat."

"Not a chance—we're going all the way. Dinner, candles, dessert, and then more dessert."

He let go of me and banged his head on the wall a few times before leaning in for another kiss. "Woman, we are gonna break the bed tonight."

"Is that a promise?"

He then took a step back, and his ocean blue eyes brightened, as if seeing me in a new light. "God, I think I fall in love with you every day," he said. "See you in a bit, sweetheart." When he opened the door, a whiff of chilly autumn air blew in. He looked at me again, then took off his jacket and hung it from the inside doorknob. "Not gonna need that right now," he said. After he closed the door, I returned to the kitchen, fanning myself with my hand, and opened the freezer door.

———

I'd lost track of how long it was taking Sam just to get sparkling cider. When I heard the knock at the door, I'd just assumed he'd forgotten his house key again. Why that boy didn't put all his keys on the same ring, I couldn't figure out. He had once rationalized something about everything having its place—that, and he made the crude joke of one bulge in his pants being enough. But I opened the door to find an Amherst police officer towering in the doorway, the smell of hickory and dried leaves wafting in the air.

"Mrs. Vanzant?" the officer asked in a baritone voice.

"Yes?"

"There's been an accident..."

That's all I remember. Local newspaper clippings filled in the rest of the details. Sam was killed by a drunk driver—a freshman student from NU. It happened around nine thirty, as Sam was pulling out of the convenience store. The car plowed into him, like he wasn't even there. A brand new Mustang. The next generation in muscle cars, an ad said. The medics found shards of glass from the cider bottle and broken window all over his body. The driver and his two buddies got out a little battered with a few broken ribs and concussions. Sam was rushed to the hospital and pronounced dead in the ER.

ELISA LORELLO

For the first three months following his death, I cried and
wandered aimlessly from room to room in our house and
stared out the windows. Dried leaves filled the backyard,
only to be covered by an early December snow, which
then turned to soggy January mush. Sometimes I slept
in his study on the faded brown leather sofa, one of the
relics from his bachelor days. For some reason, his presence seemed to be stronger in that room than any other
place in the house, even our bedroom. I could smell him
in there, that all-too familiar scent of patchouli oil and
plain soap.

I called our voice mail ten times a day just to hear his
voice—that mild tenor that reduced me to butter every
time he read to me, even sexier when he had a sore throat
and his voice took on a rasp. Over and over I listened to
the message: *Hi, you've reached the Vanzants. If you wish to
leave a message for the smart one, press one. If you wish to leave
a message for me, press two.*

The empty bed was the worst. I stayed up later and
later just to avoid going to bed and lying there, having
no one to lean my head on or brush my leg against, no
one to rest a hand limply across my chest in a protective
cuddle, all the special things that had become as regular as
breathing. Our cat, Donny Most, had always been denied
access to our bedroom. But when I started picking him
up and plopping him on the bed at night in hopes that he
would keep me company and give me someone to spoon,
he leaped off and scatted out of the room. Apparently he
didn't like the empty bed either. Even he roamed the house
looking for Sam, meowing in a drawn-out moan.

At Christmastime my mother invited me down to Long Island, but I refused to go. I couldn't leave the house, couldn't leave Sam. Instead, Maggie drove up from Brooklyn and stayed with me straight through New Year's. She didn't even ask for permission, just called and said, "I'm coming."

On Christmas Day we had takeout Chinese food. I hadn't done any gift shopping or put up the tree. But I appreciated Mags's company. Having lost her lover to leukemia fifteen years ago, she understood my grief without needing to say "I understand" every five minutes. She knew when to say nothing, when to hug me, and when to let me be.

On New Year's Eve we rented *Weekend at Bernie's*, a guilty pleasure of ours. I laughed as hard as I did when Sam mooned Governor Romney at a campaign rally on campus a couple of years ago. Then I cried in agonizing guilt.

"Don't go back to school just yet," Maggie said on New Year's Day. She placed a cup of hot chocolate in front of me, whipped cream melting down the side, and joined me at the kitchen table. "Take another semester off. They'll let you do it."

"And do what? Waste away? I don't think he'd want me just sitting around watching marathons of *Sanford and Son* on TV Land."

"I just don't think you're ready to be back in the classroom."

"There aren't any reminders of him in the classroom."

"Don't be too sure of that," she warned.

I scooped some of the floating whipped cream with my finger and licked it. "What am I supposed to do, then?" I asked.

"Stay here and write. Join a bereavement group. Or maybe just teach one section—a night class. Don't go back full time. You could even come to New York and stay with me. There's plenty to do there."

I blew on the hot chocolate, hesitantly taking a sip, and frowned.

"I'm going back, Mags. The work will do me good. It always has before."

"Losing your husband to a drunk driver is not the same as losing a boyfriend to another woman. The former is far more senseless."

On the first day of the spring semester in mid-January, I arrived at NU around nine a.m. and went to Adams Hall, briefcase in tow, feeling a strange mix of exhibitionism and invisibility as I traipsed through the narrow halls to my office—people were either staring at me or looking away, it seemed. When I reached the English department's main office, I took a deep breath and entered. You'd think I was getting ready to take the stage at Madison Square Garden.

"Morning, Kay."

Kay Mello, one of the two department assistants, picked up her head and sprang from her desk. "Oh, Andrea! How *are* you?" She pulled me to her portly body and squeezed the air out of me. She never called me Andrea. No one did, really. Except Sam.

"OK. You know…one day at a time. That sort of thing."

"I was so shocked when I got the news. We all were. You know, it's just so *sad*."

"Yeah. Well, you know. It happens."

Her perfume was so strong I thought I might gag.

"Is there anything you need? Anything we can do for you?"

"Well, um, if you can get me my mail? That would be great. I'm sure it's kinda piled up, huh. Oh and, um, perhaps you can photocopy my syllabus for me? I haven't really gotten to that. You can use the one I have on file. Just change the heading from *Fall* to *Spring*."

"Sure thing." Kay went to a bin under a table and pulled out a stack of envelopes varying in size and thickness and bound with fat rubber bands. "Your mail," she said. "I think some of them are *sympathy cards*." She said the last two words in a whisper.

At that moment, I couldn't help but wonder if I sounded as moronic to those friends or acquaintances who had lost a loved one as Kay did to me. Perhaps this could be a new academic article for me to research and write: the *kairos* of death. Surely someone had done it already.

"Thank you," I said and tried to transport the stack from her arms to mine without any stray envelopes slipping out. "I'll just go through these in my office."

"When's your first class?"

"In an hour."

13

"Well, good luck. And Andrea, no one expects you to be here. We wouldn't think any less of you if you turned around and went straight home."

"Um, OK. Thanks."

When I got to my office, I opened the door and met a dank, musty smell as well as a chill. I forcibly twisted the knob on the ancient radiator before sitting at my desk, which was covered with a thin veil of dust. Using one of the envelopes from the mail pile, I attempted to wipe the desk, but the dust just formed a wavy streak across it. When I removed the rubber bands, the mail splattered out, some pieces falling to the floor. Indeed, some were sympathy cards. The rest were from textbook publishing companies, a letter from my editor, department memos from the fall semester and winter intercession, and several pamphlets from the organizations MADD and SADD. The pile resembled the one on the judge's desk at the end of *Miracle on 34th Street*.

Before I had a chance to sort through it all, Jeff Baxter, the English department chairperson and a good friend of mine, knocked on the door as he opened it. At thirty-eight, Jeff was the youngest tenured professor to ever become chair of our department. He was also one of the first people I had met when I interviewed for the position at NU, and we hit it off instantly. His down-to-earth attitude met my pedagogical sensibility, and we often formed an alliance in faculty or administrative meetings. Outside of school, our shared enjoyment of David Lodge novels, *Family Guy*, and the New England Patriots made us and our spouses frequent dinner guests at each other's homes. I think he took Sam's death really hard.

"Mind if I come in?" he asked, already in the room.

I took another deep breath. "Hey, Jeff."

"Welcome back."

"Thanks."

"How you doin'?"

"Just got here, actually."

"That's not what I asked you."

I shrugged my shoulders and avoided his dark, boyish brown eyes, then redirected my attention.

"I don't know. I'm just sort of here, I guess. You know… one day at a time."

He sat in the swivel chair next to my desk and quickly ran his fingers through his chestnut-colored hair, revealing a few gray bangs.

"How'd your staff meeting go?"

"Actually, I postponed it to next week."

"What have you got going on today?"

"My first two classes. And getting back into the swing of things. Catching up."

"Well, I hope you don't mind if I check in with you from time to time. There's a lot going on right now, what with the Chancellor's Program Assessment Initiative and all that. You're gonna have quite a load this semester, even under sunny skies."

"I'm fine, Jeff. Really. The work will be good for me."

He gave me the Spark Notes version of the department agenda since I'd left, and recommended I read the minutes of the last three months' meetings.

"You need anything?" he asked.

Man, was *that* a loaded question.

"Not right now," I answered.

"Have a good class, then." We often said that in lieu of "Have a nice day," even if neither of us were teaching.

"Thanks. You too."

He left the door open as he left. I stood up, walked over to close it, and returned to my desk. A custodian had moved my garbage pail to the other side of the office, next to the entrance. Sitting behind my desk, I picked up each piece of mail, unopened, and flung it toward the pail until it was time for class. With the memos, I haphazardly folded them into airplanes and sailed them across. Altogether, I nailed twenty-three out of thirty-two shots. At one point, someone knocked on the door; I opened it a crack and peeked out, as if I were in an apartment alone at midnight, answering to a stranger. I saw Kay holding a thick stack of paper.

"Here's your syllabi." Her eyes darted from the mess on the floor back to me.

I transferred the stack from her arms to mine.

"Thanks, Kay. Seeya," I said, and closed the door behind her.

The discarded mail remained on the floor.

———

As class time approached, the seed of anxiety that I awoke with that morning had germinated into full-blown panic. When I entered the cold classroom—the heat was turned off in there, too—my chest pounded so loudly I could hear it, and my breathing quickened. *I'm having a heart attack*, I thought in an ironically calm manner. *My heart is going*

*to pop out of my chest, just like the alien in the movie, and I'm
going to die. My guts are going to spill out and stain my sweater.*

The students had already filled the room. The irony
of being tenured as well as a writing program director
was that you rarely got to teach the course that qualified
you to be a WPA in the first place. Thus, I had insisted
on assigning myself one first-year composition course per
semester to keep my skills and the program fresh.

"Good morning," I said, forcing a smile that probably
looked more like I was constipated (which, in fact, I was).
The students were as eerily quiet as the congregation in
the church when I finished the crappy eulogy at Sam's
funeral. Not even the heater vents uttered a sound.

"Well, OK," I said, attempting to break the ice. "I'm
Dr. Vanzant; but from the looks on your faces, you seem
to know that already. So, let's just get the elephant out of
the room, shall we?"

The students sat and either stared into their notebooks
or past me, expressionless.

"My husband was killed by a drunk driver this past
October. I'm doing OK. I'm looking forward to this class
and to doing some writing with you guys. So, let's go over
the course requirements."

I ignored the awkward silence and distributed the syllabus, reading the policies from the first two pages and
taking up all of fifteen minutes. And yet, those fifteen
minutes passed like a kidney stone. Normally, I would do
some freewriting exercises with the students on the first
day. Instead, I dismissed them. As the class filed out, one
student approached me.

"Professor, I hope this doesn't upset you, but I just wanted to tell you that my sister goes to Edmund and took your husband's class two years ago. She said he was her favorite teacher and that because of him, she loves writing now. She cried when she heard the news."

The girl's voice wavered slightly. A part of me wanted to take her in my arms and console her and assure her that it was going to be OK.

"What's your name?" I asked.

"Hayley."

"What's your sister's name?"

"Heather."

"Hayley, that's the nicest thing anyone's said to me in a really long time. Thank you. And tell your sister that I'm glad she got to know my husband. She's a lucky girl."

The tightness of Hayley's shy, nervous face softened and lightened. "Thank you, Professor. I'm looking forward to this class."

"So am I."

———

When I returned to my office, I closed the door with my back leaning against it, slid to the floor, and burst into tears. Another class awaited me that day, and I didn't know how or if I was going to pull it off. Maggie was right: Sam was everywhere, and I was a fool to think that there'd be no reminders of him here. I sat in that spot until my second class, eighty minutes later.

Five Weeks into the Spring Semester

S ITTING AT A SMALL, SQUARE-SHAPED, WOODEN
table next to a window in the library at NU, I gazed
outside, soaking in the sunlight yet feeling the wintry
draft from the window's poor insulation. My laptop's
screensaver had kicked in, patiently waiting for me to return my attention to it. The view from the sixth floor was
inspiring, giving way to the panorama of the NU campus
with all its trees and benches and grassy knolls and lawns
set against the horizon of the New England sky, perfect
for Frisbee or football throwers, nappers, and lovers,
of course.

Ever since Sam's funeral, I'd taken to occasionally
rewriting the crappy eulogy I'd delivered. About a week
after the funeral, at the Edmund College memorial service,
Sam's brother Kevin delivered a eulogy that practically
led to a standing ovation. I could hear my mother's voice
admonishing me for insisting I do the eulogy myself at
the funeral.

*Anyone who knows me knows that my love life was a train
wreck from day one. When it came to gravitating to the
good guys, my compass needle pointed south. When it came*

to sound judgments, my romantic wires always got crossed. When it came to sex, I consulted several sources throughout my life, some of which were later discredited. But Sam was the one who taught me about love.

I think the reason why Sam was such a great teacher was because he allowed people to see his flaws as well as his virtues—in fact, to him, a flaw was just as much an attribute to writing as a talent. He shared my concept of revision as embracing the possibilities that live within the flaws. His humanity came out on every page that he wrote and shared with his students, and his students loved him for it; he was "real" to them.

Sam had a curiosity for life and took pleasure in simple things. Books. Trees. A cup of coffee. A photograph. He couldn't carry a tune to save his life, but admired those who could. He was also an incurable collector. I don't remember how or when it started, but someone gave him a bobble-head doll, and pretty soon word got out that he liked bobble-head dolls. In fact, I don't think he was particularly fond of them until he started receiving so many of them—then it was just a big joke. And now the bookcase in his study is filled with bobble-head dolls.

This eulogy really blows.

As director of the freshman writing program, I'd always been busy, but Jeff was right—my workload had doubled since returning to school. In addition to catching up on the previous semester's activities, staying on top of the writing program's daily goings-on, and teaching my own course load, I needed to design and write a document detailing program assessment guidelines and procedures, implement the procedures, and report on the findings.

What's more, I also supervised the freshman writing faculty, totaling close to thirty instructors; updated program policy statements and information on the department Web site; charged a committee to research new textbook options for the following year; and attended budget meeting after budget meeting with Jeff, the dean, and other administrators. All this was followed by a two-day writing technology conference in Albany—Sam and I would've made an extended weekend of it.

I sat on two university faculty hiring committees, one tenure review committee, and three graduate student thesis committees. My assistant program director had stepped in and handled my responsibilities following my abrupt departure last semester, and I found myself repeatedly thanking her, as well as apologizing every time I delegated yet another task, many more than I would have under normal circumstances. Meanwhile, Jeff had ordered my academic advising students to be redistributed to other department faculty members for the remainder of the academic year.

One of the scholarly articles that I'd submitted for peer review prior to Sam's death had been returned to me and sat under the mountainous pile on my desk, untouched. And I repeatedly failed to return my editor's calls regarding my book proposal for a new collection of personal essays. The essays themselves still idled in a first-draft gridlock.

Work failed to serve as a refuge; instead, it backed me into a corner. What was once a passion was now a burden. Where I once displayed unwavering confidence, I now broke into a cold sweat. I did nothing well anymore, nor did I want to. As the semester dragged on, I found myself putting off appointments, delaying deadlines, and avoiding phone calls. The stack of unanswered e-mails in my virtual inbox piled just as high as the stack of paper in my actual inbox.

Most disturbing of all was how little I cared, and not for lack of trying.

CHAPTER

FOUR

F OLLOWING SAM'S DEATH, I'D DROPPED ABOUT ten pounds. Many times I entered Shaw's supermarket with a cart but rarely left with anything beyond a can of soup or a box of instant rice. At school, I designated protein snack bars as a new food group.

Cooking had become something of a ritual in Sam's and my relationship. In the way that John Lennon and Yoko Ono had taken walks in Central Park every day prior to his murder, Sam and I would convene in the kitchen, drinking water in wine glasses, and either one of us cooked while the other watched (most of the time I was the onlooker, simply because he was the better cook and I enjoyed the view), or we shared the deed—I'd season and spice, he'd slice and dice, then we'd fry or broil or bake and flip a coin to see who cleaned up. Cooking time was communion time, and the kitchen was our holy place. Our friendship blossomed while we silently stirred tomato sauce; our passion enflamed while we melted chocolate for ganache and drizzled it over warm cupcakes; our fights defused while we banged pots or chopped garlic by laying the knife flat on the cloves and pummeling it with our fists.

Food tastes better when it's prepared with love. Even charred toast or goppy pizza dough made it past our palates without complaint.

I avoided the kitchen almost as much as I avoided the bedroom.

One Saturday morning at Shaw's, I loitered up and down the aisles, eventually getting to the cookie aisle and stopping at each brand. Pepperidge Farm Mint Milanos. Nabisco Vienna Fingers. Sunshine Hydrox. Mrs. Field's Chunky Chocolate Chips. Newman's Own Organic Fig Newtons.

I hadn't bought packaged cookies in ages.

I looked at the Keebler section. Just stopped and stared at and contemplated them, in a Zen-like trance. Then I grabbed a box of Grasshoppers from the shelf and dumped them in the cart ("cheap-thrills Girl Scout Thin Mints," Sam used to call them; he was a cookie monster and never gained an ounce, the rat-bastard). Quicker now, with a stride in my step, I wheeled the cart to the dairy section, yanked a quart of milk from the shelf without stopping, and headed for checkout.

When I got home and entered the house, Shaw's plastic bag in tow, I headed straight for the den, plopped on the couch, handled the remote, and channel-surfed until I settled on a marathon of *Project Runway* episodes on Bravo. Without using dishware, I consumed half the tray of Grasshoppers in less than sixty seconds, chased by half the bottle of milk.

In a state of numbness, I lay back on the couch and watched TV for five hours straight while two stacks of essays that I'd collected at the beginning of the week remained on my desk in my home office, still unread.

Before I went to bed, I finished the rest of the cookies and milk, and the next day I did a full food shop, including two more boxes of cookies and a half gallon of milk that I devoured within four days.

CHAPTER

FIVE

April

" C 'MON IN, KID," JEFF SAID WHILE EATING
a club sandwich. He called everyone, regardless
of their age, "kid."

I've never seen anyone happy to be in the position of
department chair, and Jeff was no exception. Prior to his
appointment, Jeff used to be seen joking in the hallways
of the third floor, his loud and boisterous laugh heard
from the second floor. Since becoming chair, however, the
only time one would find Jeff laughing was at a seldom-
attended dinner party, drink in hand. The laugh increased
in volume by the third drink.

"Hey, Jeff."

He held an open snack-size bag of chips out to me. I
waved my hand and shook my head. My insides were already
churning; I knew this meeting was not going to be good.

"How you doing?" he asked.

Tired of everyone asking me that, I wanted to answer.

"OK," I said.

"You sure?"

"This is about last week's class, isn't it. The kid put in
a complaint."

"Andi, you called a student 'fucknuts' because he didn't turn in an assignment."

"No, I called him 'fucknuts' because the excuse he gave for not turning it in was stupid."

"You can't do that. You can't call your students names."

"I knew a professor at Brooklyn U who told a student to her face that she was dumb as dirt. Now that's plain mean."

"You were out of line. Besides, it's not like you to treat students in such a way. In fact, you're always the one arguing that we don't respect students enough. And that's not all. I hear you've been misplacing their papers and handing them back late, changing the syllabus without warning, coming into class late and letting them out early, not keeping office hours…"

I shifted in my seat. "I admit I'm a bit more scatter-brained than usual."

"I haven't even gotten to the faculty complaints about your committee work."

"Oh please. Like any of them should throw stones. Jan Turner is a potted plant, the key word being 'pot.'"

Normally this would make him laugh. But he didn't even crack a grin. Apparently I wasn't going to be able to quip my way out of this.

"I think you're overwhelmed and your return was premature."

"Oh, not you, too, Jeff."

"Don't you think that if I'm one in a long line of people telling you this, then you ought to listen?"

"First of all," I argued, "there is no line. No one's telling me anything. And don't you think I would know better than they would even if they did? It's my life, you know."

"Are you getting any professional help? Your insurance covers it."

"Are you allowed to ask me that?"

Jeff put down his sandwich, took a sip of Coke, and then got up and closed the door.

"Look," he started, back at his desk, "if I wasn't chair, I'd have asked you out to lunch and offered you a shoulder to lean on. But students are complaining, and that's not good, especially so soon after you were granted tenure. You know the drill; I have to address the issue. They have legitimate complaints."

I stared at the beads of condensation quietly sliding down the side of the Coke can, trying to predict where the droplets would land.

"Are you listening to me?" Jeff asked.

"Yeah, I hear you." I looked up at him for a second, then turned my attention back to the can. I heard him huff.

"You're so wicked talented, Andi. You're one of the best in this field. It won't be long before you're as well-known and as frequently cited as Elbow or Shaughnessy. Do you know how many students try to get into your class? I get tons of requests at the beginning of semesters from students wanting to get in. There's a waiting list. Your class is Studio 54, minus all the sex and cocaine."

His humor failed to elicit any reaction or response from me. For some reason, I thought he was lying to me. I felt wistful for the days when my work was a piece of cake, someplace fun to be and something fun to do, even on the arduous days.

"I don't know how I'd react if it were my wife..." he started.

I looked at him with daggers. "*Don't.* Don't you dare go there. Don't tell me I'm comin' apart at the seams because my husband died. I know perfectly well what happened. Every freakin' day of my life. So stop right there. And you don't know anything. You just don't know, and you've no right to tell me how to teach my class or what to say to my students. I'm a professional, just like you said."

"You won't be a professional for long if you keep this shit up. People don't forget around here. You're one of the bright lights here. One of the shining stars. I don't want you to lose that, and I don't want the department or the university to lose you."

"Too late," I said, feeling tears coming to my eyes. I paused for a beat. "You have no idea how powerless you really are to hold on to anything." I touched the droplets on the can with my finger, tracing them, pulling them in the direction I wanted them to go, ignoring the two tears that slid down my face.

"Will you think about what I've said? Please? Forget as department chair. As a friend? I really am worried about you."

"Yeah, OK. I'll think about it. I know you're just doing your job."

"Thanks, kid. And listen, you can talk to me anytime. My door's always open."

"Sure thing, Jeff. Seeya."

I exited his office and exhaled, glad to be out of there, trembling down the hall and back to my office. As the day went on, I thought about what he said. *I'll do better,* I told myself. *You know you love what you do. Just get that back, and everything will be OK. Everything will get better if you get back on track.*

That night I went home and caught up on reading student papers and e-mails. It felt good to finish something.

Less than a week later, as I staggered into class on time, juggling a textbook and file folder while trying to keep my briefcase from slipping off my shoulder, I heard two students talking while surrounding classmates listened and chimed in with enthusiasm. Without saying good morning, I dropped the stuff down on the desk and listened in.

"Man, I was so wasted, I'm surprised I even got up this morning."

"Dude, I don't even know how I got home."

The words hit me like lighter fluid and ignited a rage in me.

"Boy, you really are a moron," I started.

A couple of students laughed. The two boys looked at me, shocked.

"Excuse me?" one of them asked.

"You heard me. You think that's something to brag about? Do you know how completely stupid you are?" I panned across the room. "And the rest of you are just as stupid because you were cheering him on just a minute ago."

The room deadened.

"What—tell me, *what* in God's name is so cool about getting so completely tanked that you can't even remember how you got home? What is so cool about getting so wasted that you actually kill brain cells and rot part of your body away? I don't get it. I mean, I *really* don't get it."

The class sat motionless and silent, their faces awash with apathy, while I continued my rant.

"Do you have any idea how unattractive that is? Do you have any idea how *fucking stupid* you are—not only to do it, but to actually *brag* about it? My *God*, can't you have a good time without having to obliterate your senses? You'd be better off sucking on the exhaust pipe of a bus, for chrissake. Why—I mean, *why* can't you just watch a game or see a movie without having to be complete morons and drinking yourselves into oblivion? Are you all that insecure? Do you hate yourselves that much?"

"We're in college," one of the two boys said. "This is what we do. It's just part of growing up."

"Oh God, you really are that stupid if you think you can argue that bullshit logic with me. Haven't you learned anything in this class? Would you like to take a field trip to the Rhode Island correctional facility where one of your peers is doing time for vehicular manslaughter for offing my husband on a Monday night? *Ve-hic-u-lar man-slaught-er.* Kid was so fucking drunk he couldn't even say the words 'vehicular manslaughter.' I guarantee you that kid's not bragging."

Never had I sworn in front of my students. At least not to that degree.

"I thought he went to UMass Amherst," a student said to the person sitting next to him.

"Or how would you like to do a visual analysis of pictures taken at the scene of the accident? He had *shards of glass* stuck in his body. My husband."

Some of the students winced, while most of them remained expressionless.

"Do you know what speed my husband was doing? Ten, fifteen miles tops. He was pulling out of a store. You know what Satan's Little Frat Boy was doing? *Sixty.* They estimated he was doing *sixty miles* in a twenty-five mile zone. Maybe seventy or seventy-five. Wanna know what my husband was buying? Sparkling cider. We were celebrating our wedding anniversary. We don't need alcohol to make ourselves interesting to each other. We're not plastic, feckless crack babies hooked on Ritalin and porn."

Hayley, the girl whose sister had Sam for a teacher, stood up and walked out.

"I'm sorry, Professor, but that's just wrong," she said in tears as she passed me. I watched her go, and suddenly I felt as if I were outside my body, watching and wanting to stop myself, but unable to. I wanted to apologize to her, to all of them, but I couldn't. They killed Sam.

The rest of the class followed, gathering their things and walking out.

"That's right," I said. "Go. Maybe there's a bar that's still open."

The boy whom I called a moron muttered, "That's fucked up," as he passed me. The other boy looked at me and said, "I don't care what happened to you. I'm going to get you fired."

"Go ahead and try."

I trembled uncontrollably. This wasn't me. God, what was happening to me?

Leaving my briefcase and coat, I took my purse and rushed out of the building, walked a half mile to my car just as a cold, light rain began, and pulled out my cell phone once I was in the car. Shivering, I turned the ignition and cranked up the heat. My breathing was so rapid I thought I might hyperventilate. I could barely touch the phone's miniscule keypad. Maggie answered on the third ring, very professional-like.

"Oh, thank God you're there," I cried, my voice quivering.

"Andi? What is it?" she asked, alarmed.

"I think I just got myself fired."

"What happened?"

"I just went totally apeshit on my class. Yelled at them, called them names, demeaned them. I don't know what happened. This kid was talking about how drunk he was last night, and all I could see was the kid who killed Sam. The entire class. They all looked the same to me. Oh, Maggie, you were right. I never should've have come back. What am I going to do?"

Maggie paused for a moment. I thought maybe she was crying, too. Or mad at me.

"OK. You can't take back what you said. I don't think you'll get fired—you have tenure now. But this is not good. You have to go to your chairperson and tell him what just happened—he's a friend of yours, isn't he? Your students may already be lining up outside his door. They might even go straight to the dean. Then, you've got to take another medical leave, effective immediately. Offer to take it without pay, even. And apologize to your students."

"OK," I said, sobbing. My eyes burned.

"Do it right now."

"OK," I repeated. I opened the car door and stepped out. The rain had stopped as quickly as it started, and the sun looked as if it desperately wanted to reappear. The trees and bushes were budding, and the air smelled good.

"Andi?" Maggie said.

"Yeah?"

"I love you and I'm always here for you and I understand what happened. But you've got to get some help now. What would Sam say? What would he want for you?"

I didn't answer. I just cried.

"I've got to go now, but I'll call you as soon as I can," she said.

"OK."

"I love you," she said again.

"I love you too."

I turned off the phone and headed back to Adams Hall. First I went back to the classroom to get my stuff. It wasn't there. Then I went to Jeff's office, located directly across from Kay's office. His door was closed. Kay's, however, was open, and when she saw me, she picked up her phone, dialed four numbers (I heard Jeff's phone ring once), and spoke very softly into the phone. Then she looked down, as if I wasn't there, a hint of judgment glaring from her eyes as she did so. Ten seconds later, Jeff opened the door.

"Come in, Andi."

I sat in the same chair as last time and sniffled. My briefcase, textbook, and papers sat next to his desk. Kay must have retrieved them.

"I am so sorry, Jeff," I said in broken sobs. I sounded like a four-year-old apologizing to the neighbor for breaking her vase.

"I warned you."

"I know. I didn't mean to do it—it just happened. I know that's not an excuse. I'm not even trying to make an excuse. But at the time I couldn't stop it, and I'm sorry now and I think I should take another leave of absence. I'll even resign, if I have to. Just don't fire me. Please don't fire me."

"You've got tenure—you'd have to sleep with a goat to get fired. But dammit, this is wicked bad. Five students, including the two boys you blew up at, just left my office. In fact, I'm surprised you didn't run into them on your way here, and lucky for you, I might add. I even got calls from two parents whose kids text-messaged them as it was happening. I'm going to tell them why you're not fired. But as of right now, you're out of here for the remainder of the semester. Unpaid leave."

"Yes," I said. "I understand."

"You've got to get help. You can't do this on your own anymore."

"I know."

"Will you do it? Will you get help?"

"Yes."

"Do you promise? I'm asking you as a friend. You're killing me, here. You're breaking my heart. I know this is not who you really are," he said. "I miss you. We all do."

"I miss me, too."

"Do you promise?"

"Yes," I said. I meant it, too.

"OK. Do you need a ride home?"

"No."

"OK. Go home now." Before I left, he said, "You know, they weren't all mad. Some of them were actually really sympathetic."

Hearing that only added to my guilt.

"The sad thing is that I was really trying," I said, then turned and left.

I drove myself home. When I entered the house, I headed straight for Sam's study and slumped in the faded leather chair that matched the sofa, my wet face buried in my hands. When I looked up, I noticed our wedding photo sitting on the table beside me, the Mikasa frame a wedding gift. Sam in his tux and white silk necktie, beyond perfect; and me, in an A-line Vera Wang gown that fell off the shoulders, my hair in a French twist and no veil, my makeup flawless. Standing against a backdrop of New England trees spattered with autumn hues. His eyes matched the sky rather than the ocean that day, while mine matched those leaves that hadn't turned yet. We were glowing, full of love and hope and promise, death nonexistent. We didn't even use the words "till death do us part" in our vows. We said "for our lives and always."

I didn't sign up for this.

He was only forty-three years old.

I took the picture, flung it across the room, and cursed Sam to hell. The Mikasa frame broke into pieces. It was just a bottle of sparkling cider, dammit. Water would've been fine.

CHAPTER
SIX

O N A TUESDAY AFTERNOON, TWO WEEKS
after leaving the university for the remainder of the
semester, I sat in the waiting room of an office shared by
a chiropractor, a massage therapist, and Melody Greene,
a therapist who specialized in grief counseling. My good
friend Miranda, whose best friend was on one of the planes
that flew out of Logan Airport on September 11, 2001,
recommended Melody to me days after I called and told
her about the incident at NU.

"You'll love her," Miranda said. "She's very New Age,
but not flaky. She's into alternative medicine, nutrition,
you name it. And she practiced in New York City for a
while, too. The best part is that she takes insurance. She
helped me out a lot."

"With a sterling recommendation like that, it's too
bad she's not a man," I quipped. I'd gotten very sarcastic
as of late. Miranda called it my defense mechanism, no
doubt to be confirmed soon by Melody Greene.

The door opened at 2:02, and a woman of medium
height, thin build, copper hair in desperate need of a col-
oring, and a long, shapeless, paisley cotton dress escorted
her client out. Very earthy-crunchy, I thought. The short,

heavyset client held a crumpled tissue and her eyes were red and puffy. I made a silent vow to hold it together better than she had.

After the woman bid her client good-bye, she looked down at her clipboard, then up at me.

"Andrea Vanzant?"

I dropped the ragged, three-month-old *People* magazine back on the coffee table and stood up.

"That's me."

She smiled amiably, and her skin was shiny. "I'm Melody." She extended her hand to me. "It's so nice to meet you." I took her hand and shook; my grip was much firmer than hers.

She held open the door to her office, which was painted in soft, soothing aquamarine colors and smelled of lavender and ylang-ylang. I sat on one of those big round chairs that Pier One Imports usually sells to college kids for their dorm rooms. Right away I recognized it as "the client chair." Melody's chair looked more like something you might find at Office Max—a black leather, upright desk chair that actually looked more comfortable than the boat in which I tried to maneuver myself.

Melody sat and closed her eyes for a full minute, breathing deeply while I examined the layout and décor of the room. When she opened her eyes, she exhaled and was visibly more relaxed.

"So, Andrea. Tell me what brought you here. I know we spoke briefly on the phone last week, but please refresh my memory."

For some reason, I distrusted her instantly. *The hell you forgot—you just want to make me say it,* I thought.

"Well, six months ago my husband was killed, and apparently I'm not handling it very well because I was forced to take another leave of absence."

Her facial expression remained unchanged. She looked neither disturbed nor elated; she was simply serene.

"Where do you work?"

"I'm a professor of English and director of freshman writing at Northampton University."

She raised her eyebrows in response to this bit of information, as if to say, *Impressive.*

"What happened?"

The memory of the incident filled me with shame and humiliation. "I blew up at my class and cursed two of my students a few weeks ago."

She jotted something on her clipboard. *Great. It's on the record now.*

"What caused the blowup? I mean, did one of them provoke you or something like that?"

"They were talking about getting hammered, and I don't know, it's like I stepped out of myself and saw them all as the kid who killed my husband. Next thing I know, I'm ranting like a lunatic."

She continued to write on her clipboard and talk to me without looking up. "Your husband was murdered?"

"In a matter of speaking," I said, my stomach turning in knots as I replayed the memories of Sam rushing and kissing me, leaving without his jacket, the officers at my door… "It was a drunk driver."

She stopped writing and looked up at me, a look of sorrow in her eyes. "I'm very sorry, Andrea."

"Andi."

"Excuse me?"

"You can call me Andi. Everyone does."

She smiled amiably again. "OK. What was your husband's name?"

I resented her using the past tense. What the hell kind of therapist was she?

"Sam." I reached into my purse, pulled out my wallet, and opened it to a cropped photo of Sam and me on one of our weekend getaways. The edges were frayed from its constant handling. I held out the photo for Melody to see. She raised her eyebrows again.

"He's very handsome," she remarked. I nodded in agreement, fixated on the photo and visually tracing Sam's every feature: highly defined cheekbones; ocean blue eyes; short, dark, tapered hair; Hollywood straight teeth. More than handsome. And he always called *me* gorgeous…

"Rob Lowe without the teenage sex video," I said. She laughed.

"I was more of an Emilio Estevez gal until he did all those *Mighty Duck* movies."

The corner of my mouth twitched upward. She earned a point for that one.

"Why did you associate your students with the drunk driver?" she asked.

"Because he was a freshman at NU, I guess."

She nodded and gestured as if to compliment me for my insight. "How awful," she said. I nodded.

"Andi, if the incident with your class hadn't happened, do you think you would have come here on your own?"

"I don't know," I shrugged. "Maybe."

She then fired off a barrage of questions: how much sleep did I get; what kinds of food did I eat, and how often; did I have any physical ailments—stomach pains, high blood pressure, allergies; did I have any suicidal thoughts; did I hear voices or have hallucinations; did I believe in ghosts; was I religious; had I ever been in therapy before, et cetera. I answered each question in a very rote tone, as if they passed along a conveyor belt for my quick inspection. She then conducted an inventory of my family history, both medical and mental. Any alcohol or drug abuse in my immediate family? Heart disease? Cancer? Allergies? Mental illness?

"My brothers are musicians," I answered wryly. "Never did drugs, though. At least not that I know of. But my brother Tony sometimes talks to his guitar and speaks of it in the third person."

"As long as he doesn't leave his estate to it, I'd say he's fine."

Nice comeback.

I wondered if we were gonna get to any therapy anytime soon. Finally, she finished the inquisition.

"Well, I'm looking forward to working with you. Is there anything in particular you'd like to work on? I mean, would you like to set some long-term goals?"

Set some long-term goals! Was she nuts? I had enough trouble getting up in the morning.

"Well, I'd like to not scream obscenities at my students anymore."

"Anything else?"

I stared at the floor, searching for an answer. What could I possibly want that didn't involve going back to that crucial moment and handcuffing Sam to the staircase banister rather than letting him walk out the door?

"Will I ever feel normal again?" I asked.

She answered, "You'll never go back to the way it was before Sam was killed."

Great. My hopes, the size of a hot-air balloon for the split second after my question, deflated and bitterly collapsed after her answer. Why bother, then?

Melody read my body language and empathized. "But you will find the ordinary world again. If you choose it, that is. Everything is a choice."

"Not everything," I argued. "I didn't choose *this*. I didn't choose to lose my husband."

"But you can choose the way you respond to it. You'll see."

I looked at her skeptically. What did she mean by "the ordinary world"? I wondered.

Time was up. Melody opened the office door and escorted me out, just like the previous client. The waiting room was empty.

Later that evening, Miranda called to see how it went.

"OK, I guess. A lot of questions. I thought there'd be more...I don't know...more therapy, I guess."

"That's just the first day. It's like you with your students, doing icebreakers and asking them to write about where they went to high school and stuff. She just needs to figure out where you're at. You'll see. It'll get better."

"I hope so."

"It really does get easier," she said. "I know it sounds like I'm patronizing you right now, but trust me."

"I guess," I said, not wanting to show Miranda the depth of my disbelief. Sam was more than a best friend. He was my lover, my partner, my *husband*. Aside from the loss of a child, could any loss feel worse? Could it really get easier? I so longed to go back to a time when I at least believed that such things did.

"In the meantime, just fake it till you make it," said Miranda.

If she only knew what crappy advice *that* was.

CHAPTER

SEVEN

June

S INCE LEAVING SCHOOL, I'D GAINED TEN
pounds and couldn't get out of bed before eleven
o'clock, so I'm not sure how well the therapy was working.
I liked Melody, though, and seeing her gave me something
to do once a week. The rest of my time consisted of going
to the lake on the Edmund College campus and feeding
the ducks, sitting in Perch (Sam's and my coffee shop
hangout), rereading all the books we'd read together, and
watching a lot of TV. Neither of us had ever considered ourselves couch potatoes, but we had our must-sees: episodes
of the British version of *The Office* on the BBC; box sets
of *The West Wing* and *Boston Legal* series; *The Daily Show* and
The Colbert Report right before bed; baseball and football
games, especially during the playoffs; and tennis Grand
Slams. Now I watched marathons of sitcoms, talk shows,
reality competition shows, just about everything but Fox
News. I hadn't realized how much crap repeated itself, as
if all TV viewers suffered from short-term memory loss.
Over and over and over and over again.

Maggie and I called each other at least twice a week,
and she often tried to coax me to do more productive
things with my time.

"Make something good come out of this," she'd say. "Travel. Go see your mom or your brothers. Hell, come see *me*. Or write. Start those journal articles you've been wanting to write. Talk to your editor and work on that new collection of essays."

"I just don't have the desire to write anymore, Mags. All my energy has been sucked out of my body. There doesn't seem to be any point to it."

"What does your therapist say about it?"

"She's very into goal setting. And lists. She tries to get me to make a list of things to do for the day, the week, the month...that sort of thing."

"And are you doing it?"

"What's on the list? Sometimes."

"What's the point of you going to therapy if you're not going to apply it?" she asked, a hint of frustration lingering.

"Well, we talk. She asks me a lot of questions."

"What does she say about your lack of motivation?"

"She hasn't really said anything yet."

The operative word was "yet." Sure enough, at our next session, when Melody asked me if I'd achieved anything on my goal list, I answered her with the same blasé attitude as I had with Mags.

"Andi," she said in a professional tone. "I'm growing concerned about your lack of activity and effort."

I gave her the same excuse I gave Maggie.

"That's what goal-setting is for," she said. "It's to get you over that hump and recharge your batteries. You have no energy because you're working so hard to avoid the pain of grieving. You're shutting yourself down as a form of damage control. The leftover is for survival—just enough to get through the day."

My insides tightened and felt heavy. "So what am I supposed to do—have another meltdown? I've already had at least one, thank you very much. And that one was in the classroom."

"And why did you have that meltdown?"

"I already told you what that was about," I said, agitated. "My students were talking about getting tanked like it was something glamorous. I couldn't stand there and let them dis my husband like that."

"But they weren't dissing your husband. They were being young adults getting a taste of freedom for the first time. They were looking for validation to justify their behavior. And they were behaving that way in response to the fear of all the change taking place in their lives."

"You sound like *them*."

"Who is '*them*'?" Melody asked. "The students?"

"You're rationalizing using the 'kids will be kids' logic. It doesn't fly with me. I didn't need to get tanked at their age. I didn't need booze and pot to be validated."

"What did you need?"

Her question cut off my fury. What did I need?

I traveled back to my nineteen-year-old self: *A girl with big hair and little confidence, yo-yoing with her weight. A virgin submerged in the shame of her sexual inexperience, gone into hiding. Forlorn, hidden, hardly recognizable. God, she looks so desperate, so lonely, so...*

"I needed to be touched," I answered, my head down, voice withdrawn and regressed, surprised the words came out at all. Melody didn't respond right away. She seemed to be waiting for me to cry; and yet, even though I felt the urge to do so, my eyes didn't water.

Finally, she spoke in a soft, placid tone. "Andi, the response to loss is a response to whatever is unresolved in *us*, whatever losses are called up from our unconscious to be relived."

"What does that mean?"

"It means you're not just grieving the loss of Sam."

"Great," I said. "As if that's not enough."

"All the losses of your life—even the ones that seemed insignificant at the time, like losing a competition or a favorite toy—are going to resurface."

"Should I start making a list?"

"This is an opportunity for you. It's a wonderful opportunity, really. You can finally acknowledge those losses, and *choose* how to respond to them. And you can make choices other than *not* responding, or pretending like everything's OK."

"You mean, faking it."

"Yes. I don't think faking it works for you."

"Tell Miranda that," I said.

"So, what's another choice you can make?" She sounded like a school counselor.

I didn't answer her. The responsibility of choosing was too big, too overwhelming.

"Think about it," she said. "Why did you react the way you did to those boys? It was completely out of character for you, yes? You told me that you're the one who fights for students' rights and respect, that you took pride in that. So why would you, in turn, choose a response of complete disrespect? What were you really reacting to in that moment?"

I stared at the floor, my head swimming in confusion, trying to access the answer that lay in waiting on the tip of my tongue. Did I not know it, or did I not *want* to know? In that moment, a wave of terror broke on top of me, and I gripped the sides of the boat-like chair.

"Oh God, Melody. How could I have done it? How could I have fucked up like that? I mean, my career was the one thing that I always held together. Before Sam, my love life was a train wreck. But my career was always on track. I had complete confidence. And I was *good* at it—I'm cited in conference papers and scholarly articles. Nedra Reynolds would come up to me after a conference session and say, 'Great stuff!'"

As if Melody knew these people.

"Even Peter Elbow, the Paul McCartney of rhetoric and composition, once introduced me as 'The Next Big Thing.' I was trying so hard to get that back."

"The important thing is not to get stuck in what I call 'The One Wrong Move' syndrome," she said. "You've got to accept it, forgive yourself, and move on. Don't let it paralyze you. Otherwise you'll never heal."

I looked at her, dejected, my insides fluttering with fear. How was movement possible when I'd all but thrown my career away, and the one who'd turned my love life into just plain ol' life was gone?

"I've lost everything," I said, defeated.

Melody nodded as if I'd just told her it was raining outside.

"So," she said, a hint of optimism in her voice, "what are you going to do about it?"

———————

Later that evening, I sat in Sam's study with yet another draft of his eulogy in my lap. Donny Most curled his plump, orange-and-white body beside me on the sofa and purred lackadaisically. He, too, now spent the majority of his time in this room. As I read through the draft and rewrote above crossed-out words and sentences and crammed notes in margins, I thought about what Melody said about getting stuck in One Wrong Move. No matter how many times I revised it, even if I turned the eulogy into a prizewinning piece of writing, it could never make up for the crappy draft I'd written and read at the funeral, no more than a leave of absence or a lifetime of therapy could make up for what I'd said to those students that day.

I could almost hear the thunder of powerlessness so heavy I thought it would bury me alive as it collapsed on me yet again, while the incessant ache for Sam tortured and wrenched every muscle in my body.

Too late, I thought. I was paralyzed for life.

July

I WAS SPRAWLED OUT ON THE SOFA IN THE den watching a Yankees–Red Sox game while the air-conditioning unit whirred obtrusively. Hideki Matsui had just hit a triple, putting the Yanks up seven to four in the bottom of the fifth inning. One out. All of Yankee Stadium roared and jumped to their feet in the midst of the heat.

Sam and I used to watch these rivaled games with a fierce, often arousing competitive edge. The winner had to "console" the losing opponent by performing some kind of pleasurable act: cooking a certain meal, a backrub, oral sex, you name it. One time Sam made me wash his car.

A forceful knock at the door jolted me as I flashed back to the night Sam was killed. Tentatively creeping to the door, some part of me expected to see the police officers on the other side, waiting to address me: "Mrs. Vanzant?"

I cracked the door ajar, then pulled it open when I saw Jeff, a milkshake in each hand, one of which he sipped.

I exhaled a sigh of relief. "What are you doing here?" I asked, taking a step back to let him in.

"Here, take this—I can't feel my fingers anymore."

"Thanks." I took a sip. Strawberry-banana.

Dressed in tan Dockers shorts, sneakers without socks, and a faded, moth-eaten, 2004 Red Sox World Champions T-shirt, Jeff looked like he should be out barbecuing rather than sipping milkshakes. He'd cut his hair extra-short for the summer, almost crew cut style. I didn't like it. I had donned a pair of Sam's ripped jeans—they fit me now—and transformed them into cut-offs, accompanied by a heather gray NU T-shirt, size large.

"What's up, kid?"

"Matsui just got a triple," I reported.

With that news, he headed straight for the den, cursing. I followed behind.

"Damn," he said, fixated on the screen. The new Yankees rookie was at bat.

"You never know, they might pull through. It ain't over till it's over."

He smirked at me, knowing my appeasement was a sham. The rookie grounded out to third and ended the inning.

"Sorry about the pop-in, but I was out running errands and realized I haven't seen or spoken to you in too damn long, so here I am."

"Bullshit you had errands. During a Yankee-Sox game?"

"Sox-Yankee game."

I cocked an eyebrow at him. He smiled. Jeff was good-looking. Not like Sam, but attractive nonetheless. Except for the crew cut.

"OK," he confessed. "I came to see you."

"I'm flattered," I said. "Really."

"You should be. So? What've you been up to?"

I shrugged my shoulders. "Nothing much, really. I get up. I do whatever. I go to bed."

He ambled from the den to the kitchen so as not to let the game distract him.

"That's it?"

"Pretty much. I'm bored out of my skull, actually."

"How's the shrink working out?"

"Fine. I mean, I like going."

"Made any progress?"

"Hard to tell."

A moment of silence passed between us. We both sipped our milkshakes. Mine gave me goose bumps every time I swallowed.

"Getting out much?" he asked.

"You mean, socially?"

"Yeah."

"Not really," I said.

"Why not?"

Sam and I weren't social butterflies, but we'd dined with friends at least twice a week, together or separately. We had friends like Jeff and his wife Patsy, with whom we hung out in couples, as well as our own friends, like Miranda (and Maggie, in New York) for me and Sam's best friends George and Justin. Occasionally we'd either attend or host a dinner party consisting of our colleagues—we often liked to combine Edmund faculty with NU faculty and watch them try to one-up each other like competitive cousins. During the first few weeks after the funeral, they'd all called or dropped by to "check in" on me. By Christmastime, with the exception of Maggie and Miranda, I'd started avoiding their calls. By January, they'd pretty much abandoned me. I didn't take it personally. My guess was that they felt the way I did: that to face each other was to face the conspicuous absence of the man we so dearly loved, a man who livened up dull parties, who was our best buddy, thoughtful and funny and all-around great guy.

"Everyone fell off the face of the earth. Or maybe I did and they stopped looking for me," I said.

Jeff looked at me earnestly. "I owe you an apology."

"For what?"

"I cut you loose after the incident at school, and I didn't mean to. I guess I figured you needed time. Or maybe I did, I don't know. I didn't like seeing you that way."

"I don't blame you. Besides, I didn't see it as you cutting me loose. You did your job."

"But to not call you all this time? I'm your friend first. At least, I should be."

"You have other priorities," I said.

"Friends should be a priority. Life is too short."

Had he really been thinking of Sam today, and that's why he dropped by? Regardless, his words touched me, and my eyes misted. I slurped my milkshake, then kissed him on the cheek, my lips cold and puffy. I suddenly realized how much I missed hanging out with Jeff. Hell, hanging out with anyone, really—laughing, shooting the breeze, entertaining, feeling free and light and happy.

"Apology accepted," I said.

He blushed. "Anyhoo, Patsy and I wanna have you over for dinner next week. So pick a day, and 'no' is not an option."

Jeff never liked to leave anything up in the air. I picked Wednesday.

"Perfect." He looked out the kitchen window. "When was the last time you cut the grass?"

"I don't know how to use a mower," I replied sheepishly.

He looked at me as if to say, *Typical girl.*

"What can I say?" I said. "I had older brothers, then a string of apartments, then a husband who actually loved doing it, the freak."

He laughed and looked at me in a moment of recognition; even I felt the split second of normality.

"Well, I'm sure he'd be freaking out if he saw his beautiful lawns in such condition. Geezus, you've probably got lions and tigers grazing back there and don't even know it."

"Oh, please—it's not *that* bad! I paid a neighborhood kid to do it about a month ago. Then again, maybe it was closer to six weeks..."

"Well, I'm gonna do the front now, and come back tomorrow to show you how to use the mower and help you with the back."

As he went out to the garage, the condition of the rest of the house suddenly came into sharp focus: dishes piled in the sink, leftover Chinese food cartons lining the counters, a mountain of laundry covering the washing machine, bed unmade, dust bunnies procreating in corners, and paper everywhere—books, magazines, newspapers, syllabi and handouts and student papers from the last two semesters, unfinished essays, you name it—atop just about every table and chair in the house.

What a freakin' mess.

While Jeff mowed the lawn, I triaged the kitchen counters and wiped them down. I then searched the fridge for something to serve him as a thank-you: a slice of leftover pizza, three eggs, half-empty jars of peanut butter and jelly, and frozen waffles. Lots of cookies, though.

About fifteen minutes later, he reentered the house without knocking, sweaty and covered with grass clippings stuck to his calves and ankles.

"Now I know why Sam liked moving the lawn," he said. "That machine is wicked awesome."

I couldn't help but smile; Sam was a stereotypical guy when it came to electronics and power tools.

"Yeah, he used to go on and on about it, but I never listened to him. The neighbors probably envied it, though."

"He was a lucky guy."

"Not lucky enough."

I could tell Jeff was as sorry for what he said as I was for what I'd said.

"So," I pressed on, "I still make a kick-ass PB and J. Go in and watch the rest of the game while I fix you one. Yanks are still up, bottom of the seventh."

"Thanks, but I should go before Patsy thinks I actually drove out to Fenway. Besides, the Sox are gonna lose. Rain check for tomorrow?"

"Suit yourself."

He helped himself to a glass of water, and turned the faucet on and off to inspect the washer. "Tell you what. I'll do a run-through of the house tomorrow and see if there's anything else that needs fixing."

"That would be great." I put my arms around him and hugged him tight. "Thanks," I said. "For everything."

"No problem," he replied, squeezing me. "It's long overdue." We let go and I dabbed my eyes. "You gotta start living again, kid. You and Sam were like a pair of gloves.

I've never seen a better couple. But you were also individuals, with lives of your own—that's what was so great. It's as if you buried that with him. You need to get that back."

"We'll see."

Jeff kissed me on the cheek. "See ya tomorrow."

A cheer erupted in the background, signaling yet another home run for the Yankees. He shook his head and cursed again, while I gave him a cocky smile as I closed the door behind him. It'd been a long time since I'd smiled like that, since I'd felt a man's presence around the house, since I'd looked forward to company. How grateful I was for Jeff. Best of all, the Yankees won that day.

CHAPTER
NINE

I'D BEEN UP UNCHARACTERISTICALLY EARLY— since seven thirty—cleaning the house. Jeff's visit had inspired me. He kept his word and showed up around eleven o'clock, attired almost exactly the same as the day before, this time a different Red Sox World Champions T-shirt. We went out to the garage where the mower was waiting, Jeff carrying an opaque container of gas for which I reimbursed him.

"Sam never showed you how to do this?" he asked.

"Oh, he showed me once, when he first got it. But I'm the type of person who needs to be shown something repeatedly. You know, I like my hand held for the first couple of tries."

"No wonder your students love you so much."

I grinned. "Anyway, I obviously wasn't as into it as he was, so we just kind of agreed that mowing the lawn wasn't going to be my thing. Actually, I offered to take out the garbage from then on in exchange."

"And did you honor that vow?"

"More or less, yeah."

He looked at me with mock envy. "The perfect marriage."

The mower was a beastly John Deere ride-on. New Englanders loved their ride-on mowers, even if they had a patch of grass no bigger than a blanket. Jeff showed me how to work it, cutting the first couple of lines in the backyard and then instructing me to get on and do one by myself. I felt like I was twelve and back in the go-carts at Action Park—the brakes went out on my cart and I slammed into another girl's cart in front of me. She got a gash in her foot, and her dad was actually nicer to me than my own was about the accident. *"Did you see what you did?"* my dad scolded. *"I told her I was sorry!"* I replied, shamefully pleading for mercy. *"Lay off; she didn't mean it,"* my brother Tony said. Tony always came to my rescue, even when I didn't want him to.

I hadn't had time to go food shopping, but Jeff was content with the peanut butter and jelly sandwich I made for him and a cold Sam Adams, which he brought with him. We sat outside on the back deck, admiring our collaborative grass-cutting accomplishment. I drank a Coke, also uncharacteristic of me.

"Have you thought about coming back to school?" he asked after taking a swig of beer.

I looked at him, incredulous. "You're serious?"

He nodded.

"I thought you were going to ban me for another semester."

He shook his head after taking another swig. "Actually, I'm having a meeting with Jerry next week to discuss otherwise."

Jerry Donnelly, the dean of the College of Humanities at NU, had always been one of my biggest fans, but I doubted that he'd grant Jeff's request to have me back so soon. Jerry was more politician than educator, and often made decisions based on reputation, how it made the college look. In an age of public screwups, my blunder was not so high profile; however, I'm sure the NU grapevine had done its work in terms of exaggerating, mutilating, and fictionalizing the actual account of the story. For all I knew, word on the NU street was that Professor Vanzant went apeshit and threatened her students with a knife while telling them to go fornicate themselves while watching porn.

"Good luck," I said.

"There were extenuating circumstances," he said, presenting the case as if I were the dean himself.

"I hope that's not your opening statement. 'There were' is so passive, a zonker."

"What good are you doing anyone by being out of commission? You're not an NBA player with shoe contracts who used an ethnic slur; you're a damn good teacher who made a mistake."

"You're right—I'm not an NBA player. I have an even more important job and leave a greater impression on young minds."

"It was a *mistake*, kid."

"It was more than a mistake. It was an injustice to those students."

"They'll get over it. If you were a naturally mean person, then I'd be less tolerant. And so would they. But geezus, Andi—Sam was gone, what, four months?"

"Five and a half." And two days, to be exact.

"That's not a long time. I think you gotta give yourself a break."

"How would they know I'm not a naturally mean person?"

"Take a look in the mirror," he said.

I stood up and took his plate and empty beer bottle.

"I don't know," I said, entering the house. He followed me.

"Are you afraid to come back?"

The words hit me in the stomach. Damn right I was afraid.

"I just don't know if I'm ready," I said.

"Why don't you talk to your shrink about it and I'll talk to Jerry, and we'll find out where everybody stands."

———

After he finished changing washers and tightening nuts and bolts and checking my fuse box, I walked Jeff to his car and hugged him as I did yesterday, thanking him.

"It was nice to have a man around the house the last couple of days, even if it was *you*," I said.

"You'd have preferred a male hooker instead?"

My jaw dropped and I gasped. *How did he find out?*

"What's that supposed to mean?" I asked, my voice wavering between defensiveness and concealment.

"Relax, kid—it's a joke. Geez, you look like you've just seen a ghost. I'm sorry. I didn't mean to offend you."

He knew nothing, I realized. But the fucking coincidence!

"It's too soon," I lied, immediately feeling guilty that I'd just used Sam's death to hide something that had nothing to do with him.

"I'm really sorry," he said again.

"Forget it," I said. "If you can't joke around with your friends, then who can you joke with? Besides, it's time for me to start moving on, don't you think?"

Jeff bid me good-bye and said he'd call following the meeting with Jerry. As he drove away, a shiver ran up my spine.

CHAPTER
TEN

I SAT IN MELODY'S OFFICE THE FOLLOWING WEEK listening to the soft, tinkling sound of her new rock fountain nestled in the corner. It was one of Sam's favorite sounds.

"I'm bored out of my skull," I complained. "I've read and reread all the books we own, watched every episode of every crap show on TV, and it's too damn hot to sit outside and feed the ducks."

Melody grinned in approval. "That's good. It means you're ready to stop living in a state of flux. So what now?"

The question stood before me like a black hole waiting to suck me into its eternal oblivion.

"Jeff asked me about coming back to school."

"He's your friend who runs the department, right?"

"Yes."

"How do you feel about it?"

I squirmed in my chair. "I don't know, Melody. Since I left in April, my assistant director, Jackie, who's been the interim director of the writing program during my absence, occasionally calls me with an administrative question. And for a split second, when I answer her I feel a charge of electricity, like the way it used to be."

"Do you miss it?"

"I guess I do. I mean, it's always been a lot of pressure, but it was something I used to thrive in. But this past semester, it just felt like I was buried under a pile of bricks the whole time. I'm afraid that if I go back that'll happen again, and I'll handle it even worse than I did before."

"What if you just go back to teaching, then?"

I took a sip of water from my Dasani bottle and glared at her.

"They won't let me go back into the classroom."

"How do you know that? You can't be the first teacher who's had an outburst."

"I called my students 'feckless crack babies hooked on Ritalin and porn.'"

Melody winced.

"Yeah," I acknowledged her gesture. "It's harsh. Unforgivable."

"It's not unforgivable. I don't think there's anything that's unforgivable. Isn't there something you can do? A formal apology?"

I shook my head. "No one's accountable for their actions anymore. I harp on my students all the time about responsibility, and taking the consequences of their actions. Say what you will about the guys involved in Watergate thirty-something years ago, but they all paid for their mistakes—most of them either wound up doing time or resigning. These days, if you fuck up you get a promotion, a commuted sentence, increased media coverage, and a book deal. You get 'Brownie, you're doing a heckuva job.'"

Melody cocked her head slightly to the side. "You don't think you've taken responsibility or accepted the consequences? You voluntarily left your position, yes? You offered to resign."

"I never should've gone back to begin with. I should've taken another semester's leave, like my friend Maggie and everyone else told me to do."

"It's futile to 'should' on yourself," she said.

"Whatever," I replied in an obstinate tone. "The point is that my behavior shouldn't—*ought* not to be rewarded with a finger-wagging 'don't do it again.'"

"I don't think it is. Everyone deserves a second chance. From what you've told me, this was an isolated incident. You don't have a history of incompetence or abuse. You've been an advocate of the student body. Even now—you're advocating on their behalf, considering *their* well-being by questioning your return. You're living up to your lessons of integrity by being the example. And let's not forget that you were under emotional duress."

"What, have you been talking to Jeff?"

"Andi, your husband was killed by a drunk driver."

As if I needed reminding.

"Let's not use Sam as the get-out-of-jail-free card," I said. "Let's not insult him like that."

"Aren't you already doing it? Isn't that your reason for sleeping in, for watching mindless television and rereading the books that the two of you used to read together? Isn't that your excuse for not moving on?"

Shit, man.

"I can't go back into the classroom, even if they let me," I said after a bout of silence.

"Why?"

"Because I *hate* them."

"Hate who?"

"All of them. Those *kids*."

I always resented teachers who called their students "kids."

"They bitch and moan and take no responsibility and get drunk every night and have no regard for anyone outside their calling circle or their Facebook page."

"It's not about them and you know it," said Melody. "It's about the one young man who made some despicable choices that night."

"Unforgivable choices," I added.

"You think he's unforgivable?"

"He'll never get my pardon." I took a swig of water so forceful it splashed.

"So be it," she said.

I looked at her, bewildered. I had expected her to advise me to make the effort to try.

"So, if going back to the university isn't an option, then what is? Have you ever considered doing something completely new and different?"

"Like what?" I asked.

"You tell me."

I gazed past her and fixed my stare on the new rock fountain.

"I can't think of anything."

"There must be something...when was the last time you saw your family?"

"Not since the funeral. I didn't go home for Christmas."

"Give them a call."

"My brothers are usually on the road. My mother..." I drew in a breath and exhaled a huff. "I can only take my mother in small doses."

I'd shared some of my experiences with my mother in previous sessions with Melody: her systematic destruction of my self-esteem during my adolescent years by criticizing my body; her lack of consolation every time I broke up with a boyfriend; her lack of affection (and affect) since my father's death.

"Things are different now, Andi. You may find that you and your mother have a lot more in common now. You both lost a spouse."

"I'd prefer that we both knitted or something."

She ignored the quip. "Think about it."

"My mother has always treated me as her rival rather than her daughter."

"And why is that?"

"I have no idea."

"Andi, think about it. You were born in the wake of the women's lib movement, and you had a father and mother who came from a male-dominated society."

"So?"

"So, think of what that must have been like for your parents. Here is their little girl, precocious and free. Your father wants no part of it. He wants to rein her in, keep her under his thumb. He probably wanted to do the same with your mother. But she was conflicted. She probably wanted to be the good wife and mother that she was instructed to be, but she probably also wanted to be the new, liberated woman that was screaming to get out. You weren't burdened with that choice. So rather than nurture you, she resented you. You took the path that she likely wanted for herself."

I listened to Melody, astounded.

"Your parents probably had no idea how to raise you. And your brothers got caught in the middle. They tried to protect you from both sides."

I sat there, dumbfounded. It was as if my entire life had suddenly come into focus, and it all made sense. As if I'd just been absolved of a crime for which I'd been convicted, even though I'd been innocent all along. And then I began to cry like a little girl.

Later that evening, after a dinner consisting of a grilled cheese sandwich, canned soup, and four handfuls of chocolate chips, I went into the living room. Second only to the kitchen, the living room had been the social center of the house. I remembered the first night Sam and I made out like horny adolescents on the floor in front of the fireplace, when he wanted to wait to have sex, the gentleman. And later, how many times we did make love on that very spot… Since his death, the space had become desolate, like so many other places in the house.

The last rays of sunlight formed beams across the floor and spotlighted the photographs sitting on the banquet table against the wall. I perused them like paintings at the galleries and museums I used to attend in New York, and stopped at one of our many wedding photos. There I stood between my brothers, who had reluctantly surrendered their ripped jeans and biker jackets that day in exchange for sleek, black tuxedos with white silk shirts and matching silk ties in Windsor knots. They were clean-shaven, their hair neatly groomed, as if they'd spent a day with the *Queer Eye* guys. They looked so handsome, pinup perfect for a couple of Italian musicians in their forties.

I'd practically worshiped my brothers while growing up. All my friends had crushes on them. Boys envied their guitars and talent and the fact that they got all the girls, while the girls gushed over their looks. They'd sheltered me to a fault. I know that now. But back then, I reveled in their overprotection and accepted it as a substitute for the love and attention I so desperately craved from my parents. Could it be that my parents had never wanted me?

I meandered into my home office and sat at my cluttered desk, digging through the top drawer in search of my address book. It bulged with Post-its and envelopes with return addresses circled and MapQuest directions to places that Sam had insisted I save. I opened it and flipped a couple of pages, then picked up the receiver of the vintage, push-button office phone, complete with extension lights at the bottom that still lit up when the phone rang.

Joey picked up on the second ring.

"Hey, Joey." My voice wavered; I had expected voice mail.

"Hey, And. Long time." He sounded happy to hear my voice. "Everything OK?"

"Yeah. You know. The usual." I decided to get right to it. "Whaddya think about coming out here for a visit? I need an excuse to finish cleaning my house."

"That'd be great! I haven't had a break in ages."

"I was thinking of inviting Tony, too. I mean, when was the last time the three of us got together without Mom or spouses?"

"Geez, I can't even remember." He paused for a few beats to mull it over. "I know Tone's got some gigs in Connecticut in the coming weeks. How about next month? I could meet him and then we could drive up together."

"That works. We could barbeque. That poor grill hasn't seen any action since Sam—" I stopped myself, "—since last summer."

Joey ignored the slip. "Let me call Tony and call you back. I gotta ask him about the MIDI files he sent me last week anyway."

"OK. Call me back even if you get his voice mail."

"OK."

Twenty minutes later, the phone rang. I was still sitting at the desk.

"It's all set," Joey said.

We finalized plans. "Bring the guitars," I said.

"You got it. This is gonna be fun," he said after a beat.

"Yeah. I'm looking forward to it."

"Mom is so gonna kill us when she finds out that we left her out."

"So don't tell her. See you soon."

When I hung up the phone, I glanced at the clock on the desk: 10:14 p.m.

"What the hell," I said out loud, and picked up the receiver again. I dialed Melody's office number. When her voice mail picked up, I spoke with a rather superior tone: "I'll have you know that I just made plans with my brothers for them to come visit me next month. At my house. So there." I hung up. Then I cleaned until midnight.

For the first time in ten months, I had something to look forward to. And for the first time in just as long, I smiled—albeit alone—in mere anticipation.

August

T HEY ARRIVED IN MID-AUGUST, GUITARS AND duffle bags in tow. I unexpectedly bawled like a baby when I saw them pull into the driveway, and practically knocked them over when I ran out to the car to hug them. But they were cool and let me get it out of my system. Neither of them said a word about my weight gain; then again, they had seen me yo-yo with my weight for most of my young life. In fact, the six years with Sam was the only time I'd maintained a decent weight—I'd looked and felt good. What's more, when I was with Sam, I didn't think about my body, didn't have the obsessive preoccupation that took up so much of my time and energy in the past. I'd accepted it as it was. Besides, *all bodies are beautiful...*

Joey and Tony and I spent most of our time in the kitchen or out on the deck, grilling. One evening, they took out their guitars and started playing all the old Beatles songs we used to sing as kids, in three-part harmony. By the fourth or fifth song, several of the neighbors, including the adolescents, had wandered into the yard or peered over the fence to watch the free show. One of them shouted a request: "You know any Dylan?"

Tony scowled but acquiesced, and the two of them did a flawless Bob Dylan impersonation of "Like a Rolling Stone" without the harmonica part. After that, requests came left and right. And after all the applause and invitations to play at future parties, we looked at each other and knew we were done sharing ourselves with them. My brothers said thanks, packed up, and went into the house, much to the crowd's disappointment. "What a treat," I heard an older woman, who lived two doors down, say. It wasn't until well after midnight, when I lay awake in my bed, Sam's absence omnipresent, that I realized that during the entire jam session, I'd enjoyed myself so much that I'd forgotten to miss him for the first time. The revelation resulted in a mix of accomplishment and guilt.

Best of all was how much I *laughed* that week. And although there was always a hint of sadness looming in the air, like a cloud of dust, I felt a sense of comfort amid that cloud. For the first time since Sam's death, our house felt like *home* to me, the empty bed notwithstanding.

On our last evening together, the three of us sat out on the deck, Joey and Tony drinking Sam Adams while I drank birch beer, the citronella candles casting soft orange glows on our faces and protecting us from the nasty New England mosquitoes. The night air was chilly, and the salty scent of the distant sea wafted occasionally with the breeze.

"Do you guys remember Dad dying?" I asked.

They looked at each other, then back at me, a little wary of indulging me in a heavy topic of conversation, one that could put a damper on the entire week.

"Sure," they said.

"What do you remember most?"

"The suddenness of it," Joey said. "It was out of the blue."

"Me too," said Tony. "I just remember being in shock."

"Do you remember grieving it? Because I don't remember grieving it."

"Actually, I don't remember a lot of that time," Joey said. "But a few years ago, I dug out some songs that I wrote back then. They were all really sad. I must've taken it out on the music."

"Oh, I definitely channeled into the music," said Tony. "I played so much blues back then. It was the only way to get it out. Mom wouldn't talk about it. At least not with us."

"Yeah, Mom was just so out of it," said Joey.

I looked out at the bench swing in the yard, seeing Sam and me sitting on it during summer nights, clasped hands in each other's laps, saying nothing and looking at the sky, rocking rhythmically. The image then morphed into me at thirteen years old:

I come home from school to find both Joey and Tony sitting on the couch in the living room, which we only use for company. Quiet. Pale as ghosts.

"Whose car is in the driveway?" I ask.

"Aunt Jane's," either Tony or Joey says.

"Why is Aunt Jane here?" Every fiber of my being already knows that the answer is not something I want to hear.

"Dad had a heart attack at work today."

"Where is he?"

"He's, um..."

"Where's Mom?"

"Upstairs with Aunt Jane."
He's dead. I know it.

I couldn't remember who first said the words. I couldn't remember the funeral, other than the sea of black—strange, that was just about all I remembered of Sam's funeral. That and the crappy eulogy, of course. But who eulogized my father?

"They were our age, weren't they," I said as I came out of my reverie. "I mean, as old as we are now."

My brothers did the math between them. "He had to be in his mid-forties, I guess. Mom's a couple years younger," said Joey. He then added, "Wow," at the realization.

Yeah. Wow.

"My God, he was just a couple of years older than Sam. I never realized how young he was. To die of a heart attack, especially."

And Mom was my age—she was me.

"He had hypertension that he ignored. Probably saw it as a sign of weakness if he couldn't suck it up. He was stubborn that way," said Tony.

"But don't you think that's the type of thing we should talk about? Especially if it's genetic. You guys see a doctor regularly, don't you?" I asked.

"You doin' OK, And?" asked Joey. "In general, I mean."

"Yeah, I guess so. I'm seeing a therapist, and my friend Jeff is trying to get me to go back to school—he's the department chair." I paused. "It'll be a year, soon."

"Hard to believe."

I took a swig of birch beer. "You're tellin' me."

We sat quietly and looked up at the stars.

"Do you think Mom and Dad wanted me?"

They both looked at me in shock and spoke at the same time. "How could you even think such a thing? Of course they did!"

"They treated you both differently," I said. "Don't pretend you never noticed. You've protected me—and them—long enough."

"You may have been a surprise," said Tony. "I really don't know. But you know how they were raised. They didn't talk about things like that. They loved you, Andi. I think you just…I don't know. You were the only girl, and you had a fire in your eyes when you were really little. I think it scared them. Where they came from, a fire like that spelled trouble later on in life. They just went too far to keep you safe."

I nodded my head. Just like what Melody had said.

"Then why did it feel like love from you but oppression from them? You guys at least hugged me and let me tag along with you."

"How could we not?" said Joey. "You were so cute. But we wanted to keep you safe, too. You were our precious jewel. I know that's all sexist now, but we just didn't want anyone to hurt you. And neither did Mom and Dad. They just fucked it all up the way parents do."

I couldn't help but laugh, my brothers joining me.

"How's that for therapy?" said Joey.

"I wouldn't put it on a fortune cookie," I said. With that, my brothers picked up their guitars again and broke out into the Beatles' "Oh Darlin'." I swooned, tears streaming down my cheeks.

***

They left the next day. We held each other, in tears, and I begged them not to go. I felt like a child seeking their brotherly protection from the big bad world all over again. It'd been ages since they'd had their little sister all to themselves, they said. We exchanged genuine I-love-yous, and as they drove away, I reentered the empty house, restored to its former state of sullen silence. I'd become so used to that hollow feeling before they'd arrived that I never even noticed it. But now that they were gone, it physically hurt. I took the leftover pizza crusts, crushed them in a plastic bag, and headed to the lake at Edmund College to feed the ducks, who were grateful for the bounty but oblivious to me sitting on the bench, mourning for what I'd lost as well as what I'd never had.

A few days later, Jeff called to tell me that everything was "squared away" with the dean. "You'll take unpaid course waivers and focus solely on directing the freshman writing program. And you'll have one performance evaluation. Come January we'll check in again. Fair enough?"

"Are you sure?"

"The dean's behind you all the way. So is most of the department, with the exception of the usual grotesques. Face it, kid: we can't live without you."

I hesitated. "I don't know…"

"Kid, I'm not gonna let you do any damage to yourself or anyone else. I promise. Mainly 'cause Jerry'll beat the shit out of me if you do."

I smiled; he suddenly reminded me of my brothers.

"I thought you said he was behind me all the way," I said.

"He was after I suggested the unpaid waivers. Besides, if Jerry can't at least *threaten* to beat the shit out of me, then he starts moping around and brings in his banjo."

"Eek," I shuddered at the thought. I'd heard Jerry Donnelly play the banjo. "OK," I said in a surprisingly confident voice. "See you the day after Labor Day."

"I can't wait, kid. Welcome back."

October

L IFE MOVED AGAIN.
When I returned to school, I found myself
refreshed—the workload no longer felt like a heavy blanket trying to suffocate my grief, but rather was like a sieve
that I could pour myself into and strain out the unwanted
muck. What's more, if Jeff's visit that day of the Yankee
game was the crack in the wall, then my brothers' visit
broke the floodgates open. They had awakened my craving
for *company*. I started spending more time with Miranda,
and Jeff and Patsy had me over every other week. Heck, I
even made dinner for them at my place one day. I had to
take away the chair where Sam would've sat—seeing the
empty seat was too much for me.

Still, I couldn't shake the feeling of living in someone
else's skin, or on a backwards planet. Anything but an
ordinary world.

I saw Melody twice during the week of the anniversary of Sam's death, which was also our sixth wedding
anniversary.

"So, it's been a year," she said.

"Yeah," I replied. You'd think she said "nice day."

"How does it feel?"

"Well, considering that I went through it in a semiconscious stupor, it doesn't really feel like anything special."

She let out a cynical laugh. "Were you always this sarcastic?"

"I used to be. Actually, I was just uptight."

"When?"

"Awhile ago. Before I met Sam."

"What softened you up? Or who? Was it Sam?"

"No. It was New York, of all things. And Devin."

"Who?" she asked.

"This guy I knew when I lived in New York."

A flood of memories suddenly washed over me: Versace suits. Sienna eyes. Vibrators.

"Were you dating him?"

"Sort of. It was a complicated relationship." I paused and looked at the poster of a coastal beach with a sunset on the wall behind her. "Wow…Devin. I haven't thought about him in ages."

"Tell me about him."

"Well, when I met him, he was an escort. He knew a lot of the women that I worked with, if you get my drift. We sort of had an arrangement. I shared my expertise in writing, and he shared his expertise in sex. He was an unusual escort in that he didn't actually go all the way with his clients."

I felt silly saying the last part—it sounded so junior high.

She looked surprised. "Why didn't he go all the way?"

I shrugged. "Don't know. And yet, that didn't seem to bother any of them. He was very popular."

"What made you form this arrangement? Did he come to you, or did you seek him out?"

"I called him."

"You thought you didn't know enough about sex?"

"I thought I didn't know anything about sex."

"Why?" she asked.

I paused for a minute, trying to decide whether I really wanted to go back to this place. Sure, Melody was my therapist, but my old, self-conscious behaviors kicked in and I worried what kind of nutcase she would think I was if I told her the truth.

"Well, I was inexperienced," I answered.

"In what way?"

"In the way that I'd never technically had intercourse with anyone until Devin."

Melody's eyes widened. That was enough to get me to pull my knees to my chest and curl up in the chair in attempt to get lost somewhere in it.

"Was that a choice you made?"

"To not have sex, you mean?"

She nodded.

I shrugged my shoulders. "Do we really have to talk about this?"

"Why do you feel uncomfortable?"

"Funny, Devin used to push my buttons like this. He was determined to make me less inhibited, less self-conscious. And he succeeded, too. Or, I succeeded. I don't know. Anyway, when I met Sam, I wasn't so worried about it anymore, and we had a *fabulous* sex life."

"Whatever became of Devin?"

"His name is David, actually. Devin was his escort name. He left the business, moved to Boston, and bought an art gallery. He was a real art buff. Talented, too. The guy could make you look at Picasso in ways Picasso never saw it."

"Did you keep in touch?" she asked.

"Sam and I went to one of his gallery shows—I mean, I didn't know Devin was going to be there. That was a total shock. We met for coffee a couple of weeks later, and that was that. This was all years ago. Sam and I weren't even married yet. But I would occasionally look for him on the T or the streets whenever we went to Boston. We never went back to his gallery, either. I don't know why. Sam didn't know anything about the nature of my relationship with Devin."

"You never told him?"

"Not exactly. I mean, I never gave him specifics. He never put Devin and David together as the same person."

"Why didn't you tell him?"

"Didn't seem to be a need to."

Melody contemplated this. I expected her to push me on the subject, the way Maggie had countless times. *I can't believe you've never told him! What if he finds out? Things like that can wreck a marriage, you know,* Maggie would say.

"What good comes out of it?" I would shout back.

Instead, Melody asked, "Why didn't you and Devin keep in touch?"

"Like I said, it was a complicated relationship. I had feelings for him, and then he had feelings for me…it never quite clicked, I guess."

Melody looked down at her pad. I wasn't sure if she'd written anything. She looked back at me while I took a sip of water. Silence filled the room.

"When was the last time you and Sam had sex?"

The question took me by surprise, but in an instant my mind raced with thoughts about Sam's and my sex life. It was like great jazz, the way our bodies were in perfect syncopation, the way we knew and improvised and explored each other with our lips and fingers, the way we so thoroughly lost ourselves in our lovemaking, be it through bouts of heavy breathing or moaning, or giggles and laughter when we were especially playful. It was hard to believe that I had gone so long prior to knowing him without having known such pleasure, that I'd been so afraid. Then again, maybe I had just simply been waiting all along for Sam, even though Devin was my first.

Never in my wildest dreams had I imagined that sex could be like this, or that *I* could be so free, so uninhibited, so secure with my lover, my best friend, my Sam.

I'd occasionally wondered how much Devin had to do with this, or whether it was Sam's doing simply because he was just so good in bed, so caring and accepting and wanting and respectful and appreciative of my body and me. God, how my body hungered and ached to feel his heat, his firmness, his hands and lips and body intertwined with mine…

I wiped my mouth with my hand, feeling a hot flash followed by a punch in my gut.

"You wanna hear something really stupid?" I asked. "We decided not to do it for almost a week, to wait until our anniversary celebration night. We thought it'd be fun to get so horny and frustrated that we wouldn't be able to keep our hands off each other and would just ravish each other that night. It was working, too. I was so ready to jump his bones—forget dinner and the damn cider.

We were gonna do it all night and then play hooky the next day. Do you know how pissed off I am that we did that? Do you know how idiotic I feel?"

"How could you have known?" she asked.

"That's just the thing—how does anyone know?" I looked away, wistful. "It's such a cliché, but we take life so for granted."

"Have you had any kind of sexual stimulation since?"

"Are you kidding? I haven't had any kind of stimulation, period. I'm a blob. I eat Malomars at nine p.m. and watch TV all day and surf the Net occasionally. I've all but stopped reading and writing."

I paused for a moment in reverie, my breath seemingly stuck in my throat, before uttering, "Sex with Sam was fucking fabulous," more to myself than Melody, who seemed to ignore this utterance and asked her next question.

"You don't masturbate?"

There was a time when the word *masturbate* would've made me want to crawl under the chair in which I was sitting.

I shook my head. "Too much work. Besides, I don't want to be touched."

"Because if you did, then you'll have to feel. And you don't want to feel anything, do you," she said.

Bull's-eye. The truth smacked me right in the middle of my chest like a poison arrow.

I nodded slowly, my eyes watering. Again, silence filled the room, and this time it entered my gut and squeezed tight.

Say something.

"So, Andi. You made it through this week. You made it through a year since Sam's death and your wedding anniversary and you're still here."

"Barely," I said.

"But that's your choice. Tell me: if Sam hadn't gone out for that sparkling cider, if that car hadn't hit him, what would you have done? What did you have planned for your sixth year of marriage? Surely you must have thought about it. What possibilities had entered your life?"

I pondered the question.

"Sam wanted to start traveling. He wanted to start writing novels, too. He was feeling burnt out with both nonfiction and comp, I think. He seemed restless. He put in a request for a sabbatical."

"That's what Sam wanted. I asked what *you* wanted."

I sat and stared at nothingness. I honestly couldn't remember.

"I don't know," I finally said.

"You didn't have any goals, any plans?"

"I was content. Everything in my life was good. I had tenure, money in the bank, publications, a home, friends, a cat, and a man I loved who loved me back. What more did I need?"

"Well, start thinking about it now. What do you want to do?"

"I want to get the last year of my life and my husband back."

"You can't. So what else is there to do?"

"Wait for the next year, I guess."

"If that's all you want, then so be it. But I'm not going to enable your inertia in the meantime. And if you don't want anything for yourself, then why don't you do Sam the honor of fulfilling the things *he* wanted to do. Because no doubt he was including you in his plans."

I felt myself get hot, humiliated in a way.

"Are we done?" I asked.

Melody looked at her watch. "We are." She stood up and opened her arms to give me a hug. We usually ended the session with a hug. "Happy anniversary," she said. I fought the urge to cry, and lost. I could feel the warmth of her hug this time.

CHAPTER

THIRTEEN

---

*S*EX *WITH SAM WAS FUCKING FABULOUS.*

Sex with Sam was fucking fabulous because Sam was fabulous.

I always wanted to draw him, or have a portrait made of him that would capture the contours of his cheekbones, the soft turn of his lips, the light lines of crow's feet that appeared whenever he smiled. And he smiled a lot. He was one of those guys whose little bit of gray hair made him look distinguished, mature, well-read, and well-lived. He was fit and active and loved being a New Englander. And he had the bluest eyes of any man I'd ever known. Ocean blue. Blue as the Long Island Sound on a summer's day. Blue as Buzzards Bay. I could've drowned in the depth of those blue eyes.

He made me horny as hell when he read to me. And he made me laugh constantly.

But Sam's perfection was in his willingness to embrace his own flaws. I think the reason why he was such a great teacher was because he allowed people to see his flaws as well as his virtues—in fact, to him, a flaw was just as much an attribute to writing as was talent. He shared my concept of revision as embracing the possibilities that live within the flaws. His humanity came out on every page that he wrote and shared with his students, and his students loved him for it—he was "real" to them.

I reread the eulogy. I'd have to delete "fucking" despite its alliterative appeal and ability to function as both an adjective and a verb in this particular context. Couldn't say it in a church, though. And how appropriate was it to talk about my sex life? There was no way I could talk about that in front of my brothers or my mother. There was also no way I could say "horny." Hell, thank God my father wasn't alive to hear me use such words. My father could never tolerate such profanity, especially when uttered in public in front of his wife and/or children. It wasn't even a matter of tolerance, now that I think about it—he was practically phobic. Never mind that my brothers heard—and said— a lot worse in the dives where they played or basements where they practiced. Never mind what I heard on the school bus. I, on the other hand, found profanity to be delightfully versatile rather than plebeian. So did Sam. It appealed to our inner wordsmiths, lovers of language and form. *"There's an expletive for every occasion,"* he used to say. He would love its use in his eulogy, no doubt. He loved what he called "juxtapositions of texture," a phrase he stole from a Mel Brooks interview. Whereas Brooks did it with image and music on film, Sam did it with words and contexts. "Horny" and "church" were juxtapositions of texture, he would think. He'd be stifling his laughter were he actually listening to that eulogy. Hell, he might have written it himself: *My wife would get horny if I read the fucking telephone book to her...*

ELISA LORELLO

I e-mailed this latest version of the eulogy to Maggie and then looked at the time. Seven thirty p.m. An eternity before bedtime. Time passed so slowly in a state of grief. There was so much of it. Where was all this time when our loved ones were alive?

Nothing to do. Nothing to watch. Nothing to read. Nothing to write. Nothing to say. Donny Most nestled himself in the corner of the old sofa in the study. I flopped next to him, and he looked up from his nap for a moment, as if contemplating whether to crawl on my lap and snuggle with me tonight. We had become each other's consolation buddies. He decided against it and rested his orange head back down on his white paw, closing his eyes again. Oh, to be a cat. They slept away the days in wonderful contentment without anyone criticizing them for wasting their lives.

I wandered around the drafty house. The cool, New England autumn wind whistled and rattled the old storm windows. The foliage had peaked early this year. Sam and I had both wanted an autumn wedding. Last year's dead leaves still covered parts of the backyard.

I entered our bedroom and stared at the deserted, unmade bed.

Sex with Sam was fabulous.

Devin. David.

What had become of him? I wondered. What would he think if he saw me now?

I went to the closet and opened the door to look at myself in the full-length mirror. Sam's Edmund College hoodie, my size twelve jeans, and a pair of his thick socks covered the layers of flesh that had returned to my body

88

after a six-year hiatus. *I was this heavy when I met Devin*, I thought. *Maybe heavier.* Despite Devin's assertion that all body types were beautiful, I thought that if he saw me today, he'd scowl.

Geez, Andi. You really let yourself go. What a shame. Who'd wanna sleep with you looking like that?

My husband died, Dev, I'd say.

So? What kind of excuse is that?

"When was the last time you had sex?" I heard Melody ask.

I padded across the room to my dresser and opened the top drawer, where I kept my lingerie. It all sat neatly folded, waiting for me to fit into it, to be sexy and desirous again. Off to the side and at the back of the drawer, an old gift box with a frayed ribbon around it sat hidden. My vibrator. The one Devin had given me. I hadn't used it in ages. Since before I got married. Didn't need it once I left New York. Its leopard-skin exterior had faded. I wondered if the batteries still worked, if there were batteries still in it.

As I picked up the box, a pink envelope appeared.

What's this?

My name was on it, in Sam's handwriting. I opened it to find one of his handmade greeting cards.

Happy Fifth Anniversary. You know what that means... said the outside of the card in bold, colored type. I opened it and a second, smaller envelope fell out. I put it to the side and read the card. **...Time to hit up our friends for more gifts!**

My laugh pierced the silence.

I opened the other envelope and found airline tickets and a note.

Andrea, amore mio,

> *Time to be adventurous and indulge in the pleasures of the world. First stop: Rome.*
>
> *I love you more than mere words will ever describe.*

Buon Anniversario,

Sam

The tickets were for the week of spring break this past year. So, *this* was his surprise for our anniversary! A trip to Rome! I had completely forgotten! And it was right under my nose (or my vibrator) all this time! How could I have not seen it? That clever, stupid, rat-bastard!

I laughed hard, and then I backed up and fell on the bed, weeping.

CHAPTER FOURTEEN

"GO!" MAGGIE EXCLAIMED THE NEXT DAY when I called and told her about the hidden treasure.

"I can't."

"Why not?"

"Because the tickets were for seven months ago."

"So? They're probably refundable or transferable. Tell them what happened. They'll probably feel sorry for you."

"Who would I go with?"

"Yourself!"

"I can't go to Italy by myself," I protested.

"Why not?"

"I'm afraid to fly."

"Take a Dramamine or a Xanax."

"I don't know how to speak Italian."

"Isn't your cousin an Italian teacher? Call him. Or call that guy you told me about in the foreign language department, the one who always shows up at the foreign film festivals and NPR pledge drives at school. You know, the one that you once said was cute and wanted to hook me up with?"

"Piero?"

"Yeah!"

"What about the house and the cat?"

"Dammit, Andi!" Maggie yelled. I looked at the phone, taken aback. Maggie never yelled at anyone. She didn't like confrontation, especially if she was the initiator.

"Mags—"

"Stop it! Just stop it! You're being a victim. The problem with grief is that it's so self-absorbing. You act like you're the only innocent one, like it's only ever happened to you. You think you're the only one who got screwed? What happened to the woman I knew in New York? You used to ride the subway at midnight after a movie and coffee with Devin. Remember him? Remember that? Remember how you used to be?"

I found it coincidental that she brought up Devin before I had a chance to tell her about my conversation with Melody.

"That was a long time ago. And that wasn't exactly me, either. I was faking it—remember *that*?"

"You weren't faking all of it. Certainly not these last six years. Listen to me. Don't disappear. Look at *me*, Andi. I thought I'd never get over losing James. And you wanna talk about a senseless death? Leukemia is senseless. Leukemia at age thirty is incredibly senseless. Why do you think it took me so long to get back into the dating game? And trust me, every day I wish I could get back all that lost time. *Every day*. So just stop it."

"What, you're telling me to start dating?"

"I'm telling you to start doing *something*. And stop sending me revisions of that damn eulogy. Going back to work was a step in the right direction, but you're still living unconsciously. Wake up. This is not what Sam would want."

I got angry. "I hate that. I hate when people presume to know what Sam would want," I snapped.

"Fine, then. It's not what *I* want. It's not what your students want. It's not what your friends and family want. It's not what Rhetoric and Composition wants. We *need* you. Please," she cried.

I paused for a long beat. "I'll think about it," I said, and hung up moments later.

"She doesn't understand," I said aloud, and immediately felt ashamed of myself for even thinking such a thing, much less saying it. Maybe she was right about self-absorption. I felt ugly at that moment.

Melody agreed with Mags all the way. Maggie even called the travel agency herself and explained the situation. They said they would transfer the tickets to any date I wanted. Miranda offered to house-sit and look after Donny Most. I rebooked the trip for the week of spring break next semester.

Sometimes I even found myself looking forward to it.

Five Months Later
March–Spring Break

I'D SPENT THE LAST FOUR MONTHS TRYING TO learn conversational Italian without much luck; all my intermediate Spanish from my college days kept creeping in. Piero let me sit in on his Italian 101 class whenever I wanted. He had a glorious accent, which, I noticed, distracted many of his female students and one of the males who was gay. They all swooned while he conjugated verbs pertaining to dining out. ("What can I bring you?" "Do you have any wine?" "I want to eat spaghetti and meatballs.") He was also very handsome and looked a little like Hugh Jackman with jet-black hair. One day, to my surprise, I caught myself thinking about him conjugating verbs with his shirt off.

I decided it was imperative to learn some key phrases: "Where's the bathroom?" "Where can I buy bottled water?" "No wine, please—it makes me ill." "I am trying to find my hotel, Ecco Roma." And "On behalf of my country, I apologize for Starbucks."

Miranda told me to buy cheap cotton underwear and throw them out every day so I wouldn't have to worry about going through customs with a suitcase full of dirty panties on the way home. I packed all of my jeans and Sam's shirts and sweaters and his aviator jacket—I had taken to wearing his clothes on a regular basis. It killed me to have to wash them; I didn't want to lose the smell of him. Buy shoes once you're there, Miranda said. Shoes and a leather jacket.

Melody tried to ease my mind about flying, with no success. The farthest I had ever flown was to San Francisco for a conference, and that was three years ago. I nearly hyperventilated when the plane hit some turbulence. Even Sam's holding my hand and steady voice were not enough to comfort me. Since then, I insisted on attending conferences via train if the driving distance was too far. For our honeymoon, Sam and I had driven up to Canada. On the way home, we were ready to kill each other. Funny, I had forgotten about that. Fourteen hours in the car was enough for both of us to seriously consider getting an annulment.

Melody gave me a mediation CD, a homeopathic remedy, and mantras to silently recite on the plane. I bought two packs of Dramamine, two packs of gum, and downloaded all of my Nat King Cole CDs, Italian language tutorials, and the meditation into my iPod. I also wrote my will on my laptop, but didn't get it notarized. At first, in a bout of silliness, I left everything to the cat. Then I left it all to my mother with instructions to let her sort it out.

Miranda drove me to Logan Airport. Piero accompanied us and gave me a list of places to go as well as a couple of letters to deliver for him. He also kissed me on both cheeks, which, again to my surprise, sent a quick flash of heat up my spine. Miranda hugged me. Maggie had called the night before to wish me well.

"I wish you were going with me," I practically whimpered.

"You'll be fine. You need to do this on your own."

I took two Dramamine thirty minutes before my flight was called. As I walked through the corridor to the plane, my knees weakened with panic. Just as I stepped onto the plane, I froze.

"Are you OK, miss?" the flight attendant asked. He was an effeminate man named Stefano. "My goodness, you're white as a sheet."

"Oh God, I can't do this," I said. *I'm going to pass out, I just know it.* I wasn't sure if I said this aloud or not.

"First time flying?" he asked.

"Might as well be."

Stefano took me by the arm and led me to first class and another flight attendant. Apparently Sam had pulled out all the stops when he booked the original trip—first class all the way. (The travel agency told me where he had booked our hotel stay, and my cousin, the Italian teacher, called to explain the situation. The hotel manager was so moved by the story that he not only rebooked the reservation, but comped four out of the seven days—*una storia d'amore*—a love story, he said.) The other attendant was a woman named Judy. Stefano told her I needed "extra care." She asked me if I wanted a drink. God, how I wished I drank at that moment.

"No thanks, but if you could get someone to hit me with a blunt object, I would appreciate it."

She called me "honey" and assured me that I'd be OK. I took out my iPod and listened to the meditation that Melody gave me.

I am at peace with the plane…I am at peace with the plane…I am at peace with the plane…

Bullshit…Bullshit…Bullshit…

I completely trust the flow of the universe…I completely trust the flow of the universe…I completely trust the flow of the universe…

I want to see the pilot's credentials…I want to see the pilot's credentials…I want to see the pilot's credentials…

The engines revved.

I took out Sam's picture, one of him outside of Fenway Park, before a Yankees–Red Sox game. The Sox had lost that day. He was much happier in the picture than he was after the game. He sported a devilish grin underneath his faded blue, well-worn Boston cap. I could almost hear him speak to me now: "Don't worry, sweetheart. I'll land the plane if anything goes wrong. I've watched sitcoms—it's easy." His grin comforted me.

As the plane took off, I made the passenger sitting next to me hold my hand until he assured me that we were safe and politely mentioned that he wanted to read his book. Apparently he'd had enough of Crazy Lady and her vise grip. Stefano promised that either he or Judy would check on me regularly, which they did. The movie was a Tom Hanks film—not *Cast Away*, thank God. When the meal was served, I tried to eat. Then I took a second dose of Dramamine and managed to fall asleep with an Italian language tutorial crooning to me on my iPod. *Mi chiamo Giovanni. Di dove sei?…* My name is Giovanni. Where are you from?

By landing time, Stefano and another passenger sat on either side of me, holding my hands. When I exited the plane, the same knee-weakening feeling overcame me.

"You're going to be fine, honey," said Judy.

"Don't drink the water unless it's bottled," said Stefano.

"Gucci," said the passenger. "Buy Gucci."

A driver who spoke broken English met me and took me to my hotel—Sam really had thought of everything. I took a deep, brave breath and stepped out of the airport and onto the bright, sunny streets of Rome. If only he had thought to live long enough to be here with me.

Days One and Two in Italy

*B*ELLISSIMA.

Everything—and I mean *everything*—in Italy is *bellissima*. Beautiful. The people. The cars. The flowers. The fountains. The streets. The hotels. The food. Everything.

Men looked at me and greeted me with *"Bellissima!"* (And this was me wearing no makeup, oversized sweat-shirts, jeans, and Keds.) Venders pointed to their merchandise and said, *"Bellissima,* no?" A child pointed to a pigeon pecking at seed by a fountain and exclaimed, "Mama! *Bellissima!"*

I wished Sam had booked a tour, but I know why he didn't—he would've felt rushed if he was being told when to get on and off the bus, how much free time we had, what to look at on our right, our left, above us, et cetera. We were similar in that nature—we wanted enough structure and routine to keep us grounded, but enough independence to do as we pleased. But recently, with time a boulder too heavy for me to move, my every waking minute on a schedule would've been a good thing for me, especially since I didn't know anyone and could barely speak the language.

On the day I arrived, I settled in at the hotel with registration, unpacking, adjusting to the time change, and figuring out how the plumbing and phones worked. Everything in Italy looked so organic, as if the buildings had grown out of the earth as opposed to being built—modern technology like Wi-Fi seemed to stick out like a sore thumb.

Jet lag caught up to me quickly, and I slept for hours. The anxiety from my flight had taken the rest of my energy.

The next day, I set out for my first destination: a museum. The Museo Nazionale Etrusco, to be exact. A map and my Italian-English dictionary in hand, I walked the streets and hailed a cab and tried to absorb every sight and smell and sound—hard to do when you've been living your life by making a conscious effort to be numb. Everything smelled like a combination of freshly baked bread (except, of course, when I passed a flower stand) and bus fumes to me. The museum was glorious; the architecture of the Villa Giulia alone was awesome. God, how I wished Sam were with me. I saw a sculpture that had been on loan to the Metropolitan Museum of Art years ago for an exhibit that I had seen with Devin. He had been very good at explaining the Italian artists, in particular the Renaissance painters and their use of light and tone. I knew enough to know that this sculpture was definitely not from the Renaissance.

During siesta, I took a bus to one of the piazzas, sat on the steps, and people-watched, thinking, hoping that maybe Sam would appear in a fisherman sweater and blue jeans and his Red Sox cap. He'd just walk up to me, as if the last year had never happened, and say, "Hey, sweetheart."

Then he'd take out a little box with an anniversary band in it, just like those diamond commercials on TV. And we'd kiss and everyone would applaud our love...

God, how pathetic could I get?

After siesta, I looked through my tour book for other sights but stayed within the vicinity of my hotel and window-shopped, feeling lonelier by the second.

By evening, I went back to my room, watched a little bit of television to help me with the language, and wrote in my journal. I couldn't get through two sentences without including a reference to Sam. I completed the entry, but then, after a moment's thought, added a declarative sentence in block caps.

I NEED TO GET LAID.

I underlined it twice. Then I said it out loud.

"*Buona notte, amore,*" I said to Sam's picture, which I had placed on the bedside table closest to me. I turned out the light and stared at the stucco ceiling. I actually heard an accordion in the distance.

The next day, I went to a café and wrote in my journal again. This time I attempted a list of anniversary goals, as I had been promising Melody I would do. "Stop eating crap" was the most ambitious I was willing to get for the moment. I also went window-shopping and looked at Italian fashion. The shoes were to die for. I didn't dare try anything on. Later in the day, I got blisters on the soles of my feet while trying to find another museum that Piero had recommended. My water bottle empty, map in disarray, and Italian-English book stuck at the bottom of my backpack, a cool panic began to settle into my stomach. I was completely lost. Plus, I needed a bathroom.

"*Perdona mi, donde es al bagno?*" I asked a friendly look-ing woman, realizing too late that I asked part of the question in Spanish. The woman could've easily taken me for one of those students backpacking across Europe on five dollars a day were it not for the strands of gray hair sticking to and framing my face. However, she smiled in comprehension and gave me directions, speaking slowly and enunciating as if speaking to a child.

"*Grazie,*" I said.

"Are you OK?" she asked in a heavy accent.

My backpack felt like a ton of bricks. My feet were kill-ing me. I was hot and sweaty and dehydrated and hungry and lost in a foreign city and my husband was dead.

"*Si, si. Grazie,*" I said.

Then I changed my mind. "*No, no. Cerco l'albergo, Ecco Roma?*" I said slowly.

"Ahhh," she said. She started to rattle off directions, speaking much more rapidly, but I put my hand up.

"*Un momento, un momento.*" I beckoned, using an inflec-tion that suddenly reminded me of my grandmother. "I *really* need to use the bathroom."

She offered to wait. I turned the corner, trying to remember her directions, and found two doors opposite each other. Each was marked in faded letters, but I couldn't make out the words. I opened the one on the left and walked in, mortified to find a row of urinals and a man standing in front of one. You'd think that growing up with two brothers, I would've walked in on one of them at least once, but no. I'd never even seen actual urinals. I gasped and apologized in English, but in the nanosecond before I turned away, I caught a glimpse of the man who snapped his head around, holding his fly in panic. And then I gasped again.

"Oh my God—Devin!"

"Andi?"

"What are you doing here?"

"What are *you* doing here?"

"I'm lost."

"I'll say."

I ran out of the bathroom. He called out, "Wait!" I heard the tap of running water. Seconds later, Devin rushed out, drying his hands on his shirt. He looked at me, slightly out of breath, and smiled.

"Andi!" He just stood there and gawked at me. "I can't believe it!"

I didn't know what to say or do.

"Devin," I said.

"David," he corrected.

"I'm sorry—*David*."

I shook my head to snap myself out of my daze. Neither of us moved. Then he hugged me, and I stiffened. He let go and gave me another once-over; the expression on his face turned from one of delight to slight confusion.

"Nice outfit," he said with uncertainty. I looked down at my apparel of jeans and Sam's Patriots football jersey, and my face turned the same red as the logo. "You couldn't find a soccer jersey that fit, at least?"

At that moment, the woman who offered to give me directions approached us. When she saw Devin—David—she said, "Ah, you find you lover," in broken English. He smiled at her, flashing those alluring sienna eyes and winking. She transformed into a teenager, twinkling her eyes and batting her lashes in return. It never ceased to amaze me to see the effect he had on women, that all it took was one coy little wink. He said something to her in fluent Italian, and she turned and left, wishing me a good evening. I thanked her one last time.

He turned to me. "You lost?"

"Yeah."

"Where are you staying?"

I told him.

"Ah, I know where that is. C'mon, I'll take you. You're not that far off, actually."

Dusk quickly set in as we walked through the streets together.

"Where's your husband?" he asked.

I couldn't open my mouth, just looked straight ahead and kept walking.

"Andi?" he asked.

"He's not here," I managed to spit out.

"OK," he said. He didn't say anything else.

Devin—David—was right; we were very close to the hotel. He walked me in and up to my room, like a gentleman.

"Well, here you are," he said.

"Where are *you* staying?" I asked.

"I'm at the Ritz of Rome."

I widened my eyes. "Wow." I turned the key and opened the door. "Wanna come in for a sec?" I asked.

"Sure." We entered and he looked around. "You didn't do too badly either," he said in approval.

I threw my key, purse, and shopping bag on the bed and then turned to face him. He stood tall and towering in cargo pants; a long-sleeved, navy blue henley shirt; and Italian-made canvas tennis shoes. His hair had grayed quite a bit at the temples and I noticed some wrinkles had appeared on his forehead, but he was still exceptionally handsome.

"Wow. Devin."

"David."

"Yes. Sorry. David." I froze.

"Hey, Andi?"

"Yeah?"

"Where's your husband?"

I crossed my arms and hugged myself—a involuntary behavior that Melody observed I had conditioned myself to perform whenever I had to face the painful truth. The gesture was an attempt to appease myself, to get through the moment when the world felt like it was going to crash on me yet again and this time kill me for sure.

"Sam was killed by a drunk driver seventeen months ago."

I'd seen this look on others when I'd told them about Sam: first shock, then horror, then sympathy, then terror for their own mortality. Devin—David—went through the first three, but sympathy turned into the look he used to give me when I had confronted the shame of my sexual inexperience: total compassion and warmth that would envelope me. I averted my eyes to avoid getting sucked into that warmth.

"Oh my God. Oh, Andrea," he said. He came to me and pulled me to him. "I am so sorry."

I pulled myself away from him. It occurred to me that I still hadn't used the bathroom.

"I gotta go," I said, running to the bathroom. When I finished, I washed my hands and splashed some cold water on my face. I came out to find him still frozen in the same place.

"Well, thanks for getting me back here. Small world, huh."

"Don't," he said.

"Excuse me?"

"Don't pretend with me. Don't go back to that. We've both come too far."

I shut my eyes and shook my head slowly as I spoke. "Then don't make me feel it right now. Please. I'd like to get through just ten minutes without feeling it."

We stood facing each other, him looking at me and me looking at the ground. The silence finally got to me.

"What *are* you doing here?" I asked.

"Business—I'm a buyer for certain gallery owners and patrons. And pleasure—I needed my Italy fix. What about you?"

"Second honeymoon."

He cocked his eyebrow in classic Devin style.

"Sam had intended to surprise me with this trip. It was for our fifth wedding anniversary. He surprised me by getting killed instead. I found the tickets a year later."

"How brave of you to come by yourself."

This time I cocked my eyebrow. "You mean stupid, don't you?"

"You're daring to reclaim your life. That's incredibly brave."

I sat on the edge of the bed. He sat next to me.

"Doesn't feel like that to me. Feels like I'm hanging on by a thread. Feels like I'm grasping at straws, trying to find something that makes sense and feels normal again."

"I went through that after my father died and you left. It was a double whammy. You're in the right place, you know. Rome works wonders on the soul."

I sat quietly and retreated to my thoughts. Devin—David—sat patiently, also quiet. Then I snapped out of it.

"How long are you here for?" I asked.

"As long as I need to be. How 'bout you?"

"For the rest of this week. It's spring break back home."

"Well then, looks like we have a lot to do in a short amount of time."

"*We?*"

"I'm gonna show you everything you need to see, take you everywhere you need to go, and feed you everything you need to taste."

"You're offering me your services again?"

Geez, was I *flirting* with him?

He grinned and nodded. "You bet."

"I have nothing to offer in exchange this time."

"Don't be too sure about that." He stood up. "So, what time shall I pick you up tomorrow?"

"I rarely get up before ten unless I have to."

He dropped his jaw. "Are you kidding me? Oye, Andrea!" he said, gesturing his hand demonstratively. "So much wasted time! No more. Be ready to leave at seven thirty." I looked at him in protest—you'd think he asked me to be up at three a.m. "I'm telling the desk to give you a wake-up call at six," he said. I didn't even attempt to argue this. "Wear sneakers," he added.

"That's all I brought."

"Well, that's not all you're taking home. I'll be knocking at your door with biscotti and espresso tomorrow morning. *Buona sera.*" Then he kissed me on both cheeks. "Sleep well."

"Thanks, David." I remembered.

After he left, I leaned back on the bed, looking at Sam's picture. I suddenly felt like he had eavesdropped and was not happy.

I fell asleep in my clothes and was jarred awake the following morning by the ring of the telephone at six a.m. For once, time had flown in a flurry.

CHAPTER
SEVENTEEN
Day Three in Italy

FOR THE FIRST TIME, I SAW MYSELF IN THE mirror and noticed how ridiculous I looked in Sam's clothes. Why no one had ever said anything, I don't know. Then again, I don't know how receptive I would've been if they had. Nevertheless, I became self-conscious of both my body and my clothes in anticipation of David's arrival. (I had been practicing calling him David in my mind.) But I hadn't packed anything even remotely flattering. Moreover, since I'd gained weight, I didn't own anything remotely flattering.

Indeed, at seven thirty on the dot, David knocked on my door, and I opened it to find him holding a tray of espresso and biscotti. I was dressed in the hoodie and jeans, and was putting my makeup on when he showed up. I couldn't even remember the last time I wore makeup. He watched me get ready. Then he went through my drawers and armoire.

"What are you doing?" I asked, offended.

"Looking to see what you brought."

"I packed comfortably."

"Yeah, I can see that—are these all Sam's clothes?"

"The shirts and sweaters are, yeah. The T-shirts and jeans and underwear are mine."

"Hm. At least you're not wearing his boxers."

I didn't know whether he was kidding. He opened another drawer.

"What's with the cotton Fruit-of-the-Looms?" he asked, holding one of my panties up and letting it dangle.

"My friend Miranda told me to buy cheap underwear and throw them away."

The look on his face seemed to indicate that he found the idea (or just me, perhaps) absurd.

"I didn't come here to hook up with anyone, Devin—David," I corrected myself before he could. "What's the point of wearing sexy underwear that's just going to stink up my suitcase for the rest of the week?"

"That's not the point, Andi."

"What is the point?"

He shook my underwear. "The point is that these panties say, 'I'm one step away from wearing diapers because I'm just too lazy to go to the bathroom.' They say, 'I don't have a sexy bone in my body.' They say, 'I give up.' Good Lord, didn't I teach you anything?"

"Don't start in on me already."

"You could have at least gotten the black bikinis. What's with the white briefs? Are you like, twelve, or something? You're in *Italy*, for crying out loud!"

"I don't have a sexy bone in my body."

"Do too."

I opened my mouth and stood there for about ten seconds, looking like I'd just been hit with a stun gun.

"Cat got your tongue?" he asked.

I instantly time-transported back to Devin's Manhattan loft, when he would stand in front of me with his shirt off and give me a look that would practically bore a hole into me.

"Let's see how sexy you feel after your husband gets plowed by a drunk driver," I finally blurted.

"I'm not that kind of guy," he said, with a guffaw.

"You think this is funny?"

"I think you need to start wearing some sexy underwear."

"I think you need to go to hell," I said, annoyed by his nonchalance.

"I'll get there soon enough—are you almost ready or what?"

"If you would stop ransacking my personal belongings and lecturing me on my underwear for one damn minute, I could finish getting ready."

He put the panties away, closed the drawer, and sat on the bed, grinning from ear to ear. "This is gonna be fun," he said. Ten minutes later, I grabbed my backpack, water bottle, and two of the biscotti.

"Let's go, Perillo," I said.

We started with the Coliseum. David said I wasn't ready for the really good galleries yet, and the Vatican was going to take at least a day, if not more, to cover. I found the Coliseum to be both fascinating and haunting, given what took place there, not to mention crowded as hell with tourists either clicking their digital cameras or cell phones.

"It's big," I said, looking around and feeling stupid for not having anything more intelligent or insightful to say. "And open. It never looks this big on TV."

"It's incredible…" David said, his voice trailing off. I'd almost forgotten how he got in a gallery or a museum— completely lost in his surroundings, as if he were having an out-of-body experience.

David offered to take a picture of me using my camera, and I let him, but squinted more than smiled. He then took one with his BlackBerry.

"Do you think the Stones played here back in the day?" I asked.

"It's nice to see you haven't lost your sense of humor," he said.

"Who's being funny?"

The day was sunny and warm, and pretty soon I carried around the hoodie, an extra-large Northampton University T-shirt engulfing me. David asked me if I owned anything that didn't look like something a guy in his twenties would wear.

After the Coliseum, we went to a bistro for siesta and dined outdoors. Lunch consisted of chicken cacciatore and a salad (arugula, tomatoes, and fresh mozzarella), with fresh bread on the side. Chew slowly, David instructed. The combination of flavors was spectacular; I hadn't really tasted anything in a long time. We had raspberry gelato for dessert—I thought I was going to have an orgasm right there. He watched me, a look of amusement on his face. In some ways, he didn't even look like the guy with whom I used to strip down and dance, or practice sexual positions, or discuss writing styles and revision techniques, much less act like him. David was someone I never got to know. There was something much softer about this guy, more real and genuine.

"So tell me what you've been doing for the last few years," I said. "How's the gallery?"

"Well, I sold Paris Gallery last year after doubling its patronage and profile, and went to work in another gallery in Cambridge as a manager and consultant. When I turned that one around, I became a buyer. You know, I thought I'd miss the New York art scene, but there's something really great about Boston. It's not as pretentious as New York. It has a culture all its own. I feel like I've always belonged there."

He talked about his work and his life with a vibrant ring in his voice.

"Are you still writing?" I asked.

He smiled slyly. "I was hoping you would ask that. Obviously you haven't been reading the Arts and Leisure section of the *Globe*, have you."

"I don't trust the corporate-owned media."

He sipped his wine and started coughing and laughing at the same time. "You don't, eh? Well, it's been very kind to me. I get to do a review every three weeks. In addition to that, I've been asked to write a section of an art history textbook on the Impressionists."

My eyes widened. "Wow! How'd you get that gig?"

"A former client of mine from one of the publishing companies got transferred to the Boston area and came to one of the exhibits I helped put together."

This time my mouth opened in addition to my widened eyes. "Nooooooo…"

He nodded his head slowly. "Yeah…"

"How did *that* work out?"

"She was always a cool client. I mean, I told her I wasn't in the business anymore, and that this is my life now, and she respected that. Then she put me in touch with an editor to set up the book deal."

"Anyone I know? Allison? Carol?"

"Diane."

I didn't know her.

"Do you think she told anyone back home who or where you are now?"

"I asked her not to."

"Do you think she listened?"

"I considered making her put it in writing that she wouldn't."

"Well, not for nothing, but your little contracts didn't always stick too well."

He looked at me, mildly irked, I could tell. I regretted it the moment I said it.

"I did thank her," he said.

"What do you mean?"

"You know. I *thanked* her."

It was my turn to give him an annoyed look, and I stopped regretting my own snide remark. I took a sip of water. All day I'd been wondering just with whom I was hanging out. And yet, just then, he became Devin in an instant, and it was like waking up after a long sleep. I almost wanted to say, "Oh, I know *you*. You're the charmer, the schmoozer, God's gift to women and King of the Hedonists." I wondered if he wondered who I was or if I'd changed. Then I wondered if I even knew who I was.

"I put on a lot of weight," I blurted.

He did a double take of sorts. "OK," he said.

"I was down to a size six when I married Sam. Stayed that way, too. And I wasn't even trying, if you know what I mean."

"Until the accident?"

"A few months after. I couldn't eat anything at first. Now it seems like I can't stop eating."

"Understandable," he said.

"I don't even remember tasting the food when I eat it."

"It's not about taste. It's not about feeling any of the senses. It's about shutting them down."

"You sound like my shrink," I said. I looked away from him and stared out at the people walking along the streets, getting lost in no one particular thought, forgetting time. He didn't seem to mind. Then I turned back to him. "Did you go through that when your father died?"

"I think the opposite happened when my father died. I think I started to feel everything."

"Hm." I stared out again, and then returned to him. "Do you miss your father?"

He paused for a second before answering. "I miss the relationship we didn't get to have. I regret that I didn't try to make amends with him sooner, before he got sick."

This time he looked away, wistful.

"We were both so damn stubborn." He looked back at me. "I can't even imagine what it was like for you to lose Sam, especially on the night of your anniversary."

"It sucks, that's for sure. But I'm glad I'm able to say I had the relationship that I wanted to have with him."

"I'm glad, too. You know, I wanted to hate the guy the first time I saw you together in the gallery. Wanted to punch him out for taking you away from me or something stupidly macho like that. But I couldn't. I could just tell he was a good guy, and good for you. He could give you what I couldn't at the time. It turned out I wanted to thank him instead. And I could also see how happy you were. You were so laid back and relaxed with him. You were so yourself."

"Are you kidding me? I freaked out when I saw you that night."

We both laughed at the memory. "You were a little tongue-tied, if I recall," he said. "That was really cute."

"It was mortifying."

"Still, it was obvious that you weren't the uptight, inhibited Andi I'd first met however long ago it was that we met. You'd grown into yourself."

My smile faded. "And now I've lost myself again."

"So, you'll reinvent yourself."

I looked at him and furrowed my brow, then looked away yet again, this time drifting further. "I don't want to," I said, feeling a million miles away. If he responded, I didn't hear him.

After siesta, we spent the rest of the day shopping in clothing boutiques and shoe stores. David's Italian was fluent and flawless. I wondered when he'd started learning the language. I soon found out that he was telling the sales staff, *"This beautiful woman has lost her essence and has come to Rome to get it back. She needs a dress to celebrate when she does."* Each person to whom he said this gave a response of "Ahhh!" and went right to work measuring me and finding clothes for me to try on. Everyone seemed to be having a better time than I. When I came out of the fitting room in a red wraparound top and a flared chiffon-and-silk flowered skirt to match, with a pair of Manolos that would've made Carrie Bradshaw gush with envy, I felt the same discomfort as the first time I had taken my clothes off in front of Devin—totally vulnerable and self-conscious and ashamed of my body. This time, it didn't even feel like *my* body. But both David and the man assisting us looked at me with expressions of delight, even desire. The man said something to David, who concurred.

"What'd he say?" I asked.

"He said he had no idea there was such a beautiful body hidden under that hideous T-shirt."

I rolled my eyes. "Seriously, what'd he say?"

"I am serious. Ask him to repeat it and look it up in your dictionary, if you don't believe me."

"*Scusa mi...*" I started, and in my slow, broken Italian, asked the sales assistant to repeat what he'd just said to my friend. The man did, gesturing the shape of an hourglass, practically touching my outer figure as he did so.

I didn't fully understand what he'd just said, but I believed him.

I tried on three more outfits, and then the assistant took them to the cash wrap counter. "We'll take all of them," David said in Italian. That I understood.

"I can't afford that," I protested.

"It's from me. I owe you an anniversary present. I owe you lots of presents, actually. Christmas, birthday…you're forty now, yes?"

"Forty-one."

"Let's tack that on, too, then. Anniversary and birthday gift."

"Thanks," I said, although I felt awkward about accepting the gift. If I had my way, it'd be Sam buying me presents. In fact, I probably wouldn't have needed the clothes in the first place.

David seemed to read my mind. "It's OK, Andi," he said. "It's just a dress."

"And shoes."

After that, he took me to a salon where the stylist gave me the best damn scalp massage I'd ever had, covered my grays with a soft auburn color, and finished with a haircut that was runway ready. David patiently sat nearby, looking though Italian fashion and style magazines and drinking cappuccino. When he finished blow-drying and applied the last bit of product, the stylist turned me in the chair to face David, who smiled in a way that was subtle—serene, almost. As if all was right within his world.

"*Bellissima.*"

He said this rather quietly, matter-of-factly, even. As if he'd known all along. As if I'd always been this way.

The stylist spun the chair back around, and I looked in the mirror. My eyes welled with tears.

I recognized her, too, for just an instant. And then she disappeared again.

CHAPTER
EIGHTEEN

W E WENT BACK TO MY HOTEL ROOM AROUND nine o'clock. I was exhausted; this had been the most productive day I'd had in a year and a half. David put my purchases in the closet and called room service to order something for me to eat when I curled up on the bed and closed my eyes.

"Don't bother," I said in a sleepy voice. He then lay next to me and stroked my hair, not seeming to mind that it'd been over-sprayed.

"Mmmmmmmmmm," I said, feeling myself drifting into slumber, "that feels good." I remembered when Sam would do the same after a stressful day at school. He'd spoon me and stroke my hair and talk to me until I was peacefully asleep. And somewhere between consciousness and the dream world, I thought perhaps he had come to do it again. I even felt a kiss on my cheek.

"Andi," I heard him whisper.

It's Sam! He's back! He's here!

No...pay attention. Listen to me!

Then who is it?

It's time, Andrea.

I awoke around one a.m. David was gone, to return promptly at seven thirty again.

Days Four and Five in Italy

N EVER UNDERESTIMATE THE POWER OF A
good haircut.

I awoke feeling refreshed and rejuvenated. Hell, I woke
up feeling *thinner*. Ready to jump into the day.

We spent the entire day in Vatican City. The Basilica of
St. Peter was breathtaking. The Sistine Chapel, astounding.
The lines to get in, never-ending. Once we did, however,
I stood in each structure in awe, my mouth open most of
the time, feeling incredibly small and plain. David did
the same.

"No matter how many times I visit these places, I'm
blown away as if it's the first time," he said. A Vatican
virgin, I thought. How ironic.

"How many times have you been here?" I asked.

"Six, maybe more. I've lost count."

Church bells rang.

"Wanna go to mass?" he asked.

I practically gasped. "Are you kidding?"

"No. Why would I be kidding?"

I looked at him in disbelief. "Since when do you go
to mass?"

"I started a few years ago, shortly after I moved to Boston."

The irony of this was not lost on me. "You're the only person I know who actually *joined* the Boston Diocese as opposed to running from it screaming."

"I found a nice little parish. Good people. Sensible. They live by the Gospel, not by the rules."

Who is this person talking to me? I thought.

"You're serious?" I asked.

"Yeah."

"You're a practicing Catholic now."

"*Si.*"

I looked at him, baffled, and then walked out onto St. Peter's Square, pigeons and tourists both rustling out of the way, the brightness of the sun making me squint. David followed me out.

"Why does this surprise you so much?" he asked.

I sat on the edge of the steps and took a swig from my water bottle. "I read your journal entries, Dev. I remember you writing about the residuals of Catholic guilt, and even reminding me of the damage it did to my developing sexuality."

"That was what—seven years ago? A lot's changed since then. Surely you can attest to that. Besides, I came to realize that it doesn't have to be that way. You know, all that guilt and stuff. There's another way."

"Which way is that?"

"The way of forgiveness."

I laughed out loud in contempt. "*Forgiveness!*" I said, incredulous. "Whom did you need to forgive?"

"My father, my mother, myself…"

"Do me a favor, Dev: save the homilies for someone else."

"David," he corrected, more stern than usual.

"What?"

"I'm not Devin anymore."

"Whatever," I muttered.

"No—not fucking 'whatever.' Geez, Andi. You can be so mean when you're angry, you know that?"

I got even angrier because he was right.

"You can go to mass if you want," I snapped. "I'll stay out here and feed the pigeons or something. I'm here to look at the art and the buildings—not God."

"Suit yourself," he said. He left me at the fountain and went into the church.

The nerve of him, I thought as I crumbled amaretti cookies and fed them to the birds. *Trying to preach to me about forgiveness. Trying to get me to think that there's such a thing as a loving God.* What kind of loving God would do this? I had spent sleepless nights in an empty bed wondering. What kind of loving God would let a wonderful, compassionate man die so senselessly and suddenly? A loving God *wouldn't* do it, I had concluded. A loving God wouldn't allow planes to fly into buildings, wouldn't allow drunk drivers to kill husbands after five years of marriage, wouldn't allow a wife who spent most of her life sexually deprived to go hungry again, wouldn't allow the Red Sox to win the World Series *again*. So that was it: there was no loving God. In fact, there was no God at all. We were all a bunch of overgrown primates with shaving kits and hair products.

David returned to find me writing in my journal.

"Whatcha working on?" he asked. Any trace of anger he might have had for me before was gone.

"The Gettysburg Address," I said, without looking up. "I've decided that it's too long."

"Why don't you try it in couplets," he suggested, pausing for a moment, then reciting slowly: "*Fourscore and seven years ago/we set up shop and lo/thought a good idea to be free/ and pretend you're on par with me...* Hey, not bad for off the top of my head!"

I looked up at him, squinting even with my sunglasses on, with both astonishment and incredulity. Freak boy.

"When did you read—and *memorize*—the Gettysburg Address?"

"Last year."

"Why?"

"I was dating a history professor. I wanted to impress her."

"Why are you so drawn to women in academia?" I asked, hearing a hint of jealousy in my voice.

"I like teachers. If you do something wrong, they make you do it over again."

I laughed, recognizing the Rodney Dangerfield line from the eighties movie *Back to School*.

"See?" he said with a wink. "I like it when you laugh. You're much sweeter."

David might not be Devin anymore, but he could still melt me like butter in a matter of seconds.

"Where to next?" I asked.

"*Pranzo*," he replied. Lunch. His pronunciation, rather than its meaning, made my mouth water.

———

The next day was fountains, fountains, fountains. We went to every fountain in Rome, and David was in true docent form. He lectured me on their history, gave an analysis of their aesthetic qualities, recalled their folklore, and simply gawked and gazed as he always did. He saved Fontana di Trevi for last—the most famous as well as magnificent fountain in Rome, if not Italy, and his favorite. I was running out of words for breathtaking, astounding, wonderment…the sheer magnitude was enough to render me speechless, let alone the intricacy of each sculpted figure, alive and practically speaking to me, beckoning me to jump in.

"The story is that if you throw a coin over your left shoulder into the fountain and make a wish, you will return to Rome and your wish will be fulfilled. Some say it's three coins; some say it's not over your shoulder."

He then reached into the pocket of his jeans and pulled out a handful of Italian coins, paused, and tossed three over his left shoulder. They made a barely audible plinking sound. The water rippled and bobbed, sunlight dappling on its surface and reflecting other coin tosses and wish-makers and the blue sky.

"Your turn," he said.

I looked at the fountain and the water, the hundreds of coins at its bottom, naïvely waiting for nothing. Then

I looked at David, as if he'd just told me a cruel joke, and walked away.

———

Later that evening, I changed into one of the new dresses and met David at his hotel room. He opened the door dressed in a new Versace suit. *Ciao.* I had to turn away, lest I rip the suit right off his body. "David" was an appropriate name indeed; he was a work of art. *Molto bello.*

He told me that the stars would be jealous of me tonight.

We dined and danced late into the night. The tensions of the previous days evaporated into the moonlit sky, and I felt lighter with each hour that passed. A memory of Sam and me at a wedding appeared before my mind's eye:

Sam, in his charcoal gray suit and silk tie. The one that brings out his eyes. His deep, big, ocean blue eyes. Me, in a salsa dress, ruffled just below the knees, hugging my hips. My hair in a French twist, my lips full and bright red and puckering. Sam's arms touching my hips, us dancing without a trace of inhibition, the crowd clearing the floor for us...

In the present moment, I felt free and light and unburdened, just as I had then.

And horny.

Later still, we went back to David's hotel room and came out onto the balcony, where he handed me a flute of ginger ale.

"*Per te,*" he said.

I put the flute to my lips and drank slowly and provocatively, not taking my eyes off him. God, I'd forgotten how incredible those sienna eyes were. They actually looked fiery in the moonlight.

He fed me a strawberry. I chewed slowly, letting its juice fill my mouth and slide down as I swallowed, closing my eyes as I did so. When I opened them, I stood still for a moment.

First I took his hand, and then I hugged him.

We let go and locked into a gaze. Then we kissed.

I swear, I heard something like pots and pans banging together. Or cowbells. Or gongs and triangles and whistles. He stopped and practically bored a hole into me with his eyes. Hot flashes overtook me. My breathing increased as my chest heaved, cleavage peeking out of the dress.

"I'm sorry," he said with uncharacteristic shyness. "I didn't mean to—I'm not trying to take advantage."

He picked up another strawberry, and I knocked it out of his hand, where it flew off the balcony. I kissed him again, hard and messily, like one might eat a loaf of bread after months of starvation.

We somehow navigated ourselves back into the room with the lights off, pulling off each other's clothes and kissing wildly, until we blindly hit the edge of the bed and fell over, laughing at our clumsiness. He hoisted me up and dropped me on the bed before climbing onto me. When he unhooked and slid off my bra, my muscles tightened in an old, involuntary reflex of self-consciousness, and he instantly set my mind at ease.

"Your body is fine," he whispered, and went right to work nibbling my neck. "Just like I remember it."

And that was all I needed to hear.

We made love into the early hours, and I thought I might actually die from the dizzying heights of ecstasy he was bringing me to. I had an orgasm that could've woken up the pope. Had he done this with his clients while he was an escort, he could've charged double and the women would be committing bank heists just to get ten minutes with him. And for a moment, I was thankful that he never had, that I knew something they didn't know.

At sunrise, I went back to my hotel room (ignoring Sam's picture sitting on the bedside table, waiting for me), showered and changed, went back to one of the boutiques we'd been to a couple of days ago, and bought black lace underwear and a low-cut shirt. Then I went back to David's room and pounced on him again.

I was awake and alive and soaring.

I could feel every kiss, every touch, every sensation.

I could *feel*.

And then, I wept.

CHAPTER

TWENTY

———————————————

I T HAPPENED WHEN I OPENED MY EYES AFTER
we made love again and I looked at David dreamily.
He kissed me playfully on my nose.

The reality set in slowly.

Sam used to do that. Used to kiss me playfully on my
nose like that.

I'd just slept with someone else. Someone who wasn't
Sam. Good God, I just cheated on my husband.

And then it hit me like a brick wall: Sam was gone.
He was really gone. He was *dead*. Expired. Finito. Never
coming back.

My husband was dead.

What began as sobs erupted into a wail. David took
me into his arms and held me, rocking me back and
forth, stroking my hair and my back while I cried. Then
he somehow managed to pick me up and carry me to the
bathtub, where he ran the tap and added lavender-scented
salts and soap and sponged me with a massive sea sponge
and shampooed my hair while I cried. And then he took
me out of the tub and enveloped me in the cocoon of a
plush, lily-white towel and picked me up and carried me
back to the sex-soaked sheets while I cried. He pulled

the bedspread over the sheets and gently laid me down and held me again, spooning me while I cried. He said nothing throughout.

I cried until I was hoarse and exhausted.

And then, I slept.

CHAPTER
TWENTY-ONE
Day Seven in Italy

I AWOKE HUNGRY. STARVING, IN FACT. DAVID brought me biscotti and tea. I hoisted myself up in bed and ate every bite while he watched me.

"What time is it?" I asked, my throat scratchy.

"It's nine thirty in the morning."

I sipped my tea, slightly slurping it. "I'm not keeping you from anything, am I?" I asked. "Didn't you say you had business here?"

"My business is done." He took the tray away, then sat next to me and caressed my cheek, somewhat hesitant. "You OK now?"

I nodded. For the first time, I really believed it, really felt OK. I wanted to say thank you, but the words remained stuck in my throat.

"Devin," I started, then caught myself. "I mean—"

"It's OK," he said, looking at me lovingly.

This time I caressed his cheek and ran my fingers through his hair. And then, as if touching an electric socket, I arose with a jolt.

"What day is today?"

"Saturday," he said.

I gasped. "I'm going to miss my flight home!"

"So?"

"So, what do I do?"

"Reschedule."

"Isn't that going to cost extra?"

"Look, if it's a problem, I'll take care of it."

I jumped out of bed and went hunting for my clothes, collecting them piece by piece: a shoe, a bra, another shoe, skirt, panties…where were the panties?

"I gotta pack; I gotta call Miranda and tell her not to come pick me up; I gotta make sure the cat's OK… God, I haven't called her in days. What'll she think?"

"She'll think you're having a good time—relax; it'll be fine."

"You don't understand. Miranda—she's sensitive when you don't check in. And Maggie. I promised Maggie I'd call."

"Hey, I've got an idea," he said, watching me haphazardly dress.

"What?"

"Why don't you stay for a couple more days? There's still lots to see—galleries, shops… We could even take a drive outside the city and see some of the countryside. *Bellissima*."

I stopped dressing. "What?"

"*Rimane qui*. Stay. Three days. I'm sure your friends won't mind. What's the rush to get home? You said you're not teaching classes, right?"

"But I still have responsibilities, meetings and stuff. And I'm on shaky ground as it is right now. I'm sort of on probation with the dean—it's a long story. There's also Donny Most."

David furrowed his brow. "Excuse me?"

"Our cat. His name is Donny Most."

"You named your cat after Ralph Malph from *Happy Days*?"

"Yeah," I replied, combing my hair with my fingers.

"That's cute."

"He's an orange tuxedo. Took the poor thing months to get used to being without Sam. I don't want to be away from him for too long."

"He'll live. I mean, he'll recover if you're gone for a couple more days. Your friend's taking care of him, right? It's not like he's alone and starving." David walked up to me and took my hand. "*Per favore*, Andi. Stay with me. Just a few more days. We'll go home together."

I felt afraid. I was feeling *everything* now. I suddenly remembered the day we said good-bye to each other when I left New York, how hurt he looked, how I fought to keep myself from staying. A lifetime ago.

I took a deep breath. "OK," I said on the exhale.

He grinned widely. "*Grazie*, Andi."

"You owe me a gelato, babe." Funny, Sam and I always hated the term "babe."

"Any flavor you want," he assured me.

On second thought, I don't need it after all.

CHAPTER
TWENTY-TWO

I CALLED MIRANDA AND ASKED HER TO LOOK after Donny Most for a few more days, and told her I wouldn't need the pickup at Logan Airport after all.

"Of course it's OK," she said. "How come, though?"

"Would you believe I ran into an old friend here? Talk about a small world…"

I called Jeff and told him my flight had been canceled, and the only other one I could get was in three days.

"Really?" The way he said this implied, *Are you honestly going to give me an excuse that lame?*

"Um…" I answered.

"That's what I thought," he said.

"Would you believe I ran into an old friend here?"

"More than I would the canceled flight, yeah."

"Talk about a small world."

"Just make sure you get back by Wednesday. The second Shakespeare candidate is coming to interview, and you're in charge of picking her up at the airport as well as attending the teaching demo."

"Yeah, I know. I'll be back by then, I promise."

Jeff briefed me on other agenda items before wishing me a safe flight home. "You sound good, by the way. Refreshed."

I called my mother and told her I was staying a few extra days and offered her no explanation whatsoever. Then I called Maggie.

"You are *never* going to believe this," I started. Then I told her.

"I don't believe it!"

"I'm staying on a few extra days with him."

"You slept with him, didn't you. Tell me you slept with him. Of course you slept with him—I can hear it in your voice."

"I screamed 'yes' in two different languages."

"Oh, Andi, I am *so* happy for you! This was meant to be. You'll see."

"Don't start planning another wedding, Mags. This is just Italy. Who knows what's going to happen once we get back to Boston? In fact, I don't know if I even *want* anything to happen once we're back."

"Don't worry about that now, cupcake. Enjoy the rest of Rome with Devin."

"Actually, he insists on being called 'David' now. And really, he is. David, I mean. It still takes some getting used to."

"Just be sure you call him when you get back to the States."

"Oy, Maggie…"

That afternoon, after touring yet another museum, we sat outside a café drinking cappuccinos. I scribbled a line in my journal.

"So what have you been writing all this time?" David asked.

"Well, I've been trying to make sure I've captured every aspect of the experience, for one thing. I think a good memoir could come out of this. For another thing, I've been jotting new ideas for Sam's eulogy."

"Come again?"

"I've been revising Sam's eulogy."

"What for?"

Funny—no one, including myself, had ever bothered to ask me that question, and I paused to find the answer. He didn't wait for it, though. "Did *you* deliver the eulogy at his funeral?" he asked, sounding perplexed.

"Of course."

"I guess I just assumed that you'd have been too distraught and someone else would have done it, like a relative or a best friend."

I shuddered in shame at the memory. "I insisted on doing it myself."

"Must have been something spectacular."

"It was crap, actually."

"The funeral?"

"No, the eulogy. It was a piece of crap. Total shit. A dead skunk stinks less than that eulogy."

"Come on, Andi—it couldn't have been that bad."

"If it could've, it would've cremated itself."

"What happened?"

"I was so shocked by his death, so devastated by the whole thing, I couldn't think straight. I was in a haze for days. I barely remember the funeral at all, much less writing anything remotely close to a eulogy. I just remember looking down at the words on the page and suddenly realizing I was going to have to read this shit out loud. I would've been better off reciting one of his favorite poems or reading from a book. Hell, I would've been better off doing a clog-dance at that point. Unfortunately, I didn't have such wisdom in the moment. I never should have done it. I never should have insisted."

"I'm sure people understood. I'm sure no one was expecting more."

"Are you kidding? They all were. *You* were, just now. I was. Sam was. What an injustice, to write and then deliver such a piece of crap. I might as well have spit on his dead body."

"I think you're being a little too hard on yourself," he said.

I shook my head. "I'm not being hard enough. I keep revising it in the hopes that I can have a memorial and deliver it there, or have it published someplace, or something. I don't know."

This time David shook his head. "You make it sound like it was all about *you*. Like you wanted the glory. Besides, it's not going to make up for the moment you lost. It's not going to make up for the fact that he abandoned you. Isn't that what you're really trying to control?"

I took a sip of my cappuccino, feeling irked. "You channeling my shrink or something?"

He didn't respond.

"You know, I just thought of something. Why didn't you deliver the eulogy at your father's funeral?" I asked.

"No one asked me to."

"Would you have if they did?"

"In a New York minute."

I paused for a beat. "Why didn't you offer?"

"Are you forgetting what it was like for me back then? Most of my family wasn't speaking to me. My dad and I had spent a lifetime not speaking to each another. What could I have said at that point? How receptive would they have been?"

"I don't think you would've done it if they had asked. I think you would've said no. I think you're feeling the same as me—that if given the chance *now*, you would do it."

He finished his cappuccino. "Well, it's not gonna happen, so why dwell on it?"

"Why not write one now?"

"I wrote something when I was doing a column for the *Boston Leisure Weekly*. In fact, I revised the memoir I had written under your tutelage and added to it, and published it near the anniversary of his death. So in a way, I suppose I got my chance."

"Well, good for you."

He looked taken aback. "What's with the attitude all of a sudden?"

I stood up and left the café. It had grown cloudy—the first cloudy day since I'd been there. He followed me.

"Man, I hate when you do this," he said, trying to catch up.

"Do what?"

"The minute something or someone pushes one of your insecurity buttons, you take it out on everyone around you."

"Better than what you do," I said, increasing my pace. "You rationalize it away and smooth it over. Why can't you just admit that you're not perfect?"

He stopped in his tracks. "*Me? You're* the perfectionist! You don't try a single thing that is beyond your comfort zone. And for you, 'comfort' is synonymous with 'familiar.' If you don't know what it is, you avoid it like the plague, and then you have a panic attack that someone is going to find out what you don't know."

I stopped walking, too. "Look, I'm not the one who refused to have sex with women for money and claimed it was for their benefit. I'm not the one who fucked a former client to get a book deal—no, wait…sorry—you fucked her in gratitude for the book deal. I'm not the one who waited until my father was on his deathbed before I made peace with him. Don't tell me about being evasive."

He looked wounded. Dammit, how did we always get to this place, even seven years later?

A gust of wind blew in our path. Suddenly tired, I walked over to a bench and sat on it, putting my head into my hands. Moments later, David joined me. I picked my head up. We stared out ahead and didn't look at each other.

"I'm sorry, Dev." *David*, I thought.

"Me too."

"Why do we do this to one another? Why do we hurt each other like this?"

"Because we know each other so well."

Do we? I wanted to ask.

"I don't mean to do it, you know," I said.

"I know you don't. Neither do I."

"I guess I just hate it because you're right all the time. Even back then you were."

"So are you," he said. "At least when it comes to me."

We watched a boy and girl playing together in the distance.

"Was Sam always right?" he asked.

"Not always. Thing is, when Sam was wrong, he was so sweet about admitting it that you couldn't feel good about being right."

"No gloating, huh."

"Never." I smiled. For the first time, the memory didn't feel quite as cutting as usual. "That was OK, though. We had such good makeup sex that it didn't matter who was right or wrong in the end."

"Makeup sex rocks," he said. At that point, we looked at each other and laughed. And for a moment, I could tell we were both contemplating it for ourselves. But our faces softened, and instead David took my hand and held it. We sat on that bench for at least an hour, silent, holding hands, watching the little boy and girl playing together.

I moved into David's hotel room for the remainder of my stay in Rome. We spent it walking around the city, going to galleries and shops and trattorias, and taking a drive along the countryside. I was definitely going to miss the scenery and scents and siestas. David was right about Italy being life-affirming. I finally understood what he meant about finding my soul here. The Italians celebrated life and all its pleasures in such a way that one's own life and spirit and passions could not help but be validated and awakened.

On our last night in Rome, I stood on the balcony of the hotel room in an oversized terrycloth robe and looked out at the city stretched out before me. David, in an identical robe, came out and put his arms around me from behind, and I let myself fall back into the safety of his body.

"*Bellissima*," I said, feeling a chill from the breeze. He must have felt it, too, and gave me a squeeze. "I don't want to leave here."

"La Bella Italia—she'll wait for your return," he said.

That instant, I turned around.

"Take me back to Fontana di Trevi!"

He looked at me, surprised. "Now? It's late."

"Please? Take me—I need to go there!"

"OK."

We hastily dressed and left. Other late-night dwellers strolled around the city and lingered by the fountain. I took out three coins. Without my asking him to, David left me alone. I looked at the coins, momentarily overwhelmed, not knowing what to wish for. But Sam's presence was so strong, as if he were standing, *breathing* next to me. And this time, it didn't leave me aching for him; rather, it made me feel peaceful, not alone. And I even wondered at that moment if Sam had brought me back to Devin—David—or brought David back to me.

I didn't make a wish, exactly. More like, I left a message.

How I love you, Sam. I love you so much, and I'll never really leave you. I am so grateful that you bought these tickets for us and wanted us to have this adventure. That you wanted this for me. *You gave me this gift.*

And then it came to me.

I wish to dare to envision a life without you, Sam. A different life from the one I wanted with you, I mean.

The coins made a faint plink-plunk sound as they hit the water and sank to the bottom, rippling in darkness. At that instant, a weight lifted itself from my heart. I felt warm inside, as if Sam were whispering, *"OK, sweetheart. You can go home now."* As if he gave me his blessing.

I walked over to where David was standing. My eyes glistened.

"Ready to go?" he asked. I nodded.

"Let's go home," I said. We left the fountain, arm in arm.

CHAPTER
TWENTY-THREE

DAVID HELD MY HAND DURING MOST OF THE nine-hour flight home. Although grateful for his company, it did little to ease my anxiety. I could've kissed the ground once we arrived at Logan Airport.

A car picked us up and drove me back to Northampton. My head was so full that I didn't even say two words during the drive until David pierced the stillness.

"Euro for your thoughts," he said, his voice soft and gentle.

I trembled on the inside. "I don't wanna ask it."

"The 'what now' question?"

"Yeah."

"Between us, you mean."

"Yeah."

"Whaddya want?" he asked.

"I don't know," I answered.

"Is it that you really don't know, or is it that you know and it frightens you?"

Damn him.

"It's that I really don't know what I'm capable of at this point," I said.

"Fair enough," he said. "Look, if you need some space, I understand. You're home now, where everything is a reminder of Sam. But I'm not going to lie to you. I wanna keep seeing you—as much of you as I can. Things here are different for me, too."

What did he mean by that? I wondered.

"Where do you live, exactly?" It occurred to me that I had never asked him.

"Cambridge."

I nodded and resumed my silence. When the car pulled up to the house, I stiffened.

"Nice house," he said.

"You can't come in," I replied, my voice stern. Alarmed, even.

"I've seen messy houses before."

"No, *you can't come in.*"

He comprehended the second time. This was Sam's and my house. There was no way I was ready for my lover—or whatever he was—to violate that.

"OK," he said.

We looked at each other. What was I supposed to do?

"Well…" I started.

He awkwardly pulled me to him and kissed me.

"Can I call you tomorrow?" he asked.

"Sure."

The driver opened the passenger door for me, my luggage in tow, ready to walk me to the house. I fumbled in my purse for my key, and before I could even put it in the door, Miranda appeared and exclaimed, "Welcome home!" I hadn't expected her to be there, but I was happy to see her friendly face and embraced her. Once the luggage was in the foyer, the driver went back to the car, and I watched as it pulled away. Something about not being able to see David behind the tinted window unsettled me.

After hugging Miranda close a second time, I left the foyer and entered the living room. It had been professionally cleaned, along with the rest of the house. My stomach started churning, and a wave of nausea hit me.

"Are you all right?" she asked. "You just went a little pale." I nodded, explaining that it was leftover jitters from the flight. "I hope you don't mind, I had the house cleaned. Consider it an early birthday gift."

"I've been getting a lot of those lately." I turned to her and thanked her. "It was very nice of you. I'll bet it was a pigsty, huh? I really let it go."

"I supervised, so don't worry—they didn't touch anything or throw anything away."

She understands, I thought. Still, something felt wrong, like something was missing.

"So?" she started. "Tell me everything!"

———

David kept long but flexible hours. We didn't see each other for almost a week after we got home, but he called me regularly. He was busy planning gallery exhibitions; attending meetings with prospective patrons, owners, and artists; and working on the textbook chapter. I drove to his place to meet him for dinner and a movie one night. In addition to his West Village loft in Manhattan (that he had sublet to his friend and former escort partner,

Christian), he owned a luxury penthouse in Cambridge that overlooked Harvard Square and the university. Just about every stick of furniture and artwork was new, although I recognized some pieces from the West Village loft. Dinner consisted of takeout Chinese food, and the movie was a DVD from Netflix—the classic Cary Grant film *His Girl Friday*.

"I was gonna get *Roman Holiday*, but thought it was too soon for that," he said. I agreed.

At first, I kept my distance on the sofa, but found myself inching closer, until finally he moved over and put his arm around me, allowing me to put my head on his shoulder. This was nothing like Rome—here, I was terrified to feel such affection. When the movie's end credits flickered in the darkness of the room, he made eye contact with me and then leaned in to kiss me. I pulled away as if I were sitting next to a stranger. As if I were doing something *wrong*.

"I'm sorry, I can't do this. I feel like I'm cheating on my husband."

I could tell he was trying to be understanding, but felt frustrated.

"Look, I don't wanna make you do anything you don't wanna do," he said.

"I'm confused, David. And afraid."

"Afraid of what?"

"Look, I'm just not ready, OK?"

He drew away from me and leaned back on the sofa. Come to think of it, he reminded me of Cary Grant.

"OK," he said. "Do you want me to take you home?"

"I can manage. I used to take the train back to Long Island at all hours, remember?"

He remembered. He then stood up to get my coat and purse and walk me to the door. He gave me a kiss on the cheek.

I got home thirty minutes later. Then I called him.

"Look, can we just hang out like we used to, as friends?" I asked. "I just need some time, that's all. I need to get used to the idea that there's actually someone else in my life. Someone different, that is."

"And that it's OK," he added. He sounded sleepy.

"Let's just be Devin and Andi for a while. Can we do that?"

"But we're not—"

"Please? I need to go back to something I know. I know what you said about me avoiding things that are unfamiliar, but that's what I need right now."

He took a breath that sounded somewhat like a sigh. "OK." He sounded unconvinced.

"Thanks," I said, temporarily relieved.

"G'night, Andi."

"Night, Devin."

I couldn't admit it to myself, but what had frightened me that night was that I had *wanted* him to kiss me.

May

S PRING SETTLED UPON NEW ENGLAND WITH
unusually warm weather. For the last two months,
there wasn't a day under sixty degrees. Sixty-eight was
the average. Devin (I had reverted to using his old name
again without his objection, although I had never actually
asked his permission) and I began meeting regularly in
Harvard Square, which had been Sam's stomping grounds
when he was a grad student and later became part of
our weekend routines. We used to jaunt up and down
Massachusetts Avenue or Brattle Street and split a Danish
at the Au Bon Pain and gaze at each other over coffees at
the Harvard Coop. Devin's and my dates (if you could call
them "dates"; I tended to call them "meetings") weren't
spent much differently, except for the gazing part. In that
case, I resumed my old ways of avoiding eye contact with
him. Almost eight years ago, I had tried to hide my feelings from him. Now, I was trying to hide from his feelings
for me. But we did the kinds of things we used to do as
friends: walked a lot, perused bookstores and frequented
galleries, sauntered through Radcliff or sat on the stairs
of one of the Harvard buildings, and watched students

play Frisbee or touch football. We talked baseball and movies and writing and art.

It's not that I didn't feel any yearnings for his affection or attention, or to be more than friends. But this time, *I* was the one keeping him, and myself, at a considerable length.

One sunny afternoon I sat in Melody's office, saying very little.

"You look like you're losing weight," she remarked.

"Yeah, I think I am. I'm more active these days." I told her about going to the Boston Museum of Art with Devin two days ago.

"Have you spent any nights with him since Rome?"

"Well, there was dinner and a movie that one night."

"But none since?"

"I'm much more of a homebody now. It's not like it was in New York. You can't be a homebody in Manhattan—you might miss something."

"Is he OK with that?"

"I guess so."

"So then, are you dating, or are you just friends?"

"We decided to go back to being friends," I said, avoiding eye contact.

"Both of you decided this?"

"Yeah," I lied.

I kicked off my shoes and curled up in the cushioned clamshell chair, pulling my knees to my chest while Melody's conspicuous skepticism surrounded me.

"That surprises me," she said.

"Why?"

"Andi, the two of you made passionate love in Italy."

I shifted my position in the chair.

"So?"

"So, I find it hard to believe that after sex like that you'd want to just slip back into a situation that never satisfied you to begin with. Why are you trying to cling so hard to something that you've both obviously outgrown?"

"I'm not ready," I insisted.

"Not ready for what?"

"To be with someone else."

"You mean, to *sleep* with someone else?"

I reverted to my first position in the chair.

"Yes. And don't bring up Rome. That was different. That was a fantasy, a rebound."

"Are you saying it never happened?"

I rolled my eyes. "Of course it happened. But it was different. I was sexually frustrated, that's all. It wasn't supposed to happen. I mean, it was what it was and that's that."

"So, you just used him like an escort?"

"Of course not," I said, offended. "I just didn't intend for it to happen. I mean, I didn't go looking for it. It was an accident."

"Andi, I don't believe there are any accidents or coincidences in life, and I don't think it was a rebound. You're rationalizing. You told me that when you left Rome, you were ready to envision something different for your life. Why can't that vision include a sexual relationship with a man you're obviously attracted to and whom you trust?"

"Because it just can't. I can't do that to Sam."

"What if he brought you two together?"

"Please," I said with an air of pretension, withholding that I had actually wondered the same thing that night at the fountain, if only for a fleeting moment. "Two years ago, I might have offered the same suggestion to someone else in my position. But cynicism moved in the moment the police showed up at my house. And what, the drunk driver—that was part of 'God's plan,' to get my husband out of the house and offed so I could get back together with a former escort? Come on, Melody. You can't expect me to believe that."

"I don't have answers or explanations," Melody said. "I only have possibilities. Why can't that be a possibility? And why can't you believe in a possibility?"

I took a forceful gulp from my water bottle. "I'll pass."

"Andi, you're starting to feel again, and that's great. That's important. But one of the things you're going to feel is fear, and you can't hide from it. You've got to face it head on."

"What if I'm not ready?"

"Who is ever ready? Do you think there's any woman who isn't afraid of giving birth, or any man who isn't afraid of being a father? Do you think the president isn't afraid of making certain decisions that can cost lives?"

"Not if he's a Republican."

"Stop using your sarcasm to avoid the issue. I don't think it's that you're afraid of cheating on Sam—you know he's not coming back."

Yeah, thanks for reminding me...

"But I'm still *married* to him," I insisted. "That hasn't changed just because he's gone." I still had trouble saying the word *dead*.

"Didn't you say you had a hard time leaving Devin at first? Didn't you originally want things to work out with *him*?"

"That was different. It was so long ago, for one thing. I was a different person. Back then Devin and I were each other's consolation prizes. We were comfortable with each other and used each other to a certain extent. He gave me confidence in myself and my body, and he helped me let my guard down and heal the demons of my past."

"And what did you do for him?"

"I taught him to be a better writer."

"That's it?"

I contemplated before responding. "I guess I accepted him for who he was. After all, I was the only one who really knew him."

"If it was so good between the two of you, then why didn't it work out?"

"Because we weren't totally being ourselves. I mean, he was this escort who kept all his clients wanting what they would never get from him, and I was trying to be this sexy, desirous woman who had it all together. Neither of us was willing to say to the other, 'I need to be loved by you.' And neither of us was willing to make ourselves vulnerable enough to risk being hurt or rejected by the other."

"Isn't that what you're trying to protect yourself from now?" Melody asked.

I looked at her, confused. "What do you mean?"

"If you allow yourself to be vulnerable for one second, if you allow yourself to admit that you still need to be loved, doesn't that mean you might get hurt again?"

"You think Devin's gonna dump me?"

"Did you for one minute ever think Sam would leave you?"

I said nothing and looked down at my shoes on the floor. The tips were scuffed.

Melody said, "I'm going to end today with this. You made a wish, a promise to yourself at that fountain: to re-see your life. That doesn't mean you have to turn your back on Sam. It doesn't mean you abandon him. But you have to see *him* in a new way, too."

"It's about revision," I said, the revelation coming into focus.

"Exactly," she said. "As a writer, you understand what revision is all about. You have to do the same with Devin. He's not the escort anymore who used to dangle the carrot in front of you and all the other women. He's asking for more. He's *asking* you this time. And he's willing to be vulnerable now. Is it really fair for you to string him along?"

Again, I said nothing.

"It's time to revise your life. Yours and Sam's."

I left Melody's office and stepped into the breezy spring air. I don't know what terrified me more—the blank page, or the final draft.

CHAPTER
TWENTY-FIVE

A FEW DAYS AFTER MY SESSION WITH MELODY, I wandered into Sam's study. As usual, Donny Most napped away, nestled in the corner of the leather sofa, its age and prolonged usage starting to show. I sat at the desk and turned on the computer. I knew Sam's password and typed it: vandi05. I really wasn't sure what I was doing, and I had a sick feeling inside, like I was invading his privacy. After the computer booted up, I noticed a Word file on the desktop that I had never seen before: NOVEL 1. I clicked on it and opened the file.

When Alexander first met Cassandra at the Conference of Rhetoric and Reality in New York City, he knew he wanted to marry her.

"Please God. Please let her be single."

He didn't want to talk to her at first. She was petite with short, dark hair neatly coiffed in the style of the moment, her olive skin straight out of European heritage. He knew she was way out of his league the minute he heard her speak about twentieth-century rhetoric in a twenty-first–century world. But then he decided such thinking was stupid, and took the plunge.

What was this—a romance novel?

So when she laughed at his jokes and accepted his invitation for a drink and eventually saw how he color-coded his hangers and watched football with him, only then could he get up the nerve to ask her to marry him.

So he did. And she said yes.

He loved to read to Cassandra. Loved to see her face light up just like a child listening to Mr. Rogers. And he would lose himself in her inner child and wonder, "Man, how could I be so lucky?"

I scrolled down about five pages.

Alexander picked up the letter. It was postmarked twenty years ago. Twenty years! Such a nice, even number—what were the odds? He gingerly slid his fingers under the back flap of the parchment envelope and moved them so as to preserve as much of it as possible. It opened with ease. He removed the thin paper, folded neatly in threes, the creases so tight that they were in danger of ripping the letter, its fountain-pen cursive preserved, like a body inside a sarcophagus. With slow, calculated precision, he opened it and began to read.

"Dear Son,"

Who, me?

I scrolled back to the top and read every word from beginning to end. Twice. A man receives a twenty-year-old letter from his long-lost father that takes him on a journey to Peru. What if he had received the letter when it was originally sent? Where would he have ended up? As he traces the steps based on clues in the letter, he starts to piece together the synchronicity of his life, and offers a series of stories.

Daring to envision a different life.

Sam was only about thirty-five thousand words in; and yet, I was riveted. *How come he never told me?* I thought in anger. *I wasn't ready to show you yet,* I could hear him answer. That was like him; he was protective of his first drafts, and clearly this was a first draft. Maybe he thought I wouldn't like it. Maybe *he* didn't like it. Maybe he was going to show me the day after our anniversary celebration. Surely he was going to show it to me at some point, wasn't he?

I called Maggie.

"Listen to this." I read the first couple of pages to her.

"Sounds good," she said. "What is it?"

"Sam started writing a novel. I just found it."

"You're kidding me!"

"I told you he had been thinking about it, didn't I?"

"I think you did. So?"

"So what?" I asked.

"So when are you going to finish it?"

I dropped my jaw and held out the phone before putting it back to my ear. "*Me?*"

"Yes."

"Are you crazy?"

"No—well, yeah, but not about this. Come on, Andi! This is something for you to do! Summer break is almost here. Why not write?"

"For one thing, I've never written a novel before. It's not my genre. I'm a nonfiction prose kind of girl—you know that."

"What, you can't write fiction and use what you know? Talk to Nora Ephron. You think it's a coincidence that all her characters are journalists who live in New York and cook? Heck, talk to *Sam*—twentieth-century rhetoric? You think he wasn't writing about what he knew? Besides, couldn't you tell that the description of Cassandra was totally you? Even the name—*Cassandra*? Please!"

I hadn't noticed. Why hadn't I noticed that?

"C'mon, Mags. I know rhetoric and creative nonfiction. I don't know fiction."

"Those were his areas, too, and it wasn't stopping him, obviously. Besides, fiction isn't rhetorical?"

"You know what I mean."

"You've never read a novel before?"

"Mags…"

"Andi, you're a *writer*. When was the last time you wrote something non-academic?"

"Sss—"

"Not including Sam's eulogy," she said, stopping me before I could even say his name.

"Not since the last collection of essays came out—when was that two, three years ago?"

"If you can't even pin down the date, it was too long ago."

"You really think I could do it? I mean, this is clearly a first draft, and I don't know where he wanted this to go or how he wanted it to end. What if I end it in a way that is totally bogus?"

"When you get to heaven, the two of you can argue about it over a slice of cheesecake. Come on, you can do this! It's not like you don't know his writing style. Think of it as something the two of you can work on together."

I thought about this, about what Melody had said about not only re-seeing my life, but his. Ours.

"I'll think about it," I said.

The next day, I called Devin and met him late in the afternoon at the Starbucks on Church Street in Harvard Square. I told him about the novel and asked him what he thought.

"I think you should do it," he said. "I think it would be good to immerse yourself in such a creative project. I'm surprised it's taken you this long to get back into writing, actually. I thought you would've written about the accident and the grieving process."

"It's already been done by Joan Didion. And no one can catch up to Joan Didion—she's the creative nonfiction queen."

"Who said you had to write to sell books? Who said you had to write it for anyone other than yourself? Who said it even had to be *good*?" he asked.

I could hear traces of my voice from our past tutorials echoing in his own. For sure, this guy was my former pupil.

I confessed, "I can't write anymore."

"Because of the eulogy? Geez, Andi, you've got to get past that."

"It's not that. I just can't do it anymore. I can't write. I can't teach. There's absolutely no desire."

"You can. You're just afraid of fucking up, as usual."

"Geez, Devin, you're a real ego booster, you know that? Remind me to hire you to get the Patriots revved up at halftime."

He slammed his fist on the table so hard that everyone got quiet and looked at us. "Dammit!"

Even the cappuccino machine came to a halt. He got up, grabbed his leather jacket, and walked out. Humiliated, I grabbed my own and followed him.

"Don't you ever embarrass me like that again, you hear me?" I yelled.

"Stop jerking me around, and stop jerking yourself around! I'm tired of it, Andi. I'm tired of your inertia! I'm tired of your refusal to move on with your life. I thought Italy changed that for you. I thought you were ready to take your soul back."

"Yeah? Well, you thought wrong."

"What happened to that woman who allowed herself some pleasure, who allowed herself to touch and taste and feel again? Even years ago, when you were so inhibited, you were willing to do something different. You were willing to at least *try*. Now you're just throwing it away. I can't bear to stand by any longer while you do that."

"Are you saying you don't want to be with me anymore?"

"She's not even listening to me..." he said, looking to his right as if a third party was part of the discussion.

"What the hell is your problem?" I asked.

"I don't want to pretend to be Devin anymore! I don't want to pretend like this is enough! God, Andi, when did you get so *selfish*?"

At that moment, I remembered Maggie blowing up at me and telling me the same thing, telling me how grief is so self-absorbing.

I peered at him, my brows furrowed. "Oh, you have a short memory. For how long did you string me along? 'You're my *client*, Andi.' That was the excuse you gave. And yet, even then the rules didn't apply to me. No kissing. No touching. Not unless it was part of the lesson. 'Whoa, that's far enough there, girl...' It was all under your control. Talk about *selfish!*"

"You're right. I was a rat-bastard, and by the time I came to my senses and was ready to let you in, I lost you. So let me warn you: you're losing me. You're losing me as a lover, and worse still you're losing me as a friend. Do you really want that?"

I didn't know what to say. Panic crept in and gripped my whole body. "Devin..."

"Oh, for the love of God—my name is *David!* I'm not the escort anymore. I don't even wanna *be* that fucking guy."

"Well, I'm not Andi Cutrone," I said.

"I never insisted you should be! I'm perfectly OK with you being Andi Vanzant. I'm perfectly OK with you being Sam's wife. I'm perfectly OK with you being scared out of your mind, or guilty, or whatever it is you're refusing to let yourself feel. I'm perfectly OK with Sam being a part of whatever it is that we have. In fact, I would *prefer* that he was present. At least then I'd know where I stand. You're the one who has the problem with it. You're the one trying to shut him out, and me too."

Could this be true? Had I left both of them at the Fontana di Trevi?

We were still standing outside the Starbucks, and customers inside gawked at us through the window. I wondered if they could hear us. I glared back at them, and they quickly averted their eyes.

I headed up Church Street. David walked with me. We said nothing. Harvard Square was alive and in a hurry, oblivious to our fight. Something about it reminded me both of Rome and Manhattan. But whereas New Yorkers didn't give a crap, the Romans supported us and gave us permission to fight, to be passionate about something, even if we were hating each other's guts in the moment.

And I didn't hate him.

We turned a couple of corners and then silently strode all the way down to the bridge that overlooked the Charles River. Once there, we stopped and I leaned against the wall and tried to look over it; it was almost as tall as I was. The day's weather was more typical for New England at that time of year: brisk and breezy. The wind had kicked up and stung my ears.

"What do we supposedly 'have'?" I asked.

"I thought we started something in Italy. I thought we could continue it here."

"What—you mean the sex? Hell, Dev—you can fuck any woman you want and you know it. You're a fantastic lover."

"What in the world makes you think that all I wanted from you was sex? At what point did you get the impression that I just wanted to fuck you? Are you really that much in denial? Do you really *believe* that shit?"

"Tell me what you want, then."

"I love you, Andrea. I want a long-term relationship with you."

The words took me by as much surprise as when he'd first said them shortly after his father had died.

"Don't call me Andrea."

"Don't call me Dev."

He paused before continuing. "And by the way, you didn't exactly run away when we first kissed that night on the balcony in Rome. You touched my esophagus with your tongue, if I recall."

"Well, you had finished the strawberries, so…"

"You were horny as hell that night and you know it. So don't get all high and mighty on me about my supposed conquest of you."

I zipped up my jacket, pulled the collar close to my neck, and rubbed my ears, feeling the sting from the cold. And yet, neither of us moved from the bridge. David drew closer to me in an effort to shield me from the wind. Then he looked at me, shifting from anger to compassion in a matter of seconds, his eyes glistening in twilight.

"My parents were married for almost forty-five years when my father died. And my mother grieved. She had difficulty adjusting to things, like cooking for one person—she doesn't know how to do it. She usually winds up throwing the food out because there's no one to eat the leftovers. Still, to this day. But you know what she did do? Joined a bowling league, for starters—can you believe that? You don't really know my mother, but trust me—bowling is not the first thing you would think of if you did."

"What's your point?"

"My point is that she wasn't afraid to try new things. She wasn't afraid to keep living and continue with her own life, even though the biggest part of it was gone. And for forty-five years, it was the only life she knew."

"Are you saying that because I only spent five years of my life with Sam—six, actually—that I shouldn't have any trouble moving on?"

"No—absolutely not. You know I'm not saying that."

"Besides, at least your mother and you and the rest of your family got to say good-bye to your father. You knew his days were numbered. You got to tell him the things you wanted to tell him."

He said nothing, just wistfully looked out at the water.

"Didn't you?" I asked.

"Yes, I did. Two days before he died. I told him that I loved him, and he told me that he loved me."

I wanted to take his hand, to extend the same compassion to him that he was extending to me. And yet, my own hand stayed lodged in the pocket of my jacket, refusing to move.

"I'm glad you got that chance. I didn't have that with Sam. I didn't get to tell him one last time that I loved him, didn't get to make love to him one last time, or thank him for the joy he gave me, or hold him in my arms. He went out for a bottle of sparkling cider and never came back."

Tears came to my eyes.

"I have no idea how it must feel to have someone you love ripped out of your life like that, and I'm not trying to pretend that I do. I'm not telling you to get over it or anything like that. My mother had the opportunity to join a support group—also out of her comfort zone, I must mention—when my dad was diagnosed, and fortunately she was able to foresee that her life was going to change. And someone in that group was able to show her that, although difficult, this could also be an opportunity to explore and use her life in ways she might not have previously considered. She lost her husband, but she didn't lose herself. She reinvented herself. It wasn't easy, but you should see her now."

"She's had over five years to do that."

"There's no timetable, ya know. Look..." He turned me so that we were facing each other, and touched my wind-burned cheek. "I remember that woman who was so hidden away, so ashamed of her body and afraid that she might be unlovable because of what she didn't know."

One by one, the tears slid down my cheeks.

"I also remember the woman in Rome who cried cathartically in my arms for hours—I don't think I ever loved you as much as I did for those hours, Andi. That was *you* coming out from behind the curtain, and I was so glad to see it, as heartbreaking as it was."

He tenderly smudged each tear away as it fell.

"You can't go back to the way things were, Andi. You can't be the woman you were when we first met, and you can't be who you were when Sam was alive. The only option is to move forward, and be who you authentically are, the part of you that no tragedy or childhood wound can touch."

I went into his arms, and he held me close.

"I thought I was ready in Rome, right before we left. Guess I was wrong," I said between sniffles and sobs.

"No you weren't. You just got scared and hid her away again. You need to let her out."

"How do I do that?"

"Forgiveness," he answered.

"Who do I need to forgive?"

"Sam for dying, yourself for being powerless to stop it from happening, the drunk driver…"

Something inside me started burning, not unlike the rage I felt when I blew up at my students a little over a year ago. I didn't want to talk about this anymore…how could I stop him from talking about this anymore?

I kissed him.

He smiled warmly.

"I'm freezing my ass off on this bridge, you know," I said.

"Me too. Wanna get a cup of coffee?"

"Didn't this fight begin at Starbucks?" I asked.

"Wanna get into a hot bath, then?" He moved his eyebrows up and down like Groucho Marx.

I smiled slyly and winked. "Last one in has to sponge the other."

With that, he pretended to dart off in a sprint. We crossed to the other side of the bridge, arm in arm, and went back to his place, where we enjoyed an evening reminiscent of the bathtub date from our short-lived arrangement years ago, only this time I spent the night with him in his bed.

CHAPTER

TWENTY-SIX

T HE DAY AFTER DAVID AND I RECONCILED, I took out the journal I had kept while in Rome and found the page on which I listed my "anniversary goals."

Start a book club.
Start a writers' group.
Research for a journal article about the rhetoric of death.
Get back to teaching.
Take a trip somewhere else.

First, I changed the name of the list to "Summer Goals" and added a sixth item: finish Sam's novel. Second, I put together a book club consisting of Miranda; Piero, the sexy Italian teacher; Sam's friend George from Edmund College; and Jeff and Patsy Baxter. We decided to start with an oldie but a goodie: *Catch-22*. The writers' group was trickier. David wanted in on it, but I didn't know whom else to ask. When Sam died, I'd isolated myself from so many of our friends that I felt awkward about calling them up out of the blue. Of course, I wanted Maggie to be a part of it, but she was too far away. I'd been trying to convince her to leave Brooklyn and move back to Massachusetts, where we'd first met, but she had tenure at Brooklyn U and didn't want to start over.

As for the academic article, conducting research was never something I enjoyed doing even when life was sweet and normal and predictable, but I wasn't ready to check that one off the list just yet.

Jeff and I met for lunch at one of the bar-and-grill places in Amherst to discuss my return to teaching.

"I don't know, Jeff," I said. "Every time I even think about reentering a classroom, my palms start to sweat and I get nauseous."

"Sooner or later you have to get back on the horse, don't you? The longer you wait, the harder it's gonna be. We'll ease you back in slowly. We'll give you two grad level courses: the Introduction to Rhetorical Theory class and the Robert Connors Essays seminar. No freshmen. What do you think?"

I raised my eyebrows at the mention of the second course—he knew I'd had my eye on it once upon a time—and went back to poking at my salad. "Maybe."

"Thing is, Andi, I don't know if you'll have a place to come back to if you take another semester of teaching off. The contract is pretty strict about that. You've had so much time off already."

"I really don't know if I want to go back at all."

"What do you mean, 'at all'? Are you saying you want to leave the university altogether?"

"I don't know. It was a thought."

"I actually thought you just finished a good year here," he said.

"I did."

"Then why do you want to leave?"

I sipped my water. "Don't worry about it, Jeff. Forget I said anything."

"If you leave, then what?"

"I'm not hurting for money, if that's what you mean. And I can still write, you know."

"And that's enough for you?" he asked.

"For right now, yes. It'd be nice to write something that isn't up for peer review and doesn't end up as yet another line on the CV."

"I think you've had a more illustrious career than that the last few years," he argued.

"It's getting old fast."

"I thought you loved it."

I pushed my salad away and took another sip of water. "I do. Or I did. I don't know anymore."

Jeff finished his beer. "What about that guy you've been seeing?"

"Devin?" I said absentmindedly; I was still calling him that whenever I talked to Maggie and sometimes Melody.

"Devin?" he asked, confused.

"I mean *David*," I quickly corrected.

"David?"

"Yeah?"

"Who the hell is *Devin*?"

"No one," I said, now gulping my water and spilling some on my shirt.

"Well, what about him?" he asked.

"What about who?"

"Is this an Abbott and Costello routine?"

"It's starting to feel like one," I said.

"Well?" he asked, a hint of impatience in his voice.

"What was your question?"

Jeff motioned to the waiter for another beer. I appreciated that he'd asked me beforehand if it bothered me. "I just thought it must be a good sign that you're seeing someone."

"David and I have known each other for a long time. We met when I was at Brooklyn U."

"Was he a professor?"

"No, he was an es…" I quickly coughed on my words. "…an especially resourceful guy. He's an art dealer. We were friends, and then we lost touch until earlier this year. But it's complicated, you know?"

"Look, kid, I just want you to be happy, and I want to see you around the hallways again. That place is so godawful depressing when you're not around. You always make it fun."

"I thought I made it even more depressing, since, you know…"

"Kid, your worst day doesn't match the inherent misery of some of our faculty and administrators," he said, followed by a quick eye roll. I couldn't help but laugh.

"Shit, man. You have got to get out of this role as chairperson."

He laughed with me. We clinked our glasses and toasted our fucked-up colleagues.

———— ————

That left traveling. And Sam's novel.

I remembered telling Melody that Sam had wanted to start traveling. I also remembered Melody telling me to fulfill some of Sam's goals if I couldn't think of any of my own. I knew of at least two now. I hadn't looked at the novel since I'd first stumbled across it. And yet, I also hadn't stopped thinking about it. In addition to the draft, I had found a notebook of descriptions and notations regarding characters and possible storylines and plot twists. No ideas for an ending, however. Apparently he had no idea where this was going to take him, but he seemed willing to be led. The folder also contained a Google map of Lima, a personal essay written by a Harvard grad school buddy on the currency system in Peru, and a couple of travel brochures to Machu Picchu.

Why Peru? I wondered. He had never expressed a specific interest there before. Then again, apparently Sam had kept several secrets from me.

———— ————

David and I were at his place, making spaghetti and meatballs. I still wasn't ready for him to come to my house.

"Ever been to Peru?" I asked.

"No, why?"

"Just wondering. I found a brochure in Sam's desk. I think he was contemplating a trip."

"Do you wanna go?" he asked before slurping a strand of spaghetti. He then broke off another strand and handed it to me for tasting.

"Are you inviting me?" I asked. I ate the spaghetti strand and advised him to let it cook for another minute.

"I'm just asking, is all," he said.

"I don't know. Maybe. If I did, would you wanna go with me?"

"Possibly," he answered, and proceeded to set the table.

He didn't sound gung ho about the idea. I stirred the sauce pensively and thought about brushing up on my Spanish.

———

Two days later, I printed out the draft of Sam's novel and read it carefully, making edits and underlines and notes in the margins. I wrote down a lot of questions, which I usually did when Sam (or my students) gave me something to read. I'd ask questions and then give it back to him and we'd sit and talk about it, and he was always so grateful for the insight and would tell me that my students were lucky to have me. David had said that, too, as Devin, when I had given him writing instruction.

Maggie was right—this novel was something Sam and I were working on together. Every question that I jotted in the margin was a question to *him*. Sometimes I even found myself talking to him out loud. "How do you want me to do this? Should Alexander methodically research his father's past and Peru first before going there? Or should he go to Peru on a whim and let it all unravel before him? What's the deal with this guy? What is his *story*?"

———————

I stuck the Summer Goals list on the fridge with a magnet and made an additional copy to tape to my bathroom mirror—never had I done that before.

Another new beginning, I thought. One step closer to the ordinary world.

August

I N ADDITION TO THE BOOK CLUB AND SPENDING
time with David, I spent the summer engrossed in
Sam's novel, which I decided to call *My Father's Letter.*
Part of this task involved rereading almost everything
Sam had ever written in order to study his style. Doing
so elicited an array of reactions: falling in love with him
all over again, grieving his loss all over again and getting
depressed for days, reigniting my interest in stylistics from
my grad school days, and even learning things about Sam
that I had never known. For instance, I peeked into his
childhood with his brother Kevin, who would scrape up
enough money to take Sam to see the Red Sox at Fenway
and buy him baseball cards for his birthday—how much
he looked up to Kevin, especially after their father left.
In some ways, I felt as if I were intruding, but this was all
I had left of him. Reading Sam's writing was the closest
thing I had to his actual presence. Sometimes I read his
memoirs in our bed, imagining him reading them to me.
I longed for the sound and smell of him.

Furthermore, by going through Sam's papers, memoirs, and scholarly essays (he was starting to incorporate
a lot of travel metaphors in his academic writing, I'd

discovered), I found out that he had contacted his editor at University Press and queried about getting the novel published through them, since they'd already published his two books of nonfiction. Thus, when I contacted Sam's editor myself and showed her the draft of the manuscript, she was quite enthusiastic about the project, but uncertain about University Press being the right publisher for it. Great marketing potential of a love story, though, she said—not the novel's, but mine: my husband, tragically killed, and me, granting his final wish, or some crap like that.

I actually found novel writing to be quite fun. Fiction offered a chance for things to work out that were normally beyond one's control. I was writing conversations between Alexander and Cassandra that were reminiscent of the ones Sam and I used to have, and it was like talking to him all over again. There would be no tragic ending in this story. No drunk driver, no need to pick up the pieces and blindly feel one's way back to normality. There would be no former escort to confuse things. Instead, the possibilities abounded. Cassandra could be daring in the ways I was timid and confident in the ways I was insecure. Alexander didn't collect bobble-head dolls and never left his dirty laundry on the floor. What would life have been like for him had he not met her? Or for *her*, for that matter?

———

David's and my reconciliation didn't last very long. And I still wouldn't call what we were doing "dating." "Seeing each other" was a more accurate description. Every time he got too close, I would start to pull away. And when I

173

wanted to get close, he felt as if he was being used. No matter what, we couldn't get into a groove. When we'd first met in New York, we'd negotiated and notarized our relationship right off the bat. We knew our roles, put it in writing, and then carried those roles out. Never mind that we were constantly trampling over those boundaries that we'd negotiated. Never mind that we were just playing those roles like actors playing parts, that we were faking it with each other and the rest of the world. We hid behind the false security of that contract, of those pre-scripted roles. We knew who we were supposed to be and where we stood.

But when we met the second time in Rome, we had long since shed those skins. I had become Mrs. Sam Vanzant, or Dr. Andrea Vanzant, tenured professor and director of freshman writing at NU; and he had become David Santino, gallery owner and art dealer. For what purpose did we have to be together this time? There was nothing left to teach, nothing to trade, and nothing to negotiate. This time, we had to be ourselves, and the only thing we really shared was a past-life incarnation. That, and an immense attraction to one another. If Sam and I had been a pair of gloves, then David and I were a pair of polar magnets—we both attracted and repelled one another.

David and I met at the Starbucks on Church Street in Harvard Square on a regular basis. Many times we'd bring our laptops and work on our respective writing projects (Sam's novel for me, the art history textbook chapter for him) and hardly talk to each other. I don't know if this signaled something positive—that we knew each other so well that we didn't need to entertain each other in one another's company—or something negative—that we were still avoiding the hard questions. I couldn't help but think of the dinner scene in *When Harry Met Sally*, after Harry and Sally have slept with each other for the first time and are preoccupied with their salads, crunching loudly to drown out the awkward silence.

I looked up from my laptop, taking a break from vicious click-clacking, and noticed David had stopped as well, staring at his screen in concentration.

"How's it comin'?" I asked him.

He paused to finish the thought or sentence or paragraph he was reading.

"OK, I guess," he finally responded, looking up and smiling at me when our eyes met. I couldn't help but smile in return.

"Whatcha workin' on?"

"It's a sidebar piece for the *Globe* to accompany the latest American Impressionist exhibit review at the BMFA. The exhibit isn't focusing on Monet but rather on those who were inspired by him. My piece is about why you kinda need to see Monet before you can see the other artists."

I nodded my head. Before I had a chance to say anything, David asked, "Will you read it? Right now?"

My eyes widened as I straightened my posture in my seat. "Sure."

We shuffled papers and coffee cups and crumb-riddled plates around our tiny table in the process of carefully swapping laptops. "You can read mine, too, if you want," I added.

His laptop in front of me, I took off my reading glasses, wiped them on the bottom edge of my tank top, put them back on again, and began to read:

Why We Need to See Monet

What can possibly be said about Monet that hasn't been said already? Haystacks are lovely at sunset? Lily pads look divine on cadmium water? It's all been said before.

Now, here's the kicker: Claude Oscar Monet was deemed the father of an entire movement of art, and he may never have had an original subject grace a canvas. He had nothing new to say or show. And yet, he wasn't about painting new subjects. I almost wonder if Monet cared at all about what he said, what he thought, how he painted, or what he saw in his work.

So, why this guy? Why Monet, the Father of French Impressionism? It wasn't just because his painting, *Impression, Sunrise,* provided the inspiration for which the movement was named. Rather, Monet was about *seeing.* He saw movement and color and emotion, and he invited viewers to see the world in an entirely new light. His world became their world. Better still, Monet constantly posed the what-if question. What if stones don't stand still, and boats aren't solid? What if life careens in brushstrokes of thought, dancing in chaos, and we don't even know that we're missing it (life, I mean) until someone comes along and shakes us out of our reverie? It takes courage to see what Monet saw, and the way he saw it; to allow ourselves to accept and allow the chaos of the world.

If we stand at the right distance from a Monet painting, then we see the subject. We see a world of order and form.

We see the light. If we move in too close, however, then the image dissolves, leaving us with smudges of color, as though we can see the artist's process—his thoughts and movements—right before our eyes. And then, the image disappears altogether. We've traded the aesthetic illusion of picnicking on the Seine for the discomforting truth of the pigments beneath the picture. We're confronted with the thought that nothing is stable, whole, or true. And yet, *that* is the beauty. That is the most breathtaking allure of the Impressionists—they dared to harness the chaos of the world around them, and now invite us to witness the beauty of such chaos.

And will you? Will you allow yourself to see how powerful and unerringly beautiful chaos really is? Will you allow Monet to show it to you from his own eyes? Because somewhere, between the image and the brush-strokes, exists a harmony that none of us can afford to miss.

From the corner of my eye, I could see him watching me nervously, not unlike the way he used to when I'd read the drafts of the writing assignments he'd done for me during our seven-week arrangement in New York, exactly eight years ago. At that moment the urge to cry inexplicably came over me. He had matured so much as a writer. As a person. It suddenly occurred to me that I hadn't read anything of his since the *Boston Leisure Weekly* Jesse Bartlett review that Sam had showed me years ago, before we'd gotten married. Even in all the time that David and I had been seeing each other since Italy, I'd not read any of his columns or reviews. Why?

"What do you think?" he said the split second I looked up from the screen.

"I think it's very good," I started. "You've come into your own regarding style and voice. Your writing has a rhythm now."

"I feel a 'but' coming on," he said, a hint of dread in his voice.

"Not a 'but,'" I started, "more like an 'and.' I see some things that are, well, a bit questionable for your audience."

"Like what?"

"Like the introduction. I can see you opening with that for an Art History 101 class lecture, but not your *Globe* readers. Granted, I haven't seen your other work…" I blurted this out before considering that the truth might hurt his feelings, which, I realized upon seeing his sienna eyes slightly darken, it did.

"But I can tell you have a rapport with your readers, and that's great. I mean, I felt like a regular David Santino column reader as I read this." (I hoped that would soften the blow.) "But it just seems to be a little…corny…rather than sophisticated."

Eek. That was harsh, I thought. But he took his laptop back and reread the opening paragraph.

"You're right," he replied with self-assurance rather than as someone who'd just been insulted. "Anything else?"

"I never knew that Impressionism was named after one of Monet's paintings. That was really cool to learn. I always thought it had to do with the impressions the painting style made—you know, leaving an impression other than the one you'd normally see."

The words made me sound downright stupid as I said them, especially in the presence of such an expert.

"Are you telling me that I *never* told you how Impressionism got its name?" he asked in mock outrage.

"*Mai*," I replied with a smile; David's mix of Italian and English was rubbing off on me.

"How is that possible?"

"I never asked you, I guess."

"And whose fault is that?" he playfully scolded. "You, who adores the Impressionists so."

"You slacked in your docent duties," I shot back. He laughed and winked in concession. I always loved his winks.

"Yours is fucking great," he said, pointing to my laptop. "I mean, *really* good. God, Andi, you are just so talented. Really, you are."

I blushed. "Thanks. Most of that is Sam, though. I mean, I'm just imitating his style to keep his own voice pure and intact. But it's his story."

"But that's just it—do you know how much *talent* it takes to adapt to someone's style so flawlessly like that? I couldn't do it. Hell, I can't get through my own articles without sounding like a dork most of the time."

"Your stuff was always good, Dev. Especially your descriptions. You do an excellent job of showing versus telling."

"You taught me the *craft* of writing, Andi, but you have a *gift*. Both you and Sam. I'll never write like either one of you. I wouldn't even attempt to try. And I've read both of your work."

I nearly choked on my iced chai latte.

"What?"

"I bought your books. Both yours and Sam's. I bought yours when they first came out. I even bought the textbook that you and Maggie wrote—I asked one of my clients to get it for me, back during my escort days. I ordered Sam's through Amazon-dot-com shortly after we got back from Italy."

Why? Why would he do such a thing?

"How…" I stammered, "how did you even know when my nonfiction came out? It wasn't exactly best-seller material. Heck, they didn't even stock it at the local Barnes and Noble."

"I *looked* for it, Andi."

This only added to my guilt for not having read a single word of his. For the desire to do so *never even crossing my mind.*

"I don't know what to say."

"Just tell me you'll not stop writing," he beckoned. "You can change other parts of your life, but don't change that. And don't stop teaching, either. You're a natural."

For some reason, upon hearing those words, I felt the urge to run away from everything—David, Northampton, Sam's novel, teaching—and never look back. Hell, never stop running, for that matter.

CHAPTER

TWENTY-EIGHT

M Y BIRTHDAY FINALLY ARRIVED ONE WEEK
later. Last year I sat in the dark, crying after
another binge of Keebler Grasshopper cookies and milk.
This year David took me out to dinner at Johnny Romolo's
restaurant in the north end of Boston. Afterwards, when
we went back to his place in Cambridge, he presented me
with a thick manila envelope garnished with a softball-
sized crimson bow and a pink rose.

"What's this?" I asked. "Doesn't look like a vibrator."

He laughed. "Open it, Funny Girl. Sorry it's not in
prettier packaging."

I removed the bow and rose and unclasped the metal
fastener, which snapped and fell into my hands. Turning
the envelope upside-down, I let the contents slide onto
the table: maps, a pocket-sized English-Spanish dictionary, plane and hotel reservation confirmations, and an
itinerary for Peru.

I looked at him, dumbfounded.

"You said Sam was gonna go to Peru. And the novel
you're working on takes you there, doesn't it?"

"I think he was thinking of going, yeah. So?"

"So, you're going to need to do some research. Why not do it firsthand rather than Google everything?"

"You bought me a trip to Peru?"

"Yeah."

"But, that's so *much*."

It was so *Sam*, too.

David looked hurt. "Who are you, the Gift Police?"

I didn't squeal with excitement, didn't throw my arms around him in gratitude. I just stared at the contents on the table, a knot forming in the pit of my stomach.

"You're coming with me, aren't you?" I asked.

He shook his head. "No."

I know this feeling. Dread slithers around your intestines like a snake.

"I don't understand," I said quietly.

"I think you need some time alone. You never really got that in Rome."

"So you thought you'd get rid of me by buying me a trip to Peru? What is this, *Days of Our Lives*? You're bribing me to leave you?"

"No, I'm giving you an opportunity to do something adventurous."

"I can buy my own trip, thank you." I pushed the papers toward him. "And I did 'adventurous' in Rome. Look where it got me."

I regretted the words the moment they slid out of my mouth.

"Andi, I'm not trying to hurt you."

"Is this payback for my leaving you for Sam after your father died?"

He looked at me with outrage. "Are you kidding me with this shit? This is me giving you the chance to do something your husband wanted to do with you."

"Don't presume to tell me what my husband wanted. If I want to fulfill his wishes, I'll do so myself. I don't need your help."

"Can you honestly tell me you would've booked that trip on your own?"

"Eventually," I said, aware of the stupidity of such rationalization.

"So, I sped it up for you. Look, if you really wanna pay for it, be my guest—I'll send you a bill."

He left the room; I wanted to throttle him.

"Don't do me any favors," I yelled. "And don't break up with me by telling me it's for my own good."

Just as quickly as he left, he stormed back in. "Fine—it's for *my* own good, OK?"

"So you *do* wanna break up with me?"

"No! I just think you need some time alone, that's all. You need to figure out what you want for yourself and commit to it. You used to be so committed, no matter what it was you set your mind to."

"I've had plenty of time to be alone," I said, full of resentment.

"Not in a place where Sam isn't everywhere you turn."

"That doesn't change just because the scenery does." I paused, then shifted my interrogation. "Is there someone else?"

This time he looked at me with a dumbfounded expression. Like the way Nick Lachey looked at Jessica Simpson when she asked him if Chicken of the Sea was really chicken.

"You don't get it, do you," he said.

"Get what?"

He continued with the look. "No," he finally said.

"You sure?"

"Last time I checked."

I sat on the sofa and fixed my gaze on the familiar Jesse Bartlett print. He sat next to me and lightly touched my cheek with his thumb.

"You know, leaving the way you did all those years ago was so brave. Really, it was. I couldn't admit it to myself back then, but I knew you were doing the right thing. You were taking charge of your life for perhaps the first time ever. You weren't trying to please anyone else, weren't trying to avoid anything. You were the real deal and you took a real risk. I think even then I was proud of you."

I said nothing in response.

"Your boldness inspired me to take charge of my own life in the same way for the same reasons. And it made me love you even more. It breaks my heart to see you dangling like this, Andi, as I'm sure it does for you, too. I really, really thought Rome was the starting point for you to recapture that boldness. I guess I was trying to jump-start it again for you with this trip."

I withdrew from his touch.

"You know, David, I don't understand you anymore. I mean, I don't understand what motivates you. You seem to have everything that you want. And yet, it's like there's a screw loose or something. Something's missing from the equation."

"There is," he said. "You. Us. I wanna go all the way with you."

Interesting choice of words.

I paused for several beats.

"In all those years that you were an escort, why did you never once go all the way with any of those women?"

At first, he dropped his head, and when he picked it up, his sienna eyes had turned to ash. Then he stared off past me, and I could tell that he had just transported himself back into another time and place. I imagined he was seeing the face of every client that he'd teased and pleased, every client that attempted to seduce him and get him to go all the way, every client who looked at him with longing, craving him to love her and only her, to be the only one... Only he wasn't seeing them as *clients*; rather, he was seeing them as once-innocent *women*, and was lost in sadness and shame.

He didn't answer me for several minutes. Just sat there, submerged. When he finally spoke, he was barely audible, still miles away. He sounded vulnerable, pained, almost like the night we first slept together following his father's funeral.

"I couldn't do it."

I looked at him, confused. "You were impotent?"

"No. I couldn't bring myself to cheapen them like that, or myself, for that matter."

"You let them pay you to cheapen them in other ways, though. The desperation they felt...talk about cheap!"

"I know," he said, his voice remorseful. "I sold myself, and them, into believing otherwise. That I was giving them something more valuable, more respectful by not going all the way with intercourse. That giving them the attention and pleasure they wanted was the noble service."

"I think there's more to it than that," I said after a beat, sounding rather cold without meaning to be. He sat still and quiet for several minutes before leaving the room and coming back with the Matisse journal I had given him so many years ago for Christmas. I took in a breath when I saw it, flooded with memories.

"Here," he said, opening the book to a page he was marking with his finger. Not wanting to fetch my glasses, I took the diary and held it close to my face, reading his bold handwriting, like that of a designer's or architect's:

> My father used to constantly call me a fag. God, I hate that word. That word goes first on the "most hated words list." He also thought I wouldn't amount to anything.

I stopped and looked up at him, then started reading again.

> On the night of my brother-in-law's bachelor party, when I was about nineteen, someone had hired a stripper. When she came to me, I got up and left the room. I wasn't into it because I thought it was disrespectful. Well, that did it. In front of everyone, my father called me a fag yet again and made me sit down while the stripper did a lap dance on me so he could check to see whether I got an erection. The rest of the guys were so fucking drunk that they laughed and egged him on. It was the single most humiliating experience of my life.

I stopped reading again and sat there, horrified.

"Oh my God, David. I am so sorry. I had no idea. I mean, I'd always suspected that you were trying to prove something to your father. But how could you think being an escort was the answer, especially when you found that experience so degrading?"

"Think about it, Andi—it was the *perfect* answer. I proved to him that I could get any woman I wanted. Not only that, but I could give them pleasure in ways that he would never dare to do with his own wife. I out-dicked him. And better still, I'd get *paid* for it. I'd get laid and rich at the same time. I'd *be* something. And it at least stopped him from calling me a fag, finally. I was twenty-eight when Christian and I started the business. Can you believe that? I did it for almost ten years."

A silence passed between us before he continued.

"I wasn't entirely honest with you back then, Andi. In the early years, I had slept with my clients before the guilt got to be too much. That, and I was afraid of getting caught, either by the cops or a disease. And sometimes it was just unavoidable. It would just happen."

"You wanted it to happen?" I asked, trying not to feel betrayed—after all, he and I had never been together in those days. Still, he lied to me.

"Sometimes. Sometimes not. Anyway, I didn't tell you back then because I guess I was trying to protect you, just like your brothers used to."

"You mean you were trying to protect *yourself*." Again, my words sounded colder than I had intended.

A myriad of feelings washed over me: foolishness for having been duped by his charm from the very beginning;

anger and disgust for having been used along with all those women as meaningless objects in a ploy to get back at his father; compassion for the wounded child who just wanted his father's love and respect; empathy for knowing all too well a father's rejection, especially when it came to sexuality (and growing up so fucked up as a result); guilt for my present selfishness and for the past five months.

If I had known then what I'd just found out, I wouldn't have touched Devin the Escort with a ten-foot pole. And yet, without Devin, I don't think I would have, could have, had the happy, sexually satisfying marriage I'd had with Sam. Who was sitting next to me at this moment? Devin? David? Which of them was with me in Rome? With which did I want to be?

David responded, "I convinced myself that as long as I didn't do it, then no one would really get hurt. From a business point of view, it was a great selling point. We cornered the market, so to speak. It forced us to be creative. And you know the rest—the women we serviced loved it."

"But at what *cost*," I said more as a statement than a question.

"Then you came along," he said, looking at me and smiling wistfully. "When you walked into that room, that was it for me—I fell in love with you that instant."

I opened my mouth.

"Are you saying you loved me from the beginning?"

"I tried so hard not to let it show."

"*Why?*" I asked, exasperated. "Do you have any idea what you put me through? How I fought to hide my attraction to you, when all along…" Again I wanted to throttle him. "Were you out of your mind?"

"Because then everything would have had to change, and I wasn't ready for that. Even though I tried to treat you like another client, I especially couldn't bring myself to take advantage of you in any way. And I couldn't bring myself to let my feelings out. That's why I never let you kiss me, kept you at arm's length."

"Didn't you know how *I* felt? Didn't it show?"

"I was afraid. You knew Devin, not *me*. If you found out who *I* was, would you have still wanted me? Besides, I'd been Devin for so long by then. There was no David."

"Don't you think your father would've approved of you getting into a serious relationship?"

"My father demeaned me in front of every woman I ever got serious enough with to bring home. That's why the women I slept with were nothing more than one-night stands. Nothing would've been good enough. Not even you. Until the end. When he got cancer, he changed. And it wasn't until he died, when you and I made love the night of the funeral, that everything changed for *me*. Then I wanted you to know everything. But by the time I got up the nerve to tell you, well…"

This time, I mentally transported back to Sam's and my courtship, to the night David—Devin—David and I spent together, to us saying good-bye in the driveway of my old East Meadow apartment. The guilt I'd felt for leaving him, the hesitation I'd had, for just a moment, about choosing *him* instead of Sam. What if I had made *that* choice instead?

I looked down at my hands holding the diary and studied my wedding ring. A confounded regret added to all the other emotions jumbled inside. If only there had

189

been a way I could've been with both him and Sam, I thought, but then dismissed the notion as absurd.

"Why aren't you married?" I blurted.

He too looked at my ring. "I guess I never figured out how to get that far," he answered, almost in a whisper.

"Was it something you ever wanted?"

"I don't think I ever believed I was worthy of it."

"You're wrong."

God, I wanted to love him so much at that moment, but I didn't know how to reach out to him. There was a time when I could, when I wanted to. How could I let myself be as vulnerable as he just had? As he'd been all this time? Would I, could I ever be that vulnerable again?

I wanted to at least try.

I put my arms around him and held him close to me. The warmth that I had experienced at the Fontana di Trevi had returned momentarily.

"Thank you, David. I'm so sorry about before. I'll go on the trip, but only if you come with me. Please."

He released me from our embrace. "No. You need to do this yourself. You'll see."

"What do *you* need?" I asked.

The corners of his mouth turned slightly upward, as if attempting to smile. But his eyes remained dark and wistful, even glassy. He didn't respond.

That night, I stayed over for the first time in almost two months. As we drifted off to sleep after making love, with David spooning me just like the night of his father's funeral, he murmured in my ear, "When you're in my arms, everything's OK."

A shiver ran up my spine; Sam used to say the same thing, practically verbatim, to me. And yet, coming from David, I knew it meant something entirely different.

CHAPTER

TWENTY-NINE

Last Week in August through Labor Day Weekend

T HE ARCTIC BLAST OF THE AIR-CONDITIONER
shocked my body the moment I swung open the glass
doors, and I tightly crossed my bare arms. It was one of
those rare occasions when David asked me to meet him
for lunch at one of the galleries for which he was a buyer.
The recorded sounds of a string quartet echoed faintly
in the otherwise silent space. David was nowhere in sight,
nor was anyone else. Rather than sit in one of the strate-
gically placed black leather chairs, I ambled around the
open space, stopping at no one piece of art for long. The
collection consisted of abstract motifs that looked more
like what happened when you mixed all your finger paints
together than anything remotely complementary. I made
a face and turned my head to an invisible David standing
behind me, as if to ask, *Did you select these paintings? What
the hell were you thinking?*

Just then, I heard laughter—a woman's and a man's—
and recognized the man's. I turned my head again to
see a visible David exit the gallery's office with a woman
whom I can only describe one word at a time: Tall. Tan.
Blond. Amazon. Riveting. Her open-toed stilettos came

up to my calves; her fingernails were long and curved and lacquered in gold with colored rhinestones; her toenails matched her lipstick color. She wore a strapless, black-and-white sundress with a clutch bag to match. David, of course, looked more alluring than ever dressed in his usual Versace, smiling that electric smile and flashing those sienna sparks. I didn't know which one was more breathtaking.

"Andi!" I heard David say. But my gaze was so focused on this creature that it took me a few seconds to realize that David was talking to me, that I was actually standing there.

"Andi," he said again, "this is Carmen, one of my clients."

I looked at him, agog.

"What…when…" I started, but nothing else came out, my brain on communication delay.

"She's one of my art patrons," he corrected, as if reading my mind. It then hit me why I was stunned: I thought he had meant one of his clients from his escort days.

"Carmen," he continued, "this is my girlfriend, Dr. Andrea Vanzant."

It was the first time I'd ever heard him refer to me as such.

A good foot taller than me at least, Carmen literally looked down at me, moving her eyes from my ten-dollar flat sandals to my Macy's khaki capri pants and tank top and NPR beach bag to my makeup-free face and pale skin and Target sunglasses positioned like a headband. I held out my hand, and she shook it limply, as if she had just been asked to pet a toad.

"Hello," I said, sounding mousy.

"You're a doctor?" she asked in disbelief.

"I'm a professor."

She lifted her chin rather than nod. "Harvard?"

"Northampton University," David replied for me. "She's also a published author."

I resented him for needing to justify my credentials to this human Barbie doll who made the same face I'd just made to the invisible David after eyeing the paintings, and I knew she was wondering the same thing: *You actually chose this woman? What were you thinking?*

"How sweet," Carmen replied, still looking at David.

I wanted to dematerialize.

"That's cute," I said, pointing to her clutch bag.

Carmen ignored me and took David's hand. "Darling, when am I going to see you again? I absolutely must."

"Just call," he said. "You have my number."

Holy crap, did he just *wink* at her?

She coyly smiled the way Devin's clients used to behind his back, at the mere mention of his name. "I certainly do," she cooed, "and darling, let's have lunch instead of sitting in some stuffy office next time, shall we? My treat."

"We'll see," he said. He then sandwiched her hand between his two before letting go, to which she responded with a lingering kiss on his cheek. He smiled—not his classic Devin smile, but obligatory, one that said, *It's all part of the job.* I couldn't discern whether I was outraged by her flagrant flirting in my presence or jealous of her long legs.

"It was nice to meet you," I squeaked.

Still fixated on David, Carmen uttered something like "Yes," and then left the gallery. David, seemingly naïve to her rudeness, bent down to kiss me hello and ran his hand along the goose bumps on my arm.

"Hey, are you cold?"

"I'm going to get hypothermia if you don't get me out of here," I replied.

"Hang on; I've just got a couple of things to finish up here. C'mon back with me; it's not as cold in the office. Besides, I've got my jacket there. You look nice, by the way."

"Thanks. You have lipstick on your cheek."

He wiped Carmen's puckered imprint from his face as I accompanied him into the cramped office where another sundress-clad, stiletto-shoed, paper-thin woman was sitting at the desk, on the phone. The office was as immaculate as the gallery and reeked of perfume. David pulled his Versace sport jacket from the chair she was sitting in and draped it over my shoulders. He then transferred some papers from the desk to a file folder before moving to the computer and performing a series of tasks so quickly that I didn't even have time to see what was on the screen. The woman continued her phone call and ignored me just as Carmen had. I looked at the white bulletin board above the desk and saw photos of people holding crystal champagne flutes, clad in high-end fashion and jewels and tans and frosted hair. Lots and lots of beautiful people. David was in many of the photos, mostly with women.

I felt tiny while blanketed inside his jacket.

He finally got the woman's attention.

"I'm going now, Sheila. Probably won't be back today. If Dominic calls, give him my cell phone number please?

If he doesn't make a bid on that Sorrento piece, he's going to lose it."

"Will do, hon," she said in a whisper after pulling the phone away from her lips.

Hon?

"Seeya," he replied. He didn't wait for her to respond, nor did he introduce me, nor did she acknowledge me.

"Ready to go?" he said to me.

"Sure," I said.

"Anyplace special?"

"Someplace outdoors," I replied.

"Done."

I let out a sigh of relief as I unclenched every muscle of my body the moment we stepped out of the icy gallery and into the Boston heat. For another disorienting moment, I expected to see the dense crowds and cabs of New York before readjusting. Thankfully the humidity was low, and I slid my sunglasses on before taking off David's jacket and handing it back to him. He put his arm around me and kissed me again.

"This is nice," he said as we walked together, now holding hands. "We should meet for lunch more often."

"Who was she?" I asked.

"Who was who?"

"The woman in the office."

"Sheila?" he asked.

"Yeah, Sheila."

"She manages the gallery."

"Oh," I said. "And who's Carmen?"

"I told you, a client. A patron," he corrected again.

"How long have you known her?" I asked. He looked up to the sky as he mentally did the math.

"Three years, I think? Maybe four. Why?"

"Just curious," I said.

"You don't think…" he started.

"It occurred to me, actually, yes."

He stopped in his tracks.

"Andi, how could you—first of all, a woman like that does not need an escort."

"But she would buy one just because she could," I said. "It'd be a treat for her, I'm sure. Like getting an ice cream sundae."

We resumed walking.

"Second of all, no one in Boston knows that I used to be an escort."

"That you know of. They could find out. I mean, you had that one woman—you know, the textbook rep who transferred, or whatever. And that's just the one you told me about. Besides, it's not like New Yorkers don't like art, or Boston."

"So they find out. I doubt many of them would care. Anyway, that's not the point. How many times do I have to tell you—I'm not that guy anymore."

"But you act like him when you're in the gallery. It's not just today. I've seen the way you talk and schmooze with all of them, male and female alike." I spoke matter-of-factly as opposed to being defensive.

He paused to consider this. "It comes in handy," he said. "The purpose is the same, I guess: to please them. They're spending a lot of money, after all."

Ah, I thought. *It's "business as usual." I remember that.*

"I just sometimes wonder what you see in me," I said.

I think the words even surprised me, as did the revelation that *that* was what had always kept me from making a move on Devin years ago, what had stopped me from insisting that we throw out the contract that had forbidden us to be friends, or saying to hell with the arrangement and just fucking him right there on his pristine sofa in his West Village loft. Many of his escort clients had been women in six-figure-salary positions, women who could afford an escort. But there were also a lot of women like me. Almost all of my Brooklyn U female colleagues, for example, who maxed out their credit cards just for one date; women who were rather ordinary, who used over-the-counter hair products and wore no-name clothes and costume jewelry, their fingers craving a wedding ring.

I had never seen myself as beautiful enough for his world. For *him*. Despite his telling me otherwise then, and now, I had never been convinced. And yet, I'd never once had that insecurity with Sam. For one thing, he never said things like, "You *look* beautiful." No, Sam would tell me constantly that I *was* beautiful, that when it came to me, beauty wasn't merely in the eye of the beholder but hardwired into me. This coming from a man who was the poster boy for gorgeous. But Sam didn't even have to say anything to convince me; I felt that way in his presence even if I'd just woken up. If he just said, "Good morning, sweetheart," then that was enough. And it wasn't Sam's saying that made it so; rather, I believed that I had been that way all along. For Sam, though. Not Devin. And apparently, not David either. At least not yet.

"My God, Andi. If you have to ask…" David said, shaking his head incredulously.

"If I have to ask, then what?"

"Then you must not know *me* at all."

Maggie drove up to Massachusetts for the Labor Day weekend, and we laughed incessantly. It felt good to laugh like that again. If I had had a biological sister, I imagine our relationship would be like mine and Maggie's. She was, at that time, the only person with whom I really felt at home. Even Miranda, my best friend in Massachusetts, never reached the heights of silliness with me (balanced with mutual love and respect) that Maggie did.

We sat on my deck, where my brothers had played their guitars, she and I drinking nonalcoholic daiquiris.

"Do you think I'm beautiful, Mags?"

"I don't wanna marry you or anything like that," she said, "but you know I think you're beautiful, cupcake. Why? What's up?"

"I met one of David's art clients."

"And?"

"And she made Wonder Woman look matronly."

"Oh, one of *those* nightmares," she said and took a sip. "Really, Andi, don't give her another thought. She's got more plastic on and in her than Wonder Woman's invisible jet."

"You should have seen the way she was all over him."

"How did he respond?"

"You remember the way he used to be with Allison the textbook rep?" I asked.

Maggie nodded as she recalled the mental image, and I knew that was all she needed to hear.

"Well it is his business," she said. "Being an art buyer or a dealer or whatever he is now can't be much different than being an escort. In order to keep them happy, he has to play their game."

"That's pretty much what he said," I said.

"And I'm sure they're not all like that woman. And who cares if they are? He's with *you*."

"But why me? He could have any woman he wants."

"Sam could've had any woman he wanted. Did you ever question why he was with you?"

"You wanna know something crazy? Sam used to ask me once in a while why I was with *him*. *He* was the insecure one. And Sam was different. He was never around that world of glitz and money and whatnot. He was a reading and writing geek like you and me."

"But it's not like David was born into that world. He was from Long Island just like you, and worked his way through college and all that. Devin was an illusion. You said so yourself."

I finished my daiquiri. "You're right," I said. "I'm being stupid."

"He loves you, Andi."

"I know." I tilted my head toward the sun-splashed trees and squinted.

"Let's get the hell out of here, Mags," I said. We exchanged devilish grins.

We drove down to our old stomping grounds at South Coast Community College, and afterwards even farther east to Cape Cod for a couple of days, my first time there since Sam's death. First we went to Pop's Coffeehouse. Two SCCC professors who remembered Maggie from an interdisciplinary committee joined us at our table and chatted. It took all of my strength to keep a straight face—she loathed these two excuses for abolishing tenure. Just as she gave me a get-me-out-of-this expression, I got up to buy another iced chai latte. From behind me I heard a customer call out, "Hey, Rob," to the kid behind the counter.

I didn't have to turn around to know the voice that sent a needle into my spine.

As Rob handed me my change, he called back, "Hey, Andrew. Hazelnut mocha today?"

For certain this was punishment for my leaving Maggie with the heathens.

There was no way I could avoid facing my ex-fiancé short of moving like the old Frogger video game: laterally, then in reverse, then laterally, then...

"Andi?"

Busted.

I turned around slowly, the thought of pouring my latte over his head crossing my mind as I did so.

"Hey, Andrew."

He smiled. "Wow! What are you doing here?"

"Me and Maggie are visiting the old neighborhood."

"Maggie and I," he corrected. What a dick. I stared him down as if lasers could shoot out of my eyeballs and kill him.

"I heard about what happened to your husband. I can't tell you how sorry I am."

"So don't," I said. And how did he even know I was married? I wondered.

Rob handed him a tall cup of iced coffee.

"May I join you?" he asked.

First the heathens, then the dick. Why couldn't everyone just leave us alone?

"Well..." I stalled and looked over at Maggie, who was now by herself at the table and banging her head on it.

"Never mind," he said, alarmed when he saw her. "Listen, can I call you sometime?"

"Excuse me?"

"I just thought it'd be nice if we could talk again."

"Are you hitting on me—seriously, Andrew, are you *hitting* on me?"

"I'm divorced now."

My eyes widened as I looked at his hand holding the cup, wedding ring removed.

"What happened, pumpkin?"

"It didn't work out," he said. "Did you just call me 'pumpkin'?"

"It's Latin for *shithead*," I said. This was getting fun.

"Hey," he said, offended.

"You know, I'm standing here, almost outside my body, trying to figure out how it was possible that I once loved you so much, how I could ever ache for you when you left me for your now-divorced wife. So which one of you came to your senses?"

"Forget it," he said. "I thought you could be a grown-up and clean the slate with me."

"I cleaned the slate years ago, Andrew; I also threw it out. Some things you just don't want to hold on to. See ya, pumpkin."

I walked back to our table. Man, did that feel good!

"Boy, do you suck," Maggie said. "How could you leave me like that—hey, was that *Andrew* you were talking to just now?"

"Yep."

"Serves you right."

I grinned from ear to ear. "I couldn't agree with you more!"

After our brief excursion on the Cape, we drove back to Brooklyn. I hadn't been there in ages either. We went to Junior's and the Brooklyn Museum of Art and a Mets game (I could hear both David and Sam calling me a traitor). We then went into Manhattan and met our friend Jayce and some of my other former Brooklyn U colleagues. The city looked and felt different without Devin, as weird as that sounds. I'd been here a lifetime ago.

I went out to the Island and visited my mom and brothers. Shortly after I had left New York for Northampton and Sam, Mom also moved to Northampton—on the East End of Long Island, that is. She had turned the deed of the house we grew up in over to my brothers, who converted it into a studio/stopover between their tours and gigs. Tony pretty much lived there year-round, in fact. Since their Massachusetts visit (which my mother still didn't know about), Joey was back in town after a tour with his latest jazz trio, and Tony had started his own independent record label. We all met at Mom's house one evening. After dinner and my brothers had left, I sat in the living room with my mother, both the front and back doors open to allow the night sea breeze to cool the house in lieu of air-conditioning, while the ceiling fan above us whirred lightly. Wearing matching white linen capris and a sleeveless top, her silver hair pulled back in a terry headband, Mom sat upright on the sofa and crossed her legs, while I curled up in the rocking chair beside her.

"You're looking better than the last time I saw you," she said. "You're losing weight."

"Thanks," I said. "Hey, Mom, I wanna ask you something."

"What is it?"

"How old was Dad when he died?"

She looked taken aback. "He was a few months shy of his forty-sixth birthday."

"How old were you?"

"Forty-four."

I closed my eyes and soaked in this information. Trying to picture them at that age, like Sam and myself.

"It must have been really tough for you, especially having teenagers to care for."

"Your brothers were a godsend."

I'd heard her make such remarks before: *You were such a handful. Thank God for your brothers.* I'd never understood it—I'd never been unruly or out of control. I'd never gotten into trouble at school or hung out with a bad crowd. In fact, I'd had way more books than friends growing up. The remarks had always hurt me, too; but in the wake of my revelations with Melody, they took on a whole new meaning.

"How come you have no pictures of Dad around the house?" I asked.

"They're still in storage from the move," she said.

"I don't remember seeing any at the old house either."

"What's with the third degree, Andi?"

Might as well jump right in…

"How come you never talked to us about Dad dying?"

She didn't even bat an eyelash. "What do you mean?"

"I don't ever remember talking about it. I don't even remember *grieving* it. I remember you grieving, but I don't remember Joey or Tony or me grieving, and I don't remember you ever talking about it to anyone. It was as if it happened to you and no one else."

God, did those words really just come out of my mouth?

"I guess I didn't want to upset any of you," she said.

"But even after we grew up, you still never talked about it."

"What was there to talk about?"

I rocked lightly in the rocking chair while she sat still on the sofa.

"I don't remember much about Dad. I don't remember the sound of his voice anymore. I remember things he said to me, but not the sound of his voice. I don't remember being hugged by him. Joey and Anthony were much more affectionate with me than he was."

"Your father loved you," she insisted.

"Oh, I believe that. I just don't remember him showing it."

My mother picked up the book that was sitting on the end table and opened it.

"Mom," I said, irked.

"What."

"I'm having a conversation with you, here."

"Still?"

I stood up and left the room. Then I came back. "You know, I just realized something: I'm grieving just like you. Like no one could possibly know how it feels to be cheated this way. Like life can go on, but it'll never be good again, so why bother. You know what I do remember? When Dad died, you left us too. I remember begging you to get out of bed, and you wouldn't do it. I needed you to take care of me."

"And you wonder why I don't talk about it…" she muttered. "So, you're mad at *me* now?"

"I was only thirteen years old! I thought you decided to stop loving me because of something I'd done. How could I have possibly understood?"

"So now that you're older and wiser, it's payback time?"

"I don't wanna be like you, Mom. You never got over it, did you. You let Dad's death define you in some way. Like if you let that go, you'd be invalidated somehow. You let victimhood become a part of you."

"That's ridiculous. What, is your therapist feeding you this?"

I suddenly realized from where I learned my defensiveness. It was like opening my eyes and seeing clearly for the first time.

"How come when Sam died you didn't share what you went through with Dad? My friend Miranda lost her best friend on one of the planes that flew into the twin towers. My friend Maggie lost her fiancé fifteen years ago to leukemia. The guy I told you about—David—his father died a little over five years ago. They all shared their grief experiences with me. Joey didn't. Tony didn't. You didn't. Hell, *I* didn't even think of Dad."

My mother slammed her book shut and kept it in her lap.

"What good would it have done? Would it have brought your husband back? Would it have brought your father back? All it does is bring up an old pain, Andrea. It never goes away. It just becomes a part of you, something you learn to live with, like a limp or a scar or arthritis. Get used to it."

"Isn't it good to feel that, though?"

"Why?"

"To remind you that *you're* still alive."

I was struck by this wisdom that seemed to come out of nowhere. Mom didn't know how to respond to it. I stood up again. "I'll let you read your book now. I'm gonna go to my room and write for the rest of the night."

She didn't respond.

For the first time, I saw my mother in a way that filled me with compassion. And for the first time, I saw how David and Maggie and others were seeing me—so lost, so incapable of letting go of whatever it was I was clinging to in order to keep the world from doing anything unpredictable ever again. I could finally see how it frustrated them. It had frustrated me my entire life. It wasn't that my mother—or I, for that matter—was stuck in the grief of the loss; it was the *powerlessness* that kept us from truly moving on. And their frustration was in their powerlessness to change it in order to heal me. I had been powerless to heal my mother when my dad died. She was powerless to protect me—or herself, for that matter—from her pain. We were both powerless to change the outcome of events. Call 911, give my father CPR (not that it would've helped), coax him to give up red meat, take Sam's keys and do him when he had me pinned against the wall, insist just a little harder to forget the damn cider, have the clairvoyance to tell him not to leave the house... David was right—my rewriting the eulogy had nothing to do with trying to undo the first bad one. It was trying to undo the fact that I couldn't keep Sam from dying in the first place. And if I could just get it right—use the right words, convey the right emotions, capture Sam in his wonderful, celebrated humanity—then maybe I could somehow restore *him*. Maybe, somehow, this terrible injustice would right itself.

I went into my room, closed the door, and called Jeff Baxter.

"Is this a bad time?" I asked.

"Not at all, kid. What's up?"

"I was wondering if you could approve a short leave for me."

I could almost see him roll his eyes around as he huffed into the phone. At that moment, I was just one more professor making one more demand on him. "When?"

"The week of Columbus Day."

"How come?" A split second later, he remembered. "Oh."

"Well, it's not because of that," I said. "I mean, it is and it isn't. I'm going away again."

"Where to?"

"Peru."

"Peru?"

"Yeah."

"What the hell is in Peru?"

"Research. For Sam's novel."

"I thought you hate to fly."

"I'd rather chew on my innards."

"So you can't rent a video or watch the Travel Channel instead?"

"I'm surprised, Jeff. I thought you'd be more supportive. You were totally pushing me to go to Italy, if I recall."

"I could see you in Italy. I can't see you in Peru."

"I know more Spanish than I do Italian. Besides, I'm going to have a guide."

I knew exactly how Jeff felt, because the words, and the decisiveness with which I was saying them, were shocking the hell out of *me.*

"Your boyfriend's not going with you?" he asked.

The word "boyfriend" bothered me. "Don't call him that. And no, he's not."

He huffed again. "It can't wait until spring break?"

"I suppose it could, but I'd rather not."

"Well, *bien venido,* I guess. Or did I just tell you to have a nice life?"

"Thanks, Jeff. Really. I don't want you to think I'm taking advantage of your position because we're friends."

"But you are, though, aren't you. And I'm letting you, so we're both screwed."

I laughed.

"Besides," he continued, "there's more to life than NU. You're coming back though, Andi, aren't you?"

"I'll see you soon, Jeff."

After I got off the phone with Jeff, I called Piero and asked him to introduce me to Julian, the new Spanish professor; I wanted to sit in during his fall classes to brush up on the language.

Finally, I called David.

"Hey," I said when he answered.

"Hey."

"I just want you to know that I love you."

I'd not said those words to him all this time.

He paused for a beat. "I love you too," he said softly. He almost sounded relieved, as if he'd been holding his breath for the last six months.

"I also want you to know that I'm sorry for the way I've been since we got back from Italy. I understand now what you were trying to tell me that afternoon on the bridge in Harvard Square. I get it."

"I'm glad."

"I'm going to Peru by myself," I announced. "And I'm going during the week of Columbus Day. It'll be the second anniversary of Sam's death, not to mention what would've been our seventh wedding anniversary."

"OK," he said after another beat.

"And I'm going to resign."

"What?"

"I'm going to resign. I mean, this'll be my last year at NU."

"When did you decide this?"

"Just now."

"Are you sure about this?" His doubt mixed with worry.

"Yes, I am."

"What will you do for work?"

"I have no idea. Keep writing, I guess."

Another beat. "Wow."

"Yeah."

"Shit, man," he said. I smiled to myself; he stole Sam's and my phrase.

"I'm gonna take the train back up the day after tomorrow. Will you pick me up at South Station?"

"Sure."

"I'll call you then."

"OK."

Silence set in for a beat. "You OK, Dev?"

"Shocked. Are *you* OK?"

"I'm OK. It feels like the right thing to do. Like jumping off a cliff."

He laughed. "Well, you'll land on your feet."

We bid each other good night. It was only eight thirty, but I changed into my pajamas and crawled into bed. Staring at the dark ceiling, I mentally replayed all the conversations, starting with the one with Mom. Maybe David was right about forgiveness. Maybe forgiveness didn't start with Sam or the drunk driver. Maybe it started with my mother and father.

As I drifted to sleep, I could've sworn I felt a playful kiss on my nose and a whisper in my ear. *"I'm very proud of you, sweetheart."*

October

I STROLLED OUT OF THE CLASSROOM WITH Julian, the new Spanish teacher, laughing at the lesson he'd wound up teaching: Spanish curse words.

"Hey, it was the best class participation, hands down," he argued. "And it'll be the only words they remember. They'll come in handy for you, too."

"Hey, I never cursed once in Italian," I insisted.

"Who needs to curse when they're in Rome?"

Julian was six feet tall and wore Birkenstocks with no socks, even in the dead of winter. He did not have the exotic looks of Piero (Julian was American—born and raised in the Colorado Rockies), but he had a cute vibe going on with hazel eyes, thick cowlicked hair the color of brown sugar, and a pooka-shell choker reminiscent of the David Cassidy fad back in the seventies. On anyone else, it'd look stupid. Come to think of it, it looked stupid on Julian, too, but he made up for his lack of fashion-accessory sense by being well-read and well-traveled, having visited most of the Latin American countries and parts of Europe.

Despite our opposite backgrounds and experiences, we seemed to complement each other; I couldn't help but think that he and Sam would've gotten along, too.

We'd gotten quite friendly in the last month, often going out for coffee after his morning Spanish 101 class, which I'd started attending unofficially, just as I'd done with Piero's Italian class. Julian treated me the same way he treated his freshman and sophomore students, making me participate in the same call-and-response exercises and putting me on the spot. Come to think of it, had I not been seeing David, there's a good chance I might have taken even more of an interest in Julian. With Piero, I simply wanted to have one night of passionate sex with him, and he looked more than capable of fulfilling that fantasy. I was beginning to wonder if the foreign language department was hiring their faculty based solely on looks.

We rounded the corner to my office so I could get my jacket before heading out for coffee. But as I opened the door, I nearly jumped through the ceiling when David stood up from behind my desk.

"What the hell…" I started, trying to catch my breath. "What are you doing here?" I asked.

"Surprise," he said sheepishly. He then looked at Julian, his sienna eyes growing dark like thunderclouds. "I thought we could go out for coffee or something."

"Actually, we were about to do just that," said Julian. "You're welcome to join us."

"I don't want to intrude," he said.

"No intrusion," said Julian. "We do this all the time."

David pierced me with his eyes. "Really."

I stared back at him for a few seconds, wondering what had gotten into him, when I snapped out of it. "Geez, where are my manners? Julian, this is David, my…David, this is Julian, the Spanish teacher."

Julian and David shook hands; I thought David was gonna take him to the ground.

"I'm just helpin' her brush up on her Spanish," said Julian, who must have been intimidated by David's cold stare and crushing handshake.

"And going out for coffee," added David.

"All good fun," said Julian.

"Hey, do you mind taking a rain check until I get back from Peru?" I asked Julian. "I kinda want David all to myself, especially since he was so thoughtful to surprise me, and I'm leaving the day after tomorrow." I hoped that sounded diplomatic.

"No problem," said Julian. "Have a good trip. I'm totally jealous of you, you know. If I could've, I would've gone with you and offered to be your guide for free."

"That's sweet, Julian. Thanks for all the extra help this past month. Anything I can bring back for you?"

"Hmmmm…" He paused and looked momentarily up at the ceiling before redirecting his eyes back to me. "A Peruvian chica?" he said, laughing. What a Devin thing to say, I thought.

"Won't fit in the suitcase," I responded.

After Julian left, I looked at David and raised my eyebrows.

"Well, this is a surprise. Kinda wish you'd called, though. I could've been in a meeting and you would've wasted the trip out here," I said.

"But you weren't in a meeting, were you. You were going to have coffee with Granola Guy."

"So what?" I said, irked.

"How long has this been going on?"

"How long has *what* been going on?"

"Your little coffee klatches?"

"Dev, I—" I started.

"*David,*" he said, his voice a razor.

"Are you *jealous*, David?" I asked.

He threw his hands in the air. "Finally she gets it!"

"Look, he's just been helping me with my Spanish for Peru, just like he said. Just like I *told* you weeks ago."

"You never told me about the coffee."

"So what if we've been having coffee? He's just a friend. He's a guy to hang out with, that's all. I like hanging out with people, you know. I haven't done much of it since Sam..." God, I still hated saying the word. I hated saying it out loud. "Since Sam died. Other than Jeff," I added. "You're not jealous of Jeff, too, are you?"

"Jeff is married."

"So what?"

"So, that guy wants you," he said, slightly raising his voice, pointing to the door.

I laughed incredulously. "Julian?"

"You can't tell?"

"Lower your voice, please," I said in a hushed tone. "This is my workplace, and the walls have ears."

David opened the office door and strode down the hall ahead of me before stopping and trying to regain his sense of direction; he'd never been to NU before. I followed and caught up to him, took him by the arm, and led him down the stairs and out of the building to the faculty parking lot, saying nothing until we reached my car.

"Which lot did you park in?" I asked.

"Look, Andi," he started.

"I don't wanna talk to you anymore," I said. "You show up at my workplace unannounced and you go all apeshit on me, like you caught me doing it with him in his office or something. Jealousy doesn't become you, David."

"Excuse me for wanting to do something romantic. I'll bet if Sam had shown up unannounced, you would've gushed and melted on the spot. But because it's *me*, it's inconvenient."

I balled my hands into fists and jammed them into my pockets.

"You didn't just go there," I said between clenched teeth.

He looked down at the ground. Ashamed, possibly.

"And by the way, Julian's harmless. It's not like he's some jet-setter. It's not like I'm surrounded by all these beautiful people who are dying to fuck me."

David looked up at me, his eyes still dark. "What's that supposed to mean?"

"How's Carmen?" I asked in mock sincerity.

"You think I'm fucking Carmen?"

"No, I don't. But I know how much Carmen and others like her want to fuck you, and I'll bet my salary that every time she's in your vicinity, she tries. Even via phone or e-mail."

He didn't deny this.

"Nothing's changed since the old days. At least *that* hasn't changed," I said.

"Everything's changed," said David.

"I'll say."

"Make up your mind, Andi. You either want me, or you want Devin. Or you want Sam. But you can't have all three."

"Don't you dare start handing me ultimatums!"

"I'm hanging on by a thread here, Andi!" he yelled. "Don't you get that?"

I looked at him, startled. "What do you mean?"

"Do you have any idea how I've been trying to hold on?"

"Hold on to what?"

"To you! To *us*! When I saw you in Rome, all I could think was, 'Thank you, God. Thank you for giving me a second chance with her.' And I'm sorry that that comes at Sam's expense, I really am. But nevertheless, I got it and I'm desperately trying not to fuck it up. But I don't think I can take much more of this. I can't take your little yo-yo game, and I can't stand the idea of you being with anyone else."

"I don't wanna be with anyone else," I insisted.

"But you don't wanna be with *me*, either," he retorted. "And that's what's driving me crazy."

"That's not true," I said, although I could hear Melody's voice in my head questioning otherwise.

David put up his hands in surrender. "Go to Peru, Andi. Go finish Sam's novel. Go live your life." He started to walk away.

I had to consciously think of the name before I called out, "David, wait!"

He stopped and turned around.

"Where are you going?" I asked.

"To find my car," he said with a contorted laugh, and turned around again. I sped up after him.

"Don't go," I said.

"Sorry I ruined your coffee date."

"Stop," I commanded.

Without looking at me or stopping, he called out, "I'll call you later."

———————

I didn't hear from him for the rest of the day. Or most of the following day, either. Finally, late afternoon, I called and left a message on his cell phone, my voice shaky.

"There is no way I am getting on a plane tomorrow and going to a foreign country while we're mad at each other like this. There is no way in hell I am going to let what could be the last words between us be 'stop' and 'I'll call you later.' Because you never know. Lives are torn apart by much more loving words and gestures."

Two hours later, David called me back.

"Come over now," he ordered.

I went to his place, and the minute he opened the door, he pulled me in and kissed me hard. Saying nothing about the fight, or anything else, we had makeup sex not unlike the sex we'd had in Rome. Hot. Intense. Orgasmic. And yet, it wasn't exactly as enjoyable as in Rome—more like intense enough to get lost in it. I knew we were both using it as some sort of escape and avoidance. Funny, I never thought I'd ever use sex in such a way. That I'd ever *have* sex in such a way. As we panted and moved, our bodies intertwined, I couldn't help but think about Sam. I tried to imagine that I was making love to him one last time, that we were having the best sex of our lives right before he left for the damn cider. It took all my energy to call out David's and not Sam's name.

Early the next morning, when David took me to the airport, I felt like a ten-year-old girl being dropped off at summer camp, pulled out of the protective clasp of his embrace. Sitting on the plane, waiting for takeoff and the Dramamine to kick in, I recalled the night before and felt flushed before my eyes welled up.

At least I wasn't leaving angry, I thought. At least Sam didn't leave angry that night he'd left. He'd left each of us wanting more. And for all I knew, maybe that wasn't much better.

Lima and Miraflores, Peru

J ULIAN HAD WARNED ME ABOUT TWO THINGS IN
Lima: taxi drivers and spare change. The taxi drivers
will take you for a ride (both literally and metaphorically)
if you don't get aggressive with both pricing and destination, and some illegitimate drivers have even been known
to take tourists to seamier parts of the city, where they
would be dropped off and mugged. Fortunately for me,
David employed a travel agent exclusively for his business
trips, and it was through that agent that he had arranged
for me to have a five-star hotel suite and a tour guide. The
guide's name was Manuel; he met me at the Lima airport
and drove me to my hotel. Manhattan drivers have nothing
on the Peruvians—Jeff Gordon wouldn't even be able to
keep up. Between the Dramamine and flying nerves and
bad airline food and now the slalom ride to the hotel, I
thought I might retch.

The second warning had to do with a strange phe-
nomenon of a shortage of spare change in that everyone
seemed to need it but no one seemed to have it. At least
that was the case ten years ago, when he spent a summer
touring the country. "I don't know if it's still a problem,"
he said, "but just in case, hoard it. Buy a soda with a ten

sol note. Buy a platano with a five sol note. And be care-ful—counterfeiting runs rampant in Peru."

The plane ride took twice as long as it did to Rome; to say I was happy to land was an understatement. As in Rome, I spent my first day in Lima getting acclimated and letting jet lag take over and sleeping. This time, because of Sam's novel, I had more of an agenda. I didn't want to simply be a tourist on vacation—I wanted to talk to locals, observe the culture in action, and capture sights and smells and tastes for the benefit of the reader. My Spanish was better than my Italian, and Julian had often made me converse with him in Spanish even when we went out for coffee so I could practice.

On the second day, Manny picked me up and took me to various places in Lima. The people were warm and friendly and hospitable toward me. The kids loved my iPod. The girls loved my hair. The men loved my curves. I spent hours outside watching, writing, describing every detail down to the color of the street. Like Rome, Lima's surroundings had an organic feel to them, full of browns and sepias and greens, save a burst of color here and there. I could picture Sam here, taking it all in, having a blast, getting into a game of soccer with the kids. He loved to go anywhere he could be both an observer and a participant. He wasn't afraid of the foreign.

Manny invited me to his house for dinner and to meet his wife Marta. She was striking—young and tan-skinned and lean, with tresses of hair the color of blackberries fall-ing way past her shoulders. She made a dinner consisting of *ceviche*—fish marinated in lime juice and chili peppers, served with corn sliced in cross-sections on a cob twice as thick as Long Island corn, with fat, white-yellowish kernels tasting less sweet and more starchy. Afterwards we drank *mate de coca*, a kind of herbal tea made with coca leaves, which, for some reason, gave me a splitting headache. I popped two Tylenol and washed them down with bottled water—Julian had commanded me to stay away from the tap water ("even when you brush your teeth, use bottled").

The following day, Marta took me to Miraflores, a suburb of Lima. The density of Rome or Manhattan was not found in Miraflores, where many of the older buildings were more like sprawling haciendas combined with a variety of cool, modern architecture. Julian said that many of the original buildings had been destroyed by earthquakes and replaced by more modern concrete and steel structures. Marta and I visited stores and street vendors selling art and clothes and touristy items. I thought of David when I saw the art, and bought one of the smaller pieces.

I appreciated and enjoyed both Marta's and Manny's company quite a bit, and both spoke English very well. I seemed to be more sociable than I had been in Rome. As always, I missed Sam, but in Peru the pain had decreased to more of a dull ache in comparison to the vise-grip of grief that I had experienced in Italy. Maybe it was finally getting easier.

And yet, I missed David, too. I'd called him when I arrived at the hotel, and sent him a postcard once a day, always including a new phrase I'd learned in Spanish: *No more mate de coca, please—it gives me a headache. I don't watch* American Idol. *On behalf of my country, I apologize for McDonald's.*

On the night before Manny and I were to begin our journey to Machu Picchu, Marta asked to give me what seemed to be a tarot card reading, and I obliged, though surprised, considering that many Peruvians were quite religious. I hadn't had a tarot card reading since my early twenties, when I attended what was known as a "psychic fair" at the Marriot in Smithtown, Long Island, and among other clairvoyants, fortune tellers, and aura readers, met a then-unknown John Edward, who told me that the spirit of my grandfather wanted to know why I was taking a semester off from college. All I had wanted to know was the name of the man I was going to marry. John Edward told me that my future husband's name was, incidentally, Edward; two other psychics said it was Glenn; and a tarot card reader asked me if I'd ever been a lesbian in a past life.

Marta and I sat face-to-face at the small, square table covered with plum-colored fabric. She lit a homemade wax candle and set the cards in a formation I'd never seen before, sort of like a clock face. She then turned over the first card to her top right. The pictures were colorful and artistic, almost like stained glass or mosaic drawings, with Spanish words that I didn't recognize written on them.

Marta spoke to me in English. "It says that you experience a loss that was too painful for you. Your soul mate left you for the afterlife."

I took out my wallet-sized photo of Sam, faded and full of creases and smudges where I had caressed his face with my thumb countless times, and showed it to her.

"*El amor de mi vida*," I said. "*Fue mi esposo.*"

"It says that your husband is your eternal soul mate and came to live with you on earth so that you may recognize him in the next life. He is with you always, guiding you, but you are too blinded by your pain to follow." Marta looked up at me. "If you ask him where to go, he will take you there."

Tears came to my eyes. I shivered, feeling as if Marta were seeing me undressed or reading my diary. She turned a third card.

"It says you need to be alone. It says you need to sit in…unknowing, I think you say."

"I don't understand," I said, staring at the cards. "*Yo no comprendo.*"

Without looking at the cards, she said, "There is another man in your life, yes?"

It occurred to me at that moment that there were an abundance of men in my life: Sam. Devin. David. Joey. Tony. Jeff. Piero. Julian. My dead father.

"*Sí*," I responded. "*El se llama David*," I said, using the Spanish pronunciation of his name.

"You need to not need him. You need to know how to live with yourself."

I paused for a beat to take this in.

"Do you mean that I need to learn how to live by myself without turning to him for comfort?"

"*Sí.*" She nodded.

"Do you mean I have to break up—*end* the relationship with him? *No más con el otro hombre?*" My ninth-grade-level Spanish sounded ridiculous.

Marta took my hand. "If you are truly able to let go of love, then will you truly receive it. *Be* what it is you are wanting from him."

I don't know if I buy that, I wanted to say, but instead sat silently. She turned a couple more cards, saying nothing, then spoke before turning the final card. "This man, he needs to stop rescuing you."

Was that what had been keeping us together all this time? Was it what brought us together in the first place, eight years ago? Was he rescuing me? And did I want him to? Was it something I'd come to expect from him?

"*Nunca se pregunte.* No, wait…" I knew I was using the wrong verb. *Preguntar* was to ask a question, while *pedir* was to ask for a thing or a favor…but how was I supposed to conjugate that? I gave up and spoke English. "I never asked him to do that."

Marta touched my hand again, and this time I felt a surge of energy followed by a sense of well-being. Her compassion radiated from her touch.

"David was given to you by God to heal things in your life that give you deep pain. But it is time for you to go to this next part of your life journey without him. Let your soul mate guide you instead."

"What—do you mean *this* journey?" I tapped the table with my pointer finger. "To Machu Picchu?"

Marta shook her head. "You need to do it without *him*. And he cannot need you either."

"Do what? I don't understand. *Cómo sabes todo eso?* Did I say that right? How do you know all this?"

Marta turned over the last card and smiled.

"Is OK," she said. "You are going to be truly happy again."

No way. Sure, it gets a little easier every day. I'm laughing, and having sex, and not watching twelve hours of TV while zonked out on milk and cookies anymore, but find true happiness again? Never. It died with Sam.

Marta rose, put her hands together, and bowed to me. Then she hugged me. At that moment, I felt nothing but love. And not the kind of love that I felt for Sam, or David or Maggie or my brothers, but something much greater.

"*Vaya con Dios,*" she said.

"*Gracias,*" I replied. "*Y tú también.*"

Machu Picchu

T O GET FROM LIMA TO MACHU PICCHU, MANNY and I flew to Cuzco (which is at eleven thousand feet in altitude), where I got what is known as altitude sickness—shortness of breath, migraines, dizziness, nausea, et cetera. I thought I was going to pass out from the migraine. Manny found a doctor, who prescribed *dieta de pollo*, a kind of thin chicken soup. Most of the locals drank *mate de coca* to ease the headaches, but I refused, thinking it might very well kill me. For some strange reason, a combination of Peruvian chocolate and Extra-Strength Tylenol did the trick. However, it took me a whole day to recover, postponing our journey to Machu Picchu.

The next morning we boarded the train from Cuzco to Aguas Calientes, which took about four or five hours, I think (still wiped from the altitude sickness, I slept through most of it, despite Manny tapping me on the shoulder to take in the views of the white water rapids and monstrous boulders along the riverbank—unbeknownst to me until I got home, he had taken pictures with my camera). Manny recommended I spend the night in Aguas Calientes in order to refresh and prepare myself for Machu Picchu.

Because tourism had tripled in the last ten years, hotels and souvenir shops and little eateries had sprung up everywhere, leaving us with no problem getting rooms for the night.

"I read somewhere on the Internet that the increased tourism was taking an environmental and ecological toll on Machu Picchu," I said.

He agreed. "Certainly it takes away from the simplicity of Aguas Calientes," he said.

I continued my regimen of *dieta de pollo*, Peruvian chocolate, and Tylenol.

Thank God for Manny.

————

The next morning we boarded a bus from Aguas Calientes that shuttled us up the tendril-like roads to Machu Picchu. Once off the bus, we did a lot of walking and climbing. We encountered crowds everywhere we went—a motley composite of tourists and locals ringing my ears with their languages. The locals tried to sell us oranges, handwoven bracelets or coin purses, and maps. Julian had advised me to wear well-cushioned shoes and carry a walking stick. He'd also warned me about pickpockets who target the tourists, which Manny confirmed. It was a sunny day, and hot, especially while we hiked. Fortunately, I packed a lot of bottled water and sunscreen and dressed lightly in capris and a tank top, sun visor, and Easy Spirit sneakers. All the traveling exhausted me, and I still felt lightheaded from the altitude.

But it was worth it.

The Sistine Chapel was a shitbox compared to the Incan remains of Machu Picchu. And that's really saying something. The ruins, as well as the view, were definitively awesome. The unimaginably steep, sharp-ridged, richly forested mountains that marched off into infinity; the majestic white clouds sweeping overhead; the riverbank some one thousand feet below, seen from opposite sides of the ruins—the *enormity* of it all—took my breath away and weakened my knees, altitude sickness and a day's hiking having nothing to do with it.

And the *silence*—oh, the silence! No words could adequately describe it. Never had I known such silence. It seeped into my skull and pushed every mundane thought out of my brain. It penetrated and interacted with the cells in my body. It practically paralyzed me.

As I stood still, my only movement a pivot to take in another point of view, I wept, and couldn't even tell you for what or whom or why. One had to be standing where I was to truly understand why this site was chosen as a *huaca*, a sacred place.

Manny came up behind me and rubbed my back in a big-brotherly way. "*Sí*," he said, rubbing gently, back and forth. "Is OK."

Throughout my stay, I had wondered why Sam had chosen to set a portion of his novel in Peru, what made him want to come to Machu Picchu, of all places. I still didn't have an answer, but right then and there, in the midst of that vastness, that sacred silence, I was certain that he had been searching for *something*. And it broke my heart to know that not only had he not lived to find it, but that I was no closer to finding it for him either.

CHAPTER
THIRTY-THREE

DAVID PICKED ME UP FROM THE AIRPORT AND greeted me with a bouquet of red and white roses. He then took me back to his place. The postcards I'd sent sat on his coffee table. I picked them up and flipped through them, noticing that two hadn't arrived yet.

"I read them all at least twice," he said. "The one on top just came yesterday."

He put his arms around me.

"Hey," he said. "I missed you a lot." He kissed me, and we stood in each other's arms for I don't know how long. I kept thinking about what Marta had said about David being a rescuer, about my needing to be alone, to not need him. A feeling of dread passed over me like a dark cloud. He loosened our embrace and looked at me, pushing a strand of hair away from my face. "You OK?" he asked.

"Yeah," I said. "You know…it's just the flight and everything. I'm exhausted."

"You want something to eat?"

"I just wanna go to bed."

"Want me to take you home?" he asked.

Too drained to even move, much less speak, I looked at him as if I couldn't comprehend the question. As if I didn't know what or where home was. I fell into his arms again. I didn't want to be alone in my house. Didn't want to go back to the emptiness, to the reminders of Sam. I didn't want to go back to the uncertainty of my life.

David's hands rested lightly around my waist. I took hold and moved them to cup each of my breasts and massage them.

"I missed you too," I said in a near whisper.

He leaned in close and whispered into my ear, "Show me."

I kissed him and tiredly unbuttoned his shirt while he slid his hands under my sweatshirt and pulled it over my head. He lifted me up and carried me to bed, just like a scene out of a soap opera, and we made love. The dread only grew more intense, almost into despair. I lay next to him, stroking his hair and gazing into his eyes, my own heavy and barely open.

"I do love you, Dev," I said, my words sounding sleepy.

"I know you do," he said, breathing lightly and evenly. "I love you too." He pensively gazed back at me. "What if we had met in a different way? What if I had asked you out from the very beginning?"

"I wouldn't have gone out with you. I was too afraid of you then. Besides, I had too much to compete with."

"What if I hadn't been an escort?"

"Then I wouldn't have learned what I needed to learn, and neither would you."

"And you wouldn't have met Sam."

"Don't bring him in here," I said.

"He already *is* here. He's always here. Don't you know that?"

Of course I knew that. Dammit, I knew it better than anyone else. But I didn't want him there in that moment. I didn't want him anywhere I could see or feel him or be reminded of how upside-down my life still was, or felt.

"Yes," I answered softly. "Yes, I know. I just..." I paused.

"I mean, I'm OK with that—I'm not complaining or anything. I just want you to be OK with it."

The man is a saint, I thought, amused by the notion.

My eyes grew heavy. "I just wanna fall asleep in your arms and not think about anything right now."

Marta was wrong, I decided. No—it was a scam. Manny knew my husband had died. He must have told Marta everything, including the stuff about David. I had played right into her hands by showing her the picture. She certainly had no psychic insight. To infer that Sam lived on this earth long enough to meet me so that either one of us could fulfill some mission was ludicrous, as ludicrous as the idea of a loving God, or of a former escort and his former client trying to have a real relationship. It was better when we were both faking it, I thought as I drifted off to sleep, smelling David's body on me. At least then we knew where we stood.

CHAPTER
THIRTY-FOUR

D AVID DROVE ME BACK TO MY HOUSE THE next morning. I sat in the car for a moment, silent, staring at the shapeless hedges and the lawn already covered by fallen maple leaves, some still brilliant New England autumn gold and crimson. Miranda had already left for work.

"You OK?" he asked. He seemed to be asking me that a lot in the last twenty-four hours.

I finally spoke. "Would you like to come in?"

He did a double take. "What?"

"Would you like to see the house?"

He paused for a beat, trying to shake off the shock. "Sure," he finally said.

I wasn't sure what had prompted this invitation. But my stomach fluttered once he accepted. He carried my suitcase for me while I fished for my keys in my purse. The moment I turned the knob, Donny Most greeted me with a loud meow and brushed up against my leg. I couldn't help but smile widely, as if I were exhaling after holding my breath for a long time. He circled me and barely let me take two extra steps until I scooped him up, squeezing and kissing him, while he kneaded my shoulders with his claws and put his head down, purring loudly. God, I missed him. David grinned and ran his hand down Donny Most's soft orange back.

"He's a big guy," he remarked.

"Yeah. We overfed him, I guess."

Without warning, Donny Most became restless and leapt out of my arms, landing on the hardwood floor with a thud; yet he stayed close by, curiously brushing up against David's legs.

"Do you like cats?" I asked. It dawned on me that the subject had never come up.

"Yeah, I like cats. Not as much as I like dogs...but yeah, cats are cool."

Once inside, we both took tentative steps, as if we had broken into someone else's house and were snooping around.

"Well," I said. "This is it."

David slowly and quietly moved around the living room, as if he were in a sacred place. He observed and absorbed every hue and shape and value and tone and texture, I could tell, and moved on to the other rooms the same way, occasionally asking a question about a piece of artwork or furniture or knickknack, almost in a whisper, as if needing to be reverent of the space.

"Did you do the decorating?" he asked.

"We both did," I answered. "Sam owned the house before we met, but once we committed and I moved in, it became ours—not just legally, but emotionally as well. I never once thought of this as 'Sam's house' the whole time we were married. And yet, I can't bring myself to call it 'my house' either, especially since he's been gone. It's always been *our* house."

David perused the display of photographs of Sam and me: our wedding day, our honeymoon in Montreal, on the Cape, in Boston, hiking, at the beach, and with our respective families. Among those were also new ones I had put out of Maggie and me, Miranda, and even a few of Rome. None were of David, however, and this fact was conspicuous.

"You look so different in these pictures," he remarked.

"I wasn't so heavy back then."

"It's not the weight—I wasn't even looking at your body. It's *you*. It's in your eyes. You're so happy, so at peace with yourself."

How I hunger to get that back.

"I was," I said sadly.

We entered the study. He chuckled when he saw the shelf of bobble-head dolls, which had gotten quite dusty. I explained how the collection got started. At that moment I felt a nostalgic fondness for them.

"Wow," he said, looking around and hugging himself, as if getting a chill. "He's really in here."

"Excuse me?"

"Sam. He's in this room. His presence is very strong in here."

"Yeah, I know." I suddenly wanted to leave, wondering if Sam was mad at me for bringing another man into *his* room—in particular, the only man (other than him) I'd ever had sex with, before and after marrying him. How disrespectful could I get?

"You know, I'm sorry I never really got to know your husband," David said. "I'm sure I would've liked him a lot. I liked him that one time I met him."

"We should leave now," I said, standing by the door, impatient. After he exited, I closed the door behind us, something I hadn't done since the day of the funeral.

This was a bad idea, I thought as we passed our bedroom, and quickly grabbed and shut that door before David had a chance to even peek in. I think he instinctively knew better, however, and continued straight ahead and down the stairs, back into the living room.

"Your house is wonderful, Andi. It's more than a house—you and Sam have a *home.*" (I was pleased that he said "have" and not "had.") "I've never had that before, not since I was a kid living in my parents' house. And even then I never really felt like I belonged there."

At that moment I remembered something that Sam had said the day I moved in: *Now it's a home, sweetheart.* I then remembered being in David's parents' house on the day of his father's funeral and seeing the family photographs and, at that point, a man I never really knew. And yet here, in Sam's and my house, I saw the same man I had seen at that funeral, the man I slept with that night. He had needed me that night.

Was he really that same man?

Suddenly I found myself stuck between two, perhaps even three worlds. First, the world of Sam and Andi Vanzant: a world of certainty and comfort and home and self-assurance and confidence and love. Sam and I were best friends as well as lovers, and I missed our intimate friendship on a daily basis even more than the sex. Second, the world of David Santino and Andi Vanzant: two people with undeniable chemistry, knowing each other from a past life and trying to assimilate into a new one. We loved each other—there was no denying that. But shortly after Sam and I had gotten engaged and ran into David at the gallery, I remember thinking that it was probably a good thing that David and I had never gotten together because I was never really going to know David. He would always be Devin to me, and I would always want him to be Devin. I worried that this was still true.

Which brought me to the third world: Devin the Escort and Andi the Aloof. The alluring man clad in Versace with whom I'd gallivanted around Manhattan and learned about blow jobs and discussed Aristotle and Isocrates; and me—uptight, inhibited, self-conscious. We were so guarded and unavailable to each other in those days.

Perhaps we were struggling to find the comfort of familiarity. Or perhaps the payoff that came from something familiar was bigger than the payoff that came from something unfamiliar. So which was it going to be, especially since it had already been decided for me that my world with Sam was gone forever?

"Thank you for letting me into your home, Andi," said David.

I began to cry.

He took me into his arms and held me.

"It was a big step," he said. "I'm proud of you."

"I just feel so *lost*," I cried, voice muffled, my face buried in the same blue henley he wore that first day in Rome. "Just when everything starts to look familiar again, I look around and suddenly don't know where I am."

"I know," he said, soothing me and stroking my hair. "You'll find your way. I promise. Even if it's a new road. It'll be OK."

He let go and lovingly looked into my eyes, which made the corners of my mouth turn upward in benevolence. He kissed me softly.

I walked him outside to his car.

"I'll call you in a couple of days, OK?" he said. I nodded my head in agreement.

After he left, I reentered the house, scooped up Donny Most again, and carried him into the study, where I sat on the couch and cried, stroking his fur and apologizing to Sam over and over again.

CHAPTER
THIRTY-FIVE

I SPENT THE NEXT THREE DAYS RECOVERING from the hangovers of flying anxiety, jet lag, altitude sickness, hiking, and emotional exhaustion. Worse still, I had to go back to school and be productive—having squandered that allowance in the weeks leading up to my meltdown, I couldn't afford to slack for even a minute. On the Friday following my return, I sat in Melody's office telling her all of this. Then I segued into a new conversation.

"I can't believe it's two years since Sam's been gone," I said.

"You mean, since Sam's death," Melody responded.

Melody always tried to get me to come out and say it, but I never gave her the satisfaction. "And I'm forty-two. Geez, when did *that* happen?"

"It kinda creeps up on you, huh."

"I don't feel forty-two."

"How old do you feel?" she asked.

"Some days I feel like I'm thirty-two. Other days I feel like I'm sixty-two. My brothers are taking it really hard. Joey's going to be fifty in December, and Anthony is forty-seven. The thought of their 'baby' sister catching up to them is a little scary, I guess."

"Are either of them married?"

"Both of them are divorced. It's hard to be married to a musician, especially with the kind of work they do. They're on the road a lot, and around a lot of drinking and drugs and promiscuity."

"Do they participate in those activities?"

"If they do, they never said a word to me. They don't seem to be the type, although who knows? I managed to put up a good front for a long time."

"What do you mean?" Melody asked.

"I mean, on the outside, I made sure my hair and makeup looked nice and that I wasn't fazed by the extra pounds or upset when Andrew or anyone else dumped me. And anyone would've thought I had a healthy, active sex life."

"Until Devin?"

"Yeah. Devin totally had my number."

"You hid nothing from Sam?"

"Well, I never told him that Devin was an escort. All Sam knew was that I had been sort of 'involved' with someone in New York," I said, gesturing quote marks with my fingers at the word *involved*. "I never really specified with whom or the extent to how involved we really were."

The memory flashed before me:

> *"What does 'involved' mean?" asks Sam.*
>
> *"It wasn't exactly dating. We were just sort of hanging out together."*
>
> *"How is that not dating?"*
>
> *"Well, we weren't sleeping together."*
>
> *Sam grows quiet. "But you liked him."*

"I was attracted to him, yes," I admit.

"Why didn't you sleep with him if you were hanging out together?"

"I don't know. It just wasn't that kind of relationship."

"He never wanted to sleep with you?"

"He...he didn't communicate that."

I take his hand. "Look, Sammy. It was a very shallow relationship. He was a great guy to hang out with, but he just wasn't available—I don't mean married, just...let's put it this way: even with you being four states away, you were more available and present than he was. Really," I say, "that guy wasn't the one."

"You're not going to tell me his name?"

"You gonna hunt him down and beat the crap out of him?"

He laughs. "He's not worth the bridge toll."

I put my arms around him and kiss him. "Exactly. You're the one I want, Sam."

"Why did you never tell him everything?" asked Melody.

"I've told you before—there didn't seem to be a need to. That information alone made him edgy."

"Edgy?"

"OK, pissed off. Insecure, I guess. He actually had second thoughts about marrying me at one point."

"How did you resolve it?"

"Well, I reminded him that I *moved*, for chrissakes. Relocating to a new state pretty much demonstrates commitment, I think."

Melody nodded and paused for a beat.

"Is that all you withheld from him?" she asked.

The question settled into my stomach. "Yeah, I guess so."

"Do you think he hid anything from you?"

"He never told me about the novel, or the trip to Rome, obviously, but other than that…no, I don't think so."

I grew suspicious. "Why are you asking me this, Melody? Do you think he was having an affair or something?"

"No, it's just that sometimes we see only the things we want to see."

I wanted to strangle her.

"Well, thanks a lot. Thanks for filling my head with all kinds of doubt. Now you're going to make me want to go through his drawers and read his diaries and letters and things."

"That wasn't my intention."

"What was your intention?"

"Certainly not to make you doubt your husband's faithfulness."

"Sam loved me massively. He was the only guy with whom I felt perfectly at ease in my own skin. Being with Sam was like being at home."

She looked at me curiously. "And what is being with Devin like?"

"David," I rebuked like a defiant teenager.

"I'm sorry," she said politely. "What is being with David like?"

I stared at a stain on the carpet a few feet away from me, wishing I were someplace else.

"Being with David is like being away from home," I finally responded, unsure of what it meant.

I changed the subject and mentioned Marta and the supposed tarot reading in Peru. Melody was wide-eyed. This was right up her alley, I thought. Total New Age shit.

"Apparently she went through a lot of trouble to dupe me," I said in conclusion to my story. "And I almost fell for it, too. I mean, I got caught up in it while I was there—how could you not? But I came to my senses when I got home."

I was waiting for Melody to argue with me, to tell me that this was one of those signs from the universe, or maybe from Sam himself, and that I was just using my denial to avoid going exactly where I needed to go. But she said nothing in response. In fact, she let a good ten seconds of silence pass by, making me increasingly uncomfortable. Finally, she spoke.

"Well, I guess in the end you were too smart for her."

"Yeah," I said, and pulled my feet up and curled into the chair.

———

I tossed and turned in bed that night, unable to get the session with Melody and subsequent memories out of my head.

You hid nothing from Sam? I heard Melody say.

Before we were married, Sam and I had gone on a spring break jaunt to New York and stopped at Maggie's on the way to Long Island. We met her at Junior's in Brooklyn, where Sam had his first taste of the famous cheesecake and wasn't disappointed.

"When was the last time you were here?" Maggie asked.

"It was—" I caught myself. The last time had been with Devin, sitting two booths away, when I told him about Sam and that I was leaving New York. Told him that I loved him.

"When?" Sam coaxed me to finish.

Mags and I exchanged glances, and she uttered, "Oh."

"What?" asked Sam. I jammed a forkful of cheesecake into my mouth while Maggie sipped her coffee. But he knew that look on my face and changed his question.

"With whom?"

"No one," I lied, my face turning crimson.

What a stupid, stupid thing to say.

"The guy," he said.

An hour after we left Junior's, coasting in the high-occupancy vehicle lane on the Long Island Expressway towards my mother's house, Sam had spoken less than two words the entire time while I feigned casualness. Finally, I couldn't take it anymore.

"Whatcha thinkin' about?" I asked.

"Sweetheart, tell me right now who the guy is and what he meant to you. Because I don't think you're being completely honest with me."

I froze in my seat and said nothing.

"Was he your first, Andrea?"

I couldn't remember the last time he called me by name and not "sweetheart."

Once again, my silence answered his question.

"Dammit," he muttered, illegally pulling out of the HOV lane and off at the next exit, where he drove along the service road until he came to an elementary school. He then pulled into the parking lot and turned off the car after screeching to a halt in a bus lane.

"I can't believe you'd keep something like that from me."

The parking lot lights cast a jaundiced glow on his face. He took off his glasses and squinted his eyes shut, rubbing them with his fingers and pinching the bridge of his nose.

"It was just one time," I explained, my voice quivering. It sounded so cliché, so completely lame. "His father died, and I went to the funeral, and we wound up together that night. He just needed someone to comfort him."

"And you just happened to be there."

"I told you, we were friends."

"When? When did this night happen?"

"Before I moved," I answered meekly.

"In other words, you and I were already..." he searched to find the appropriate words, "...emotionally involved. It was after you came up for the NU interview."

"It changed nothing," I insisted.

"It changed *you*," he said, raising his voice. "It changes *everything*! You lied to me! How am I supposed to trust you now? How do I know you don't still have feelings for him? How do I know you're not still *seeing* him?"

"Ask me, Sam."

He looked me directly in the eye, his own eyes pleading. "Are you?"

"No," I affirmed, my voice resolute and unwavering.

"Have you since then?"

I thought of the Paris Gallery and the Peruvian coffeehouse two weeks later. *But that was David*, I rationalized. No. I couldn't lie to him.

"I ran into him one more time, but that's it. It was at a coffee shop."

"Where?"

"What difference does it make?"

"Boston or New York?"

"Boston."

"When?"

"This past fall."

I hoped he was putting it together with the weekend lecture that Maggie and I had attended rather than our Columbus Day getaway. But he didn't venture any guesses out loud.

"And?" he demanded.

"And he saw the ring on my finger and the look on my face whenever I talked about you."

Sam shifted his attention to my engagement ring, the diamond and sapphire catching a glint, as if to make sure it was still there. As if expecting it to have magic powers and being disappointed to find out otherwise.

"That was it, Sam. I haven't seen or heard from or thought of him since. Check the phone records, if you want. Check my cell phone and e-mail. Read my diary. I'm telling you the truth."

"Why didn't you tell me then? Why didn't you tell me you slept with him even for that one night?"

"Because it was a chapter that was over and done with as far as I was concerned. *You*'re the book I wanted to read—to *write*," I corrected. "It was one unplanned night with him. But you are my *lover*, sweetheart." I softly brushed his cheek with my thumb. "He never was and could never be that. You're my lover and my best friend, and I can't wait for you to be my husband."

He stared through the window and into the blackness.

"I don't know how I can marry you if I can't trust you."

"Oh, Sam," I said, trying to fend off the arrow heading for my chest. "I think if you take some time and search your heart, you'll find that you can. I never told you about the guy because I wanted a clean break. That's all. I *moved*, after all. Don't you see? I was done with him even if you hadn't been in the picture. And I never once doubted my decision.

"I fall deeper in love with you every day. I can't say or do anything to persuade you of that except to give you my diary. Seriously. I'll turn it over to you tonight."

We sat still, staring ahead. It wasn't until I looked down that I realized we were holding hands, so tightly that the gemstone from my engagement ring dug into and left an imprint on his skin.

"We should go," he said coldly. "Call your mom and tell her there was traffic."

He started the car and left the school, heading back towards the expressway. The remainder of the trip took forty minutes, all of it in silence. Not a single word was uttered between us. Not even the radio. I stared out the window just like I used to when I rode the train to and from my old East Meadow apartment and the city.

When we got to the house, Mom could tell something was wrong.

"What did you do?" she asked when Sam was out of earshot.

"What makes you think I did anything?"

"Because he's a saint."

"And what am I, a gremlin?"

"Don't lose him."

"Butt out, Mom."

———

Two days later, before we went back to Massachusetts, we took a long morning stroll on the beach. It was Sam's first time on a Long Island beach. The dunes stretched out before us, with houses on the horizon, the Atlantic Ocean to our right, its musical waves crashing with force, yet receding with ease, as if imitating Sam's and my present dynamic. The breeze blew our bangs back, while the sun warmed our faces. This was one of the few places I felt truly at home, I remembered thinking that morning. This beach, a classroom, Sam's arms.

We padded along the flat, damp sand, holding hands, saying nothing, looking ahead, listening, listening…

Sam spoke first.

"I've decided that you were incredibly wrong to keep such a vital piece of information from me."

"Yes, I was," I conceded. "And I'll never forgive myself for it."

"Why?" he asked. "I have."

For the first time since that moment in Junior's, the knot in my stomach loosened.

"And I understand why you didn't tell me," he continued. "All those things you confided in me about your growing up. Those weren't lies."

"No, they weren't." I handed him a folded piece of pink stationary.

"What's this?"

"A love letter."

He clasped it without opening it, then stopped walking and turned to me. "I have something to confess."

I stiffened. *Here it comes,* I thought. *"I've been having an affair with my secretary, George." "I've decided to leave you and become a Buddhist monk." "I'm going to shoot you with this gun and throw your body into the ocean along with your silly love letter."*

"I didn't really think the Junior's cheesecake was all that."

I opened my mouth, shocked.

"Well gosh, I don't know if I can marry someone who can't appreciate the instant orgasm that is Junior's cheesecake."

"Maybe you killed it with all your hype."

"Maybe you're afraid you can't compete," I teased.

He gasped in mock outrage. Then he took a few steps toward me as I took as few steps back. "I can't compete?" he said, his voice a flirtatious threat. Our playful faces had finally returned from their temporary exile. "I can't compete?"

"I mean, you're good, but…" I started before letting out a squeal when I broke off into a dash as he chased me towards the surf. And as he attempted to wrestle me off my feet and into the waves, one of them crested and broke, soaking us up to our waists. We both shrieked upon contact of the cold splash, and laughed until we embraced, erupting into private tears.

"I'm so sorry, Sam. I love you so much."

"I never wanna feel like that again, sweetheart. Promise me neither of us will ever feel like that ever again."

"Promise."

We exchanged salty kisses and locked in an embrace while the tide crept in, sand and sea sloshing around our sneakers and ankles. I took deep breaths and let each one out in long sighs. Home. Sam's arms. Our world.

On the night of our second wedding anniversary, after making love, I lay in my husband's arms and listened to his light breathing.

"Sam?"

"Yes?"

"Have you had any doubts about marrying me since the Incident?"

"Not a single one."

"Have you had any doubts about trusting me?"

"None." He didn't even pause.

I sat up and looked at him. "Why?"

I was afraid he was going to think I had cause for him to start.

"Because you gave me your word, sweetheart. And because I know you."

He kissed me on my nose before I lay back down and rested my head on his shoulder. "I trust you implicitly," I said in practically a whisper.

Melody had once said something about a major loss con-
juring up all the other losses in our lives. I had almost lost
Sam before he was my husband. After that week, I never
again feared losing him, and Devin never came up again,
in thought or conversation. But in the present moment, as
I lay in bed alone, with neither Sam nor David, I couldn't
help but wonder if I had lost something that week after all.

I heard Melody's voice again: *Sometimes we see only the
things we want to see.*

Were we so afraid of feeling betrayed, of betraying
each other, that we'd built a bubble around us? We must
have. And when that car plowed into him, the bubble
burst along with its secrets and doubts and all the things
from which we'd tried to protect ourselves and each other.
Sam had kept things from me, and I from him. Was that
the mistake, or was it that we'd convinced ourselves and
each other that we'd had no secrets at all? Wouldn't it have
been better if we'd at least admitted that much?

His death was a betrayal, I realized. Only I didn't
know who the betrayer was. The obvious culprit was the
drunk driver, of course. But right then and there, it might
as well have been me. And this was my punishment. But
what did that make David, then? Was he responsible in
any way? And if so, what was his sentence?

I longed to return to Machu Picchu. Somehow, the
answers had all been there, and I'd missed them.

CHAPTER

THIRTY-SIX

November
Thanksgiving Weekend

D AVID AND I DROVE TO LONG ISLAND TO-
gether to spend Thanksgiving with our respective
families, apart from each other. He dropped me off at
Maggie's apartment in Brooklyn, and the following morning on Thanksgiving Day, Maggie and I went into the
city to catch a glimpse of the Macy's parade. In sunny,
forty-five degree weather, we bundled up and sipped hot
chocolate as we waited for the Kermit the Frog balloon
to make its way down Broadway.

Surprisingly, I found myself looking forward to dinner with my family this year, even without Sam or David.
Mags, however, wasn't too keen on her plans: dinner with
the family of the guy she'd been seeing since the summer.

"What was I thinking?" she asked as we huddled
together in the cold. "It's too soon to meet the whole
family, especially on a national holiday."

"I guess he's serious about you," I said.

"More serious than I am, I'm afraid. I'm just not as
into him." She sighed. "Maybe I'm just afraid of getting
hurt again. Maybe I never really got over James's death.
Maybe you never get over it."

"Gee, thanks, Mags. That gives me something to look forward to."

She laughed. "Sorry, cupcake. Then again, I'm also at the place where I've just grown comfortable with the idea that it's just me. I like my independence. I like having the option of *not* being in a relationship. I often think that's the place you have to get to in order for anything really good to happen to you."

"That's similar to what Marta told me in Lima," I remarked.

"Still think that was all bullshit?"

"I'm not sure whether it was bullshit; I just question whether it was an authentic moment."

"Who cares? You got the message, didn't you? Isn't that what really matters? And besides, I think it was *very* real and it just scared the crap out of you because it was exactly what you *didn't* want to hear."

"Oh, *come on*, Mags! How could she know anything about me or Sam without Manny telling her or my giving it away somehow?"

"Andi, don't stop believing in possibilities. Sometimes they're the only things worth believing in."

I thought about this as Kermit the Frog hovered above us, wavering in a gust of wind, while a high school marching band played an annoyingly perky rendition of "Can You Tell Me How to Get to Sesame Street."

———

Later that day at Mom's house, while Tony and I watched the Dallas Cowboys get their asses kicked by the Philadelphia

ELISA LORELLO

Eagles (much to my dismay since I had bet David twenty dollars against the Eagles), I called David.

"How're you holding up?" he asked.

"I ate half a turkey leg on a dare from Joey," I said as my stomach gurgled. He laughed hard. "How 'bout you?" I asked.

"My mother and sisters wanna meet you again. They want you to come over later tonight or sometime tomorrow. Whaddya think?"

"How 'bout tomorrow? I don't think I can move, much less fit behind the steering wheel of a car."

"How are the Cowboys doing?" he asked.

"They suck."

"Which means your money is going in my pocket tomorrow night."

"That may not be the only thing that goes in your pocket tomorrow night," I said with a wink, even though he couldn't see me. "I don't know what that means, but it sounds sexual, doesn't it."

"I know *exactly* what it means," he replied. I could swear he winked back. We both laughed and finalized plans. When I snapped my cell phone shut, I looked up to find Tony gawking at me, mouth open, mortified.

"I don't even wanna know what it means."

I laughed. "Get over it, Tony. Your little sister has sex."

Tony covered his ears and yelled. I laughed again. "Great sex!" I teased. "Earth-moving sex! Sex so good you'll never want to leave the house ever again! Better-than-*jazz* sex!" He ran out of the room, hands over his ears, yelling to make it stop. I almost fell off the chair, laughing.

The last time I had met David's family was on the day of his father's funeral. From what he told me, they had liked me back then and were thrilled to find out that we were now a couple, albeit under such tragic circumstances. I was surprised that they remembered me at all.

He picked me up at my mother's house in the Hamptons at six thirty. Mom opened the door; it was her first time meeting David.

"Hello," she greeted him and extended her hand. "I'm Genevieve Cutrone, Andrea's mother. Nice to finally meet you."

"Same here, Mrs. Cutrone. I'm David Santino."

"Italian?" she asked.

"All the way."

"I heard you speak it, too."

He replied in fluent Italian, and could have been condemning her to hell for all either of us knew. Yet she and I both swooned at his inflections and lacy enunciation. David's speaking Italian made me horny the way Sam's reading to me used to—I could've jumped him right there.

His eyes brightened when he saw me, and I practically pushed my mother out of the way and kissed him hello. "*Ciao, bella*," he said, eyeing me up and down.

"So, David. Would you like to come in and sit down?" asked Mom.

"I'm afraid we can only stay for a moment or two. Holiday weekend traffic and all."

She eyed him as if to say, *You'd stay if you knew what was good for you.* I raised my eyebrows and concurred. He followed me into the great room.

"Gorgeous house," said David.

"I got it at a fabulous price, just before the housing market went to hell."

"Lucky for you."

Mom took in an eyeful of David before turning to me. "He's very handsome, Andi. You've always managed to attract handsome men." Then she turned to David. "My husband had your look. Tall, dark, and handsome."

Good God, was my mother flirting with my lover? And when was the last time she had brought up my father, especially in front of someone she just met?

"Although you're more…what's that word everybody uses now…metrosexual?"

I wanted to dissolve into my seat.

"That's the word," David said, taking it in stride, easing my embarrassment with a wink in my direction.

"Yes, he wasn't one of those. Otherwise, you picked someone just like your father, Andi. You know what they say about girls choosing men like their fathers."

I cringed. "*They* don't say it, Mom. *Freud* said it. And by today's standards he'd probably be considered a quack and have his own reality show."

"Well, I'd like to thank you for sharing your daughter with me this weekend, Mrs. Cutrone." Ever the charmer.

I stood up. "Well, we gotta go." Mom and David stood up as well.

"You have keys, yes? I'm locking the door." She then turned to David and extended her hand again. "Come for dinner the next time you and Andi are in town."

"It would be a pleasure," he said, and kissed her hand. Oh, please…

As we walked out to the car, I huddled close to him. "OK, what'd you say to her before in Italian?"

"Wouldn't you like to know."

"You're mean."

"Most metrosexuals are."

I laughed loud enough for it to echo, and didn't have to look back to know Mom was at the window, watching us.

———

David drove us to Port Jefferson, where his sister Joannie lived. Their sister Rosalyn couldn't be there, but his mother, who had relocated to Florida and was staying with Joannie through the holidays, greeted us at the door. She looked less pale than I remembered. She had also put on a little bit of weight and dyed her hair dark brown, yet looked stylish in black palazzo pants and a red cashmere sweater.

"Annie?" his mother said, smiling at me.

"Andi," I corrected.

"Andi?"

"Yes, Ma," David said quickly.

"Is that short for Andrea?"

"Yes," I said.

"How nice. So nice to see you again, although David told us the tragic story of your husband's passing. I am so sorry, dear. What an awful thing to have to experience, especially at such a young age."

"Thank you, Mrs. Santino," I said.

"Marjorie, please."

"Marjorie."

She stood on her toes and kissed her son on the cheek as we entered the foyer. "Hi, honey. You always smell so nice." David blushed. We moved ahead to the living room as he handed our coats to his mother, who took them away. He was dressed in his usual Versace, while I opted for a plaid wool pencil skirt, knee-high suede black boots, and a teal sweater twinset. Joannie then came out of the kitchen with a tray of dishes and coffee cups. She looked exactly the same from when I last saw her, only this time she wore cranberry corduroy jeans and a white button-down stretch shirt. She said hello, then put down the tray to extend her hand to me.

"Amber?" she said.

"Andi," I corrected. David looked mortified.

"I'm sorry. Hi, I'm Joannie."

Just then a young girl flew down the stairs, her flaxen hair cascading behind her. She looked to be about thirteen.

"Who's here, Mom?" she called halfway down the stairs, jumping from the last three, and came to a halt when she saw us.

"Hey, Missy," David said, giving her head a tousle.

"Oh, hey, Uncle David. Wanna see what I found on You Tube? You'll like it—it's from the *eighties*," she taunted.

"First I want you to meet someone."

It took me a moment to realize that this was Meredith, the little girl with whom I had colored pictures that evening following David's father's funeral. She was barely six years old then; thus, I didn't expect her to remember me. Still, my face lit up when I saw her.

"Wow! You've grown up so much since the last time I saw you!"

"That's right!" David said as the memory came to him, and he shared it. Meredith shrugged her shoulders either out of shyness or disinterest.

"Are you going to be my new aunt?" she asked. It was nice to see her blunt honesty was still intact. I glanced at her uncle and raised my eyebrows, as he raised his arms in defense and donned a don't-look-at-me expression. Joannie invited us to sit in the living room while she served apple pie and coffee. David and I sat on the sofa together, our legs touching and his arm around me, and Joannie and Marjorie sat in chairs flanking the sofa on opposite sides, forming a conversation nook. Meredith slouched on the sofa next to David, preoccupied with her pie and milk.

"So," Joannie said, "tell me again how you met? I've forgotten."

David and I exchanged nervous glances. "We met at a cocktail party," I said. I looked at him. "Eight years ago, yes?"

"You weren't one of his…"

"Please," Marjorie interrupted, either to keep a fight from coming on or from bringing up his shady past in front of Meredith, or both.

"No," he lied, his voice curt and sharp. I almost expected him to tack on, *Well, not exactly…*

"But you got married shortly after our father passed— isn't that right?"

"Well, I left New York shortly afterwards, and got married about a year later."

"So how did you and David get back together—I mean, how did you meet again?"

Her questions felt more like an interrogation than getting-to-know-you.

"Would you believe in Rome?" I said.

"Where?"

David and I exchanged glances again.

"I turned around and there she was," he responded. I let out a small cough to stifle my laugh before taking a sip of coffee.

"Sounds romantic," said Joannie. But Marjorie squinted at David as if she knew he was withholding a crucial detail. How do mothers know these things?

"Well," Joannie said to her brother, "it's nice to see you've finally met someone you can actually bring home."

"Don't start, Jo," he said, annoyed.

"I'm just saying—"

"Say nothing."

"This pie is delicious," I interjected, and turned to David. "Wanna split a second piece with me, Dev?"

It took less than a nanosecond for me to catch myself, but a nanosecond too late to stop it from spilling out. I started to gasp but caught that too as David squeezed my arm.

"*Dev?*" said Joannie.

"Dave," he said in an attempt to yank out the foot I'd just rammed into my mouth.

"*Dave?*" she and her mother said in unison.

"Since when do you like to be called 'Dave'?" Marjorie asked.

"I heard 'Dev,'" said Joannie.

"It's a nickname," I said. "You know, like a pet name."

"Why 'Dev'?" his sister interrogated.

"You call Meredith 'Missy,'" David said.

"You always hated 'Dave,'" said Marjorie.

"She didn't say 'Dave,' OK?" he said, raising his voice.

"Who, Annie?" said Meredith.

"*Andi*," David and I said at the same time.

"What does he call you?" Joannie asked me.

"Cupcake," I said. Which was, in fact, the name Maggie used from time to time.

"*Cupcake*? That is so degrading," said Joannie.

"I don't call her 'cupcake.' I don't call her anything."

"I *love* cupcakes," said Meredith.

"Me too," I concurred.

"Shall we start over again?" David asked.

"Who's on first!" I said.

Meredith hopped up. "Do we have any chocolate cake left?"

I hopped up, too. "Can I help you look?"

"Sure." With that, I followed her into the kitchen.

Almost two hours later, as I was coming down the hallway from the bathroom, David ambushed me from the opposite direction, pushed me into a dark room, and closed the door behind us, kissing me hard at the same time.

"Cupcake?"

I laughed and then quickly covered my mouth. "I am so sorry," I said softly. "It just slipped out. Do you think she knows now?"

"They never knew my escort name."

"Well, how far-fetched can it be, then? You'll think of something, schmooze-boy."

"Well, you're off the hook for now, Hot Lips—"

"See? You do have a pet name for me."

"—but next time I'm gonna have to kick the crap out of you."

"I didn't know metrosexuals could do that."

He laughed and kissed me again, making an "Mmmmmm" noise. His mother was right; he smelled really good.

"Ever do it in someone else's house?" he asked. He had me pinned against the door and moved his hand along my thigh and up my skirt while my memory flashed to Sam doing the exact same thing right before he went out for the damn cider.

"Sam and I did it in his office at school one time."

I wasn't sure if I was getting more turned on by the memory or David's present moves.

"Wanna do it now?" He kissed me again and touched me. I started breathing heavily.

"Won't we be missed?" I asked, undoing his fly.

"They're doing the dishes."

"Where are we, anyway?"

He started grinding me. "I think it's the guest room."

"You *think*?"

"I hope it's the guest room."

"Isn't your mother staying in the guest room?"

"Shut up." He kissed me hard again.

Shortly thereafter, we came out of the room, got our coats, and said our good-byes, both of us trying to hide our elation. I felt flushed and kept fixing my hair, convinced it had become tousled and unruly. David had to take my hand away and hold it.

"It was so nice to finally meet you again, Andi," Marjorie said.

"Yes," I said. "I had a wonderful time." David squeezed my hand.

"Come any time," said Joannie.

With that, David and I exchanged glances one last time and burst out laughing. "We will," we said in unison.

When we pulled into the driveway of my mother's house, he leaned in and kissed me again—I could still taste the apple pie and coffee on his tongue.

"Have I told you lately how great a lover you are?" he asked in a dreamy voice.

I smiled slyly. "Tell me again."

"You're fantastic."

"I had a good teacher."

He returned the same sly smile. "Thanks," he said.

"You're very proud of yourself right now, aren't you."

I didn't have the heart to tell him that I had actually been thinking of Sam as the teacher. And yet, I knew that had it not been for him, for *Devin*, Sam never would have had the chance.

And I loved them both.

Christmas Eve

"COME TO MIDNIGHT MASS WITH ME tonight," David begged. "Please? You don't have to sing or pray or receive Communion. Just be with me. You can consider it a present to me."

I sighed in surrender. "OK."

I hadn't been to any church since Sam's funeral. Before that, a handful of baptisms and weddings (including my own), and David's father's funeral. Before my father's death, we hadn't missed a single Sunday of church—we'd be the first to arrive and the last to leave, and God forbid Joey or Tony or I fidgeted or talked to each other during the mass—my father would give us hell. My brothers never went for it—they found Catholicism too constraining for their nonconforming ids, even though I had argued early on that Jesus was both a rebel and a rock star in his day. After my father died, however, my mom stopped going. She ignored the phone calls from the pastor and avoided the parishioners who attempted to say hello to her in the supermarket. I suppose she blamed God for my dad's death, and I understood this all too well. And yet, since Sam's death, I was still sticking to the idea that there was no God to blame—or, at least, no God who gave a damn whether I blamed him or not.

My dread intensified with every minute leading up to midnight mass; but David rarely, if ever, asked anything of me, and I thought it'd be a good way to make amends for all my self-absorbed grief by doing something that meant so much to him.

"What made you go back to church in the first place?" I'd asked him earlier that afternoon at a café.

"I'm not sure, exactly. I was in Italy a few years ago, heard the chimes from a nearby church, and it was like they were calling me, hokey as that sounds. So I went in, and something about it felt good. Peaceful."

———

"Can we sit in the back?" I asked as we turned the corner and approached the church. It was a frosty twenty-five degrees outside, and we strode quickly and closely together for warmth.

"Sure," he said. I thanked him and took his gloved hand in mine as we entered the crowded sanctuary. My heart tightened and went into my throat; the image from Sam's funeral—the sea of black—flashed before my eyes. However, unlike the somber faces from that day, this congregation was jovial and bright, decked out in furs and wool and fleece coats, kids trying to keep their tired eyes open in anticipation of coming home to a bountiful tree, and gleeful faces all around. Some even approached David and wished him Merry Christmas. "My gallery patrons," he said of a few. Others he knew solely from attending mass each week.

We squeezed into the second-to-last pew; the church was packed. It was small in comparison to the cathedral-like structure I'd attended growing up. The pews were made of dark walnut and lined up in two rows of no more than thirty each, parted by the aisle like the Red Sea. Each pew was adorned with a wreath facing the aisle. The altar was decked out in poinsettias and a live Douglas fir with white lights and homemade ornaments and a large crèche off to the side. Bright red carpet and gilt trim and stained-glass windows outfitted the rest of the church. A choir rang bells and sang carols, and the procession to the altar was grand. And yet, the mass itself was simple, humble even. The celebrant walked to the center of the altar, away from the lectern, and talked *to* the parishioners rather than *at* them. He shared rather than preached, making me feel welcomed back rather than judged for having been away for so long. David was right about this not being the mass we grew up with.

We held hands throughout most of the mass. I watched him intently as the liturgy progressed, trying not to stare at him, but I couldn't help it. I watched him make the sign of the cross, recite each prayer, sing the responsorial Psalm, sit and stand with purpose as opposed to obligation or involuntary habit. I watched him listen intently to the readings and the homily, and as the organ played "What Child Is This" and the choir sang so angelically and the celebrant prepared the consecration of the Eucharist, I watched David, the peaceful gleam in his eyes—he was so present—and realized I was *falling in love* with him. What

I had previously thought to be falling in love, when he was Devin, was a lie, I had decided long ago. No doubt, I'd loved him all this time, but this was different. It felt different from the way I felt when I fell in love with Sam, but I knew what I was feeling in that church, and it simultaneously terrified and touched me.

A long time ago I questioned whether it was possible to be in love with two men. What if Marta was right, and Sam had orchestrated this whole thing from heaven (or wherever he ended up), and David was the guy with whom I had always belonged? But Marta had also said something about my needing to be alone, to not need him or anyone else.

I closed my eyes and prayed:

Dear God, help me! Show me what to do. Show me where I need to go and who I need to be with. Dearest, darling Sam, forgive me. Forgive me for falling in love with another man, and sleeping with him. If you come back to me, I'll leave him. I'll leave him this instant if you appear to me. It never would've happened had you not died. I swear to you, Sam, I was perfectly content to spend the rest of my life with you—you know that, don't you? Please...

David leaned in and whispered to me, "Sweetheart, are you OK?"

I stiffened.

No. He wasn't allowed to call me that.

I ached to beat it out of there at that moment, but couldn't move. How could I possibly be in love with David? How could there ever be anyone other than Sam? If there was a loving God, then how could he mess with me like this? What the hell kind of answer to a prayer was that?

Don't cry, don't cry, don't cry, don't cry...

When the mass ended, I practically pulled David out of the pew, my knees feeling weak, legs momentarily unsure of how to move on their own. During our rushed walk down deserted streets in the dark, cold night, I was oblivious as David rambled on about the service, the choir, the lights, and so on.

Finally, I spoke. "Don't ever call me that again, OK?"

"Call you what?"

"Sweetheart."

"When did I call you sweetheart?"

"In the church—don't you remember?"

"I honestly didn't realize I said it. Are you OK? One minute you looked fine—well, actually you looked tense throughout most of the mass. But then you closed your eyes and went white as a sheet, and then you just sat there trembling for the rest of the service."

"It was just—forget it. Just don't call me that, OK?"

"I'm sorry. I guess it was too much to ask you to do this tonight."

"It's OK," I said.

———

It was almost two in the morning when David came into the living room with two cups of hot chocolate. The room glowed in the gold lights on the Christmas tree we'd put up together a week following Thanksgiving. (I still couldn't bear to have one in my house.) In addition to the lights, we hung Crate and Barrel and Pier One Imports ornaments as well as delicate baubles that he had bought from Italy, Spain, France, and Mexico.

He wanted to exchange gifts, but I was too tired.

"Please? Just one present each?" he pleaded like a six-year-old. I could barely keep my eyes open, but gave in.

"OK, Dev. You first."

I handed him a gift; his face lit up with delight as he examined it from all sides in the shimmer of the tree lights. He ripped the paper and pulled off several layers of bubble wrap to discover the piece of artwork I had bought for him in Peru. You'd think I'd given him a Mr. Potato Head.

"I'm gonna play with it for real tomorrow," he said mischievously.

"It *is* tomorrow."

"Good. Then I can get to it sooner. Your turn." He reached under the tree and handed me a meticulously wrapped, medium-sized box. I looked at it, then him, my insides quivering; he was all smiles. Slowly and carefully, I slid off the silky bow and tore the shiny paper. The suspense was killing him, I could tell. I opened the box to find clouds of tissue paper. Fumbling through, my hand felt something solid, like sifting through the sand to find the buried treasure—and everything in my gut told me that this was buried treasure.

I lifted the find: a petite velvet box. My stomach leapt into my chest, while my heart started pounding loudly.

Oh God.

With the box nestled in the palm of one hand, I creaked it open with the other. The square-shaped diamond dazzled even in the dimness of the room, just like David's eyes, while the pure platinum band seemed to be struggling to hold its weight.

Shit, man.

"Oh, Devin," I uttered under my breath.

Shit! Of all the times to slip!

"David."

I looked up at him; his look of anticipation and excitement had faded.

"Is this what I think it is?"

"Do you like it?" he asked.

"It's absolutely stunning," I answered, breathless.

"I know it's probably too soon, but I've been thinking about it for a while now."

"So, it is…" I couldn't even bring myself to finish.

"Andi, I love you and I want to marry you," he spat out, his words wobbly. "Believe it or not, I knew it when we were together in Rome. But obviously, there was no way I could say anything then."

I took my eyes off the ring long enough to see him— really see him—completely vulnerable and wide open, exposing his heart to be sabotaged. *Don't do it, man*, I wanted to warn him. *I can't guarantee your safety.*

"I don't know what to say, except that I didn't know. I mean, I didn't realize—"

"I understand." He moved in even closer to me and took my hand, still clutching the box. "Andrea," he said softly. His hand was shaking fiercely—I'd never seen him like this before. "Will you…"

I yanked my hand away and backed off as if he were some guy making an unwanted pass at me.

He looked wounded, the arrow hitting him right in the heart. Bull's-eye.

"I'm sorry. God, I'm so sorry," I said. I couldn't bear to see the look of bitter disappointment in his eyes.

I started to cry more out of guilt than anything else— guilt for betraying Sam, for hurting David, for always taking one step forward and two steps back. As I buried my face in my hands, I could feel the weight of the rings on my left hand, and Sam's wedding band on a gold chain around my neck, close to my heart. And then I looked at them, the diamond and sapphire engagement ring and engraved wedding band perfectly nestled together. To remove them would be to steal a precious stone from its glass case in a museum, or the Baby Jesus from the crèche.

I had taken steps to move beyond Sam in every way that I could—I laughed out loud; I traveled alone; I picked up where he left off in the novel; I let a man into my body and my life and my house; I grieved and grieved and grieved.

But those rings weren't going anywhere.

"I can't take these off," I cried, showing David my hand, my voice full of remorse. The hurt that was creeping into his body was torturous to watch, as if I were making actual stab wounds with blood gushing out.

"I mean, I *won't*. It's not that I don't love you—in fact, I think I've finally fallen *in love* with you. But *this*," I said, holding up the box, "this scares the hell out of me, and I don't know if I can truly move beyond my husband and give you what you so deserve, which is one hundred percent of me. I don't think there's one hundred percent of me to give anyone ever again."

David leaned in close to me. "Look, I know it's Christmas, and I know you're tired and scared and we probably should've talked about this first. But don't say no yet—please don't say no. Just think about it—can you do that?

"You don't have to wear this ring. You can keep Sam's rings on. In fact, we don't even have to get married at all—"

"Are you listening to yourself?"

"Please, Andi, *please!* I can't lose you again! I just can't. Less than one hundred percent of you is ten times more than any other woman."

"No! Don't settle. I used to settle. Look where it got me. It made me cling to men who left me at the first sign of dissatisfaction. It made them disrespect me and me resent them. It made me need to hire an escort to teach me all the things I should've learned when I was a teenager."

He stood up. "You make it sound like you're ashamed of what we did together. Like I'm one of those guys."

I stood up as well. "You were! Look how long it took for you to let me in. By the time you did, it was too late. In the meantime, however, you knew how I felt and you strung me along. You never let me be who I wanted to be, who I actually was."

"That is so untrue. Especially since Rome. Andi, I've let you be afraid, distant, guarded, confused, a total mess, and I've let you run away and come back more times than I care to count."

"And why in the world would you want to spend your life with a basket case like that?"

"Because I love that basket case! I've loved you from the moment I first saw you. Talk about never getting over something, about never moving on... Why do you think I've had nothing but short-lived flings and one-night stands for the last god-knows-how-long? Hell, why do you think I moved to *Boston*? Because when you went to Sam, I missed the boat and I knew it."

What was he saying? Had he really moved to Boston to somehow be closer to me? The confession was too much to take in at the moment.

"I think you love the fact that I give you the same payoff all those women gave you for so many years. They needed you to fill something in them that they couldn't fill for themselves, and you took pleasure in giving it to them. But you never gave them *everything*. You just did a good job of making them think you did. You never gave them the thing *you* needed most yourself. I never could figure out who or what you were trying to save, but it was *you*, wasn't it. You never could fill *you*."

Tears filled his eyes. He crossed to the other side of the room, and I followed him.

"Your father never loved and accepted you the way you needed him to. And yet, you tried so hard to give it to the *women*. What did you see in them that you so related to? Did your sisters never approve of you, either? Your mom? Or was it that *they* never came to your rescue when your father dismissed you the way he did?"

"Shut up!" he yelled. "You're one of them, you know. Hell, you were the *ultimate*—you needed more saving than any other woman, and I met some pretty miserable, fucked up women in my day, believe me."

There was a time when those words would have sent me into a rage; but I felt unfazed by it in the moment, as if I were impermeable to such coldheartedness.

"You're right," I said. "You're absolutely right. So what good is a relationship that's based on needing to be saved? Why do you think it didn't work out the first time around? I didn't need you anymore, Dev. I'd gotten to the point where there was nothing else to hide. You helped me confront and heal the shames of my past. You took away my anxieties about my inexperience by giving me a safe place to gain that experience. I will always be grateful to you for those things. Without them—without *you*—I couldn't have had the wonderful years I had with Sam, or been the confident, experienced, comfortable friend and lover and wife I was to him. And I never would have been able to receive all the love he had for me."

He refused to look at me.

"Dev, I am so glad I chose the wrong door that day in Rome. Maybe on some cosmic level, it wasn't even the wrong door. But I don't know who I want you to be—Devin the rescuer, or David, who I sometimes don't really know. I want to be fun-loving, easygoing Andi Vanzant again. But to be her, I need *Sam* back, and I can't, and I get so paralyzed by the powerlessness of that. So what's left?"

"I don't know."

I put my arms around him. We held each other, and I felt his damp cheek brush up against my own.

I stood on my tiptoes and spoke softly into his ear. "I'm not going to say no to you, OK? But there's no way I can say yes right now, either."

"I understand." He sounded like a boy who hadn't gotten the puppy he wanted.

He let go of me and took a few steps back. I held out my hand—my left hand—and lightly touched his cheek.

"I'm so sorry, David. I know this wasn't what you wanted tonight. I'm sorry I ruined it all for you."

He said nothing.

"Do you want me to go?" I asked.

"It's almost three thirty a.m."

"Do you want me to sleep on the couch?"

"I want you to come to bed with me," he said.

"Are you sure?"

He hugged me again, tightly.

"Please."

Leaving the ring in its box on the floor, amidst gobs of crumpled tissue paper and ripped wrapping, David turned off the tree lights, and the room went black. He followed me to the bedroom, where we crawled into bed and didn't bid each other good night or fall asleep. Five hours later, I got up, got dressed, and went home. He didn't try to stop me.

CHAPTER
THIRTY-EIGHT

W E DIDN'T SEE OR SPEAK TO EACH OTHER for the rest of the week. I thought about calling Melody; about driving down to Brooklyn and showing up on Maggie's doorstep; about flying to Rome and going back to the Fontana di Trevi to make another wish; about finding a fortune teller to ask what happens next.

Instead, I called Miranda and invited her out for coffee at Perch on the day before New Year's Eve. She patiently listened to me tell her the story, beginning with the midnight mass and ending with the proposal and my noncommittal answer.

"You're looking for the ordinary world," she said.

"Dead giveaway, Rand. Melody's influence."

She raised her eyebrows and nodded in a proud way.

"I know, but she's right. You're just looking in all the wrong places. When I heard that one of the planes that hit the towers was from Logan, I knew—I just *knew* that Jade was on it. And I knew my life had just turned upside down, and all I wanted was to go back to the day before."

"Yeah, unfortunately I know that feeling," I said, nodding in validation. "Never mind the day before. I wanted to go back to the hour before—hell, the very *minute* before Sam walked out that door. Still do."

"But you get what Melody means, don't you? Good or bad, we are in this world. We live. We go on. That's a blessing."

I contemplated this.

"So, do you think you've found your ordinary world?"

"I think I have, but it's new and different. You make a new world, a new normality for yourself. And it includes your loss and all the pain and senselessness that go with it. But it also includes *grace*. You learn a way of being in the world without your best friend. But it can be a world that is happy, normal, peaceful. Any world is going to include the sorrows and pains and turbulence, too. Even your world with Sam wasn't utopia. We sometimes distort that image in the midst of our grief."

Again I nodded in validation. "It's funny, but I can hardly remember the fights we used to have."

"I know. Me too."

"I don't know what to do, Miranda. I still miss Sam so much. And I love David, but it's like I want to put it all in a blender and come up with a new concoction—the familiarity of Devin with the qualities of David and the happiness I felt with Sam. I miss the world I knew."

"But don't you see, Andi? This is a good thing. You're ready to take a new risk."

"Doesn't feel like it. Feels like I'm hurting someone I really care about—*again*—and am going somewhere even less familiar than ever. How is that the ordinary world?"

"It's about making something *else*. And it's exactly what you need to do. You'll never get back what you lost. You'll never be the same, and David will never be the same, either. And if you had lived with Sam for another ten or twenty or fifty years, *he* wouldn't have been the same. People and places and things change. Only the spirit is eternal."

I stared at my muffin for several minutes before asking my next question. "Do you think you could ever forgive the terrorists?"

She took in a deep breath and exhaled, as if she'd just taken a drag on a cigarette.

"I'm working on it. Most days I want every single terrorist to eternally die a slow death. Other days it's the war that's unforgivable." She paused and took a sip of her mochaccino. "Do you think you can forgive the drunk driver?"

"You know what's crazy? Sometimes I don't think I've even forgiven Sam."

"Not crazy at all. I was furious at Jade for not having the foresight to know that something bad was going to happen when she got on that plane. The thought may be irrational, but the feeling isn't. It's part of grief."

Shifting the conversation from terrorists back to my love life seemed incredibly shallow; nevertheless, I did so. "So what should I do about David? I don't wanna lose him, but there's no way in hell I'm ready to marry him. I don't wanna hurt him again, either. I already broke his heart the first time I left."

"I think that if you're afraid to lose him, then you've got to be on your own for a little while. You've got to be at the place where you know you're going to be OK no matter what. Otherwise you're holding on to David more out of safety than love."

Miranda could tell by the look on my face that that wasn't what I wanted to hear. And yet, she wasn't saying anything I didn't already know and hadn't heard a thousand times before, either from Melody or Maggie or Marta or my own voice that kept me awake at night.

"I hate to be so cliché, but if you two really love each other and are really meant to be together, you will be," she said.

"It's the *not* knowing that terrifies me," I said. "The *if.* What if it takes too long? What if he finds someone else and marries her? What if I never fall in love ever again?"

"All the more reason to be on your own. The only way you can alleviate that fear is to confront it. Be OK with *not* knowing."

"As a writer, you have no idea how frustrating it is to not know the outcome. Even worse, to not be in control of it."

"Control is an illusion," said Miranda.

I rolled my eyes. "Geez, would you please stop being Melody?"

"At least I charge by the mochaccino!"

We both laughed and clinked our coffee cups, toasting our friendship.

———

On New Year's Eve, David and I went to a party at the gallery of an owner for whom he consulted. I watched him in full Devin mode—charming all the women, yukking it up with all the men, talking about the artwork as if they were his children. I loved seeing him in action. This was where he lived, his world. This was the guy I loved. And it was so much easier to love him from this place, from afar.

Despite our estrangement, he was attentive and introduced me to every person as if I were the guest of honor. We left before midnight, however. I wanted him all to myself at the stroke of twelve, I told him. He said he was happy to oblige.

New Year's Eve had never been a big deal for Sam and me. We'd split a pint of Ben and Jerry's ice cream and watch the *Twilight Zone* marathon on the Sci-Fi Channel. Our resolutions consisted of promises we'd make to each other:

"I resolve to pick up my dirty laundry off the floor and to clean the bathrooms when it's my turn," he'd say.

"I resolve to not nag you to pick up your dirty laundry and clean the bathrooms," I'd say.

We went back to David's place; how I wished we were back on the balcony in Rome. We listened to Sarah Vaughn on the stereo and danced slowly for a little bit. His arms felt strong and protective. Then we turned on the TV to watch the ball drop in Times Square as the crowd drunkenly counted down the final seconds to midnight in happy anticipation.

Ten.

Nine.

Eight.

Seven.

Six.

Five!

Four!

Three!!

Two!!

One!!!

Our eyes met—those sienna eyes, mixed with love and sadness, were reflecting my own green eyes, mixed with love and sadness.

That was it. That was the ordinary world. A world of sadness and joy. Loss and love. Agony and ecstasy. Coexistence.

I wasn't there yet. But I could see it.

I kissed him. Kissed him again and again. I wanted to make love to him, to feel our bodies pressed against one another, to know that feeling of certainty, that for that moment, all was right in our world, and the world was ours.

It was my turn to take care of him for the night; to make him feel like he was the only man in my life; to make him feel cared for and protected and safe; to make him feel full. I gave him everything he wanted that night. I gave him all of me—all that there was of me to give. Because I knew what my resolution was going to be. It was going to be for all of us: Sam, David, my mother and father, my brothers, Maggie, Jeff, my students, Miranda, and most of all, *me.*

It was time for me to go. And I was going to be OK. I was sure of it.

CHAPTER

THIRTY-NINE

January

TWO DAYS LATER, WHILE SITTING IN THE Starbucks on Church Street, I announced my plans to David.

"I'm going away again."

His eyes widened. "Where?"

"First to Hawaii, I think. Someplace I've never been."

"For how long?" he asked. I heard a note of worry in his voice.

"That'll be spring break. Then I'm thinking of something bigger for the summer. Europe. Back to Italy, and then Spain, France..."

"Alone?"

"Yeah. I'll have to cut some corners, though."

"I'll give you some contacts if you need places to stay."

"Thanks, Dev—sorry; David."

"It's OK." He looked down at his mug, and then at me. "You know, I have a confession to make. I actually love when you call me Dev. I don't know why. I guess because you're the only one that ever did. It's something just between us that no one else can share or relate to. And I guess it's also a good cross between Devin and David. But sometimes I worry that you still think of me as Devin."

"When I think of you as Dev, I think of the best part of Devin."

"Which part was that—the sex or the writing?" he asked with a wink.

"The friendship," I replied.

He blushed. And in the split second before he looked back down, I saw his eyes become glassy.

"What comes after all this traveling?" he asked.

"I don't know, but…" The words got trapped somewhere in the back of my throat. "I need some time away from you."

He stiffened.

"How much time?"

"I don't know."

He stood up and rushed out. I ran after him, calling him.

"God, don't do this to me again," he said when I caught up to him. "I can't take it—I really can't take it."

"Listen to me—will you please listen to me? Let's go somewhere and talk. Can we do that?"

We walked to the Harvard Chapel—a glorious sanctuary of fountains and flowers and tranquility. Sitting in the back of the chapel, we spoke softly.

"We haven't talked about Christmas Eve." I spoke barely above a whisper.

"What's there to talk about? You turned me down. What more do you want to say?"

"I didn't turn you down. But I realized something that night—rather, it was something I couldn't deny any longer. I don't want to *need* you, David. I've lived by myself before. But I've never lived *with* or *for* myself. I want to know what it's like to be my own best friend.

"When I left Massachusetts after I broke up with Andrew, I really didn't like living with myself. I constantly felt lonely, even when you and I were spending so much time together."

"I wasn't exactly fully present to you back then."

"But it wasn't your job to be present, nor was it your job to keep me occupied or keep me from having to live alone. And since Sam died, I've been living in his shadow. And you're trying to take care of me all over again."

"Are you saying you *want* to be alone?"

"I want to be able to live in solitude, yes. I want to know what that's like."

"So then, we can still be friends, yes? We can still see each other."

"No."

He put his head down and pinched the bridge of his nose where his brows met. I put my hand on his shoulder in a comforting way.

"There is no one who makes me feel as safe and secure as you do, Dev. The only other person ever to do that was Sam, except I didn't need that from him. I was safe and secure enough in my own being. Which, when you think about it, is ironic, isn't it? I felt that on my own, but lost it when I lost him. But that means I don't need him, or you, to give it to me. I need to recover it on my own. Does that make sense?"

"No, it doesn't. I have no friggin' idea what you just said. And what do *I* do in the meantime?"

"I think you need to stop rescuing the world. I think we both need to be on new terms with each other. We each need to find our own ordinary world."

"Our what?"

"A world where we know each other. Where I'm sure of who I am and want to be, and where I don't have expectations of you to be someone you aren't."

"Why can't we find that together?"

"Because we distract each other too easily. And because I need to figure it out for myself. Look, this doesn't have to be a breakup. Call it a separation."

"Oh, because that makes me feel so much better."

He pushed my hand off his shoulder. I then took his hand and clasped it into my own.

"This isn't like the last time. I'm not leaving you for another man. You deserve so much more than what I've been able to give you. Didn't you say that about yourself when you saw me with Sam? You said you were happy because he could give me what you couldn't at that time. Well, that's the way I feel right now."

"Do you have any idea how much it hurt the first time you left? And how long do you expect me to wait for you?"

"I don't know how long it's going to take. If you meet someone else, so be it."

We sat together in silence, looking at our interlocked hands.

"I am so afraid of losing you. I'm afraid you'll never come back," he said, his voice breaking on the last word.

I nodded. "All this time, I've never really been here."

"I mean—" he started.

"I know what you mean," I interrupted. "And if you think this doesn't terrify me, you're wrong. But remember what you told me in Rome? You told me that I was daring to live a different life. Now we both need to take that risk.

To envision a life without the other and know we're going to be OK. If there's anything I've learned, it's that there are no guarantees. We can get married and the plane could go down while we're on our way to our honeymoon. Hell, Sam just went out for a bottle of sparkling cider."

Another stretch of silence passed.

"Can I see you at all? Can I call you?"

I shook my head, and a tear slid down his cheek.

I turned to him. "Let me tell you something: you've made my heart flutter from the moment I met you. That's never gone away. Every time I see you, my pulse rate goes up."

"Yeah, well, I'm not exactly the Rock of Gibraltar around you either, despite appearances. Andi, I'm just so in love with you."

"Then let me go so that I can learn to not only be in love with you but also be fully present to you."

"Isn't that a catch-22?"

"Might be. Fucking annoying, huh."

He laughed. We were, after all, in a chapel, and I covered my mouth the second after the expletive mixed in with the scent of incense.

"I think now's a good time to get out of here," he said.

We walked back to my car while snowflakes fell in that wonderful, silent, serene way that snowflakes do, and embraced tightly. Déjà vu all over again.

"Letters?" he pitched in a last-ditch effort. "It's a dying art form."

"I taught you about the genre, did I not?"

"Yes, you did."

"Good. You can practice your prose. Think of them as the journal entries you used to do for our weekly sessions. But don't send them."

He forced a smile and held me tight. Then he began to sob. "I don't wanna let you go."

I cried too. "I don't wanna let you go either. We'll both be OK. You'll see."

He kissed me hard, followed by a caress across my cheek, then embraced me one last time before I finally got into my car and drove home.

For the second time in my life, I left David Santino behind as I drove off to the next chapter of my life. The first time, Sam had been on the next page, waiting to begin the book of our life together. This time, I had no idea who or what would be waiting for me, if anything at all. And yet, when I got back to my house, Sam was there, present as always. My cowriter. And somehow, I knew he approved.

CHAPTER

FORTY

A Year in Review

O N THE FIRST DAY OF THE SPRING SEMESTER in mid-January, I entered Jeff's office and handed him a letter of resignation, effective at the end of the academic year. He begged me to reconsider. I told him I would think about it, but he and I both knew I was done. And I also knew that he wanted what was best for me.

When spring break arrived, I went to the island of Maui by myself, just like I said I would. Just relaxed and read and wrote on the beach for six days. I barely even went sightseeing. Shortly after that, I received news that *My Father's Letter* would be released at the end of the year. I had gotten a publishing deal while the work was still unfinished, which was rare for fiction. But Sam and I, being published authors and known in our field already, had a little bit of clout in that regard. A buzz was already circulating for the story outside the novel—Sam's tragic death and my picking up where he left off, literally and metaphorically. I insisted that we be credited as coauthors: a novel by Sam Vanzant with Andrea Vanzant. Despite all the work that I had done, it was still Sam's novel as far as I was concerned.

When the spring semester ended in May, I celebrated my resignation with a trip to Italy. This time, Joey, Tony, and my mother stepped off the plane with me, and the four of us spent two weeks touring Venice, Florence, Rome, Naples, Capri, and back to Rome, taking lots of pictures and eating until we busted a gut. Surprisingly, we all got along (with the exception of occasional annoyances typical of traveling with family). Even Mom and I got along. We threw coins into Fontana di Trevi and made wishes together—we even *hugged* afterward.

La Bella Italia. Magic.

When I wasn't hanging out with my family, I spent most of my days sitting in outdoor cafés and bistros, writing; it seemed to be all I ever wanted to do anymore. I wrote travel essays about all the places we visited. I even recounted trips Sam and I had taken to New Hampshire and Vermont and Maine and Cape Cod and Boston. I wrote letters to Sam's brother Kevin, to Maggie, Miranda, Jeff, Piero, Julian, and Melody. I wrote to David, too, but didn't send the letters. I did break my rule once and sent him a postcard from Florence; I didn't write anything on it, however.

After Italy, Joey and I went to Spain for a couple of days. We arranged to stay with contacts of David's, all very hospitable and cordial and gracious. In Madrid, we looked at the architecture and museums that both David and Julian had told me about. From there I headed to London, on my own again, where I visited all the traditional tourist sights without the assistance of tour guides.

My fear of going out into the foreign world had subsided quite a bit. I stayed for four days.

───────────

When I came home, a package awaited me. My mother had sent me a box of photos, all of my father—photos of his youth, wedding photos with Mom, family photos with my brothers and me. Indeed, my father had been tall, dark, and handsome, and so much younger than I remembered. I studied his features and saw that I resembled him in some ways, although I looked more like my mother. She had the same glimmer in her eyes that I had in all my photos with Sam. She must have really loved my father. And yet, it couldn't have been easy for her either.

Every night I went through the photos, one by one, scrutinizing them with such curiosity and contemplation, and even framed a few. It was during those nights that I finally grieved my father's death, and made peace with him, too. Then I called Mom to thank her for sending them.

"You have no idea what that meant to me, Mom. Thank you so much."

"He would have liked seeing you interact with your brothers in Italy. I don't think I even realized how close the three of you were until then."

"It was a great trip. I'm glad you were with us."

Mom paused. "I'm sorry it didn't work out with you and David."

"Me too," I said. "I miss him."

"Maybe you can try again?"

"Maybe."

She paused again.

"You know, Andrea, you have a lot to be proud of, the way you've worked so hard to get past your husband's death while still keeping his memory alive. And doing it all on your own, too."

I took in a breath, a lump forming in my throat. "I wasn't exactly alone, but I know what you mean. I didn't have children to worry about. You're the one that had it so tough."

"Still," she said. "You didn't let it stop you from moving on. I'm proud of you," she said after a beat, her voice choked with emotion.

Tears filled my eyes as I also choked up. "Oh, Mom," was all I could say.

———

Shortly after my return from Europe, I went back to NU to speak to Jeff. It turned out that I might have been too hasty in my resignation, I told him—I wanted to teach again. Part-time.

"Not comp," I said more emphatically than intended. "But I was wondering if there was something in the creative writing program, or even just an upper-level course in rhetoric."

"I'm sure we'll find something for you to do," Jeff said. "NU takes good care of its own. Trust me—the door didn't slam behind you."

"Just one course," I reminded him again.

"One is all you'll need."

Meanwhile, Miranda suggested that our book club read *Man's Search for Meaning* by Viktor Frankl—a much heavier read than most of our selections, but we all decided to go for it. I vaguely remembered reading it in college for a psychology class; I also remembered needing to put it down because I couldn't see past my tears to read the words clearly. This time I wept again with the same intensity and empathy, but I also had an epiphany that I shared with Melody.

"Frankl says that between stimulus and response, one is free to choose. Do you know what that means? It means I can choose the way I respond to Sam's death, to my mother's behavior, to my students' writing. And when I think that that's how he survived the concentration camps, when he realized that that was the one thing *no one* could take from him, that one essential freedom…"

My eyes welled up from the magnitude of the moment. So did Melody's.

It was what Melody had been trying to tell me all along. In the face of powerlessness, *that* was my ticket to freedom. I could choose to be eaten alive by grief, to spend the rest of my life living in fear of that powerlessness and the unknowable; or, I could respond differently. Not react—*respond*. I could either keep Sam alive in me and others, or bury him along with his physical body.

I could choose to forgive, too.

Forgiveness wasn't a one-shot deal, I learned. Rather, it was a lot like the revision process; it involved re-seeing a person or a situation in different ways, of looking past the surface errors and finding the real meaning, finding truth. Once accessed, that truth could be transformed into compassion, understanding, love.

The hardest person to forgive was the drunk driver. He would've been graduating college by now; instead, he was serving time for manslaughter. He fucked up his life and knew it. Hell, he fucked up *my* life, and all this time I'd assumed he didn't give a shit about that.

Since Sam's death, I had written so many letters to that kid. Angry, hate-filled, horrid letters in which I wished his own death on him. The truly frightening flaw in humanity is our capacity for cruelty—we all have it. Thank goodness I had never sent any of them. Thus, my first step in forgiveness was to destroy those letters. As they burned in a pile of leaves in my backyard, my anger raged right along with the flames. I wanted to kill him myself. And then I cried cathartically, once again, for the loss of my husband, my best friend, our life together. But I also realized that this kid had taken his own life, too, metaphorically. We all lost something.

I began writing letters again, and this time I sent them. Some began angrily but moved towards a gesture of willingness. *I'm willing to learn to forgive you.* Willingness was always a good starting point, whereas hate and bitterness and resentment took up too much energy. Sam had come to realize that right before he died. I think his novel was the beginning of his forgiving his own father for leaving. And he had come to take a position on war that had nothing to do with politics and everything to do with forgiveness. "Imagine if we had forgiven the terrorists instead of bombing the wax out of the ears of innocent

ELISA LORELLO

people," he'd said. "Imagine if instead of a 'war on terror' we had a 'forgiveness of terror.'"

I'd been against war from day one; throughout my life, really. But I hadn't truly heard him that day. "Thank you, John Lennon," was my response. In hindsight, my ignorance and dismissal must have hurt him deeply. "Forgive *me*, Sam," was my present plea.

A few weeks later, the kid responded, expressing his utmost remorse. My first reaction was that his grammar and spelling were atrocious. My second was that of pure skepticism. *Of course he's remorseful. He's stuck in hell and an orange jumpsuit and can't even take a shit without someone watching him. Serves him right. The hell he's sorry. He's sorry Sam got killed, maybe, but not for getting so tanked in the first place.*

Choose a different response, I heard a voice within me say. I'm pretty sure the voice was Sam's.

I wrote back to the kid, one line. *Do you like writing?*

He wrote back. *No. My teachers in High School told me that my writting is terrible and the only way I would pass collage was if i cheated my way thru.*

And that's when I began to see him in a new light. Was it possible that he had gotten so tanked that night in order to forget who *he* was? Was it possible that he took to heart that the only way he was going to get through life was by cheating himself and others? No kid deserves to be told that.

He wasn't born wanting to be a drunk driver. He wasn't born wanting to kill my husband.

I wrote to him again. *Would you like to learn something about writing?*

He responded. *Yes.*

I then sent him a composition notebook, the kind used in elementary school with black and white squiggles on the cover. I also gave him his first assignment (write about your history with reading and writing) and enclosed a copy of one of Sam's literacy narratives. Thus began the long-distance tutorial by mail. How completely bizarre and ironic that my first composition student since leaving the field of composition was the one who had caused me to leave in the first place.

———————

I had also tracked down the students from the class in which I'd had the meltdown. I mailed each of them a handwritten apology. One of the boys had dropped out. Another graduated. A third e-mailed me to tell me he'd gotten wasted that same day, then woke up in the middle of the night after having a vivid dream about my husband. "I quit all of it," he wrote. "The drinking, the pot, everything. Been clean ever since. I never want to be the cause of someone having a nervous breakdown like you did that day."

I cringed upon reading the words "nervous breakdown." Students can be quite perceptive.

Hayley, whose sister had had Sam for a teacher, came to visit me in my office one afternoon.

"Thank you for your note. I'm so glad you're doing better," she said. "I had heard so many good things about you as a teacher. That's why I tried so hard to get into your class. If I could, I'd take another one, but I'm graduating this semester."

I congratulated her. Then I added, "I'm sorry I ruined your expectations, and that I let you down."

"It's OK—it wasn't meant to be," she said.

My Father's Letter was released Columbus Day weekend (how appropriate) to mixed reviews, but captured a lot of attention thanks mostly in part to interviews I did with National Public Radio in Boston, the *Chronicle of Higher Education*, the *Boston Globe*, and both NU and Edmund College's campus newspapers. I also did book signings at both campuses, as well as Harvard (Sam's alma mater) and independent bookstores in Amherst and Harvard Square before hitting the road for a New England book tour that ended in Manhattan and my hometown on Long Island.

In addition to the reading, Edmund College held a small remembrance ceremony for Sam. And there I read the finished eulogy:

> *I grew up on Long Island, not far from the Walt Whitman birthplace. Back then, the house remained unguarded and exposed to the public. It looked like your typical colonial house—and yet it inconspicuously sat in the midst of commercial supermarkets and shopping centers and delis and the International House of Pancakes. Years later, after some vandalism occurred, the Town of Huntington set out to restore the Whitman house and build an accompanying museum. And a fence, too. Sadly, one can no longer see the house from the street (then again, in those days one had to be looking for it in order to see it at all).*

Every visit to every new town or city or state was an adventure for my husband, Sam. He would Google information on histories, traditions, events. He'd talk to the locals and go to the places that weren't on the tourist maps. He'd bring a camera, but would take only those pictures that best encapsulated the essence of the experience because he much preferred seeing the world through his own lens.

On one of our many weekend excursions, I took Sam to the Whitman house, now obnoxiously named the Walt Whitman Birthplace State Historic Site and Interpretive Center. He went through the museum methodically, reading every placard and perusing every document and intensely studying each artifact. A fountain of knowledge of all things Walt Whitman, he augmented much of the docent's comments with his own bits of trivia, much to my delight and the docent's dismay for being shown up.

But when we went into the actual house, Sam was awestruck. He pointed to the antiquated wooden desk—"Just think of all the words that came pouring out of him while sitting at that desk!" he said. Then he pointed to another piece of furniture. "Just think of the conversations he had there!" And so on. I sauntered through the house less inspired, although tickled by his childlike thrill.

"Doesn't this excite you, sweetheart?" he asked me. "We're standing in Walt Whitman*'s house! One of the greatest poets of all time! One of the greatest* citizens*! I've seen you more excited walking through a shoe store."*

"Sorry, Sammy," I said, "but I've seen it many times. I've been here on school field trips, when I got my driver's license, breaks from college…it's like going home to me. And all the hoopla from the museum and the fence and the preservation has

kind of taken something away from it all. I liked it better when it was more ordinary, when it was lost in its surroundings."

"But that's precisely what makes it extraordinary!" *he exclaimed. "That desk, that table and chair, this entire house—it was all once ordinary. Just one house owned by one family. How could Walt Whitman have possibly known that generation after generation was going to pass through these rooms and marvel at the greatness to come from something so ordinary? Imagine that—imagine generations to come walking through* our *house like that. Will they ever know our greatness?"*

"What makes us so great?" I asked.

"Because we're here. *Now."*

Alas, that was Sam—always willing to appreciate the past and look forward to the future without ever being absent from the now. He believed in greatness. But greatness was found in flaws. He believed that flaws, even the horrific ones, made humanity truly worthwhile. Without flawed humanity, there could be no revision. There would be only one way of seeing the world, of relating to one another, of creating a piece of art. Art that is not flawed is not beautiful, he would say. Even Walt Whitman was flawed. Perfection to Sam was the balance of strengths and weaknesses. Love and fear. Feast and famine. He was a yin and yang guy all the way.

As a writer and teacher, his own flawed humanity came out on every page that he wrote and shared with his students, and his students loved him for it—he was "real" to them. He was real because he was ordinary. And he was extraordinary because he saw greatness everywhere.

I miss Sam every day. He wanted to travel and see more of the world. He wanted to write novels. He wanted to answer the "what-if" questions that he posed to his students, his friends, me, and the world. He was not in the world—the world was in him. And what I've come to realize is that he's not left the world, he's become *the world.*

We may never have visitors ambling through our home one hundred years later, our rooms carefully preserved and roped off for protection, gawkers pointing at our couches and tables and chairs, but Sam has clearly left his mark. My heart swells to the bursting point when I think of all the students he's touched, all those who are better people, less flawed, because of knowing him, even after meeting him for a few seconds. Certainly I am a much better me. It's up to us to pass on the best of Sam to everyone we meet and know. That way, he can't and won't ever leave us, and his greatness will live on.

I could let go of that now, too.

———

Living alone did not have to be the purgatory I'd always believed it to be. I now went by myself to all the places I had gone with Sam or David—the Coop in Harvard Square, the North End of Boston, the lake at Northampton University, to name a few. I took myself to the movie theater. I took myself to dinner. I took myself to Cape Cod for a weekend. I sat in Perch with a book or my laptop, perfectly content. I strolled down Main Street in Amherst and basked in the sunlight. Indeed, I kept myself good company, and it didn't take long for me to realize that I was actually courting myself.

Miranda noticed that the sadness in my eyes had all but disappeared lately. Melody was happy to hear me talk about the future with hope rather than hollowness. I told her that I was going to end our sessions. Didn't need them anymore.

She agreed. "You've arrived," she said.

We embraced in her office, and my heart was filled with gratitude for her.

Maggie said I sounded like "the old Andi," but better. "You've learned how to be your own best friend," she said. "Magnificent." Even Donny Most curled up in my lap and brushed up against my ankles affectionately.

The ache for Sam never went away, but it became a part of me that I chose to accept and live with. And oftentimes, especially when I wrote, Sam was with me. He was good company, too. Still.

———

I fell in love again, too—with novel-writing, that is. Not long after the first one went to print, I started writing a new novel about a woman who meets several people while hiking the Appalachian Trail; its working title was *Walking*. And, like most hikers on the trail, I wasn't sure where it was going, or what else there was to do besides walk. I had discovered that hiking the Appalachian Trail was something else Sam had wanted to do. I contemplated trying the trail myself, but the idea of not being able to plug in a blow-dryer anywhere was unappealing.

The dialogue between these characters was interesting, however. It was an exploration, albeit too soon to tell of what. A lot of it seemed to stem from conversations and relationships I had or wanted to have with all the men in my life. With each new person the protagonist encountered, I felt as if I were walking with a different person as well.

It was about moving forward, really.

———

In the fall I went back to teaching at NU. Jeff gave me one course called Autobiographical Writing. The class consisted of fifteen students, all upper level, and I conducted it workshop style. I assigned both Sam's and my collections of creative nonfiction prose, and began a new series of essays—I was finally writing about Sam, and not to eulogize him. It occurred to me one day that I was writing love stories. Everyone, including myself, contributed writing on a weekly basis.

It was nice to be back in the classroom again, especially in this way. Maggie and I were even thinking about a compilation of texts for a graduate level class on the rhetoric of life, death, and regeneration. Jeff said, "Welcome back, kid."

———

I refused to date anyone but had started spending time with Julian the Spanish professor again. We'd meet after class for coffee or attend Foreign Film Fridays at NU. One night afterwards, he walked me to my car and kissed me good night. I never saw it coming.

"That's cute," I said afterwards. He looked at me, puzzled, and I grinned. "Thanks," I said. I liked him.

But I missed David. Not a day went by when I didn't think of him.

I found out through one of NU's textbook reps that the art history book with the chapter he wrote had been released, and she got me a desk copy. I read every word of his chapter. Since we'd broken up, I read every word of every one of his columns as well.

I wondered if he was seeing anyone. I only hoped that if he was, it was serious and not some fling, even though I was contemplating a fling with Julian. He and I went out on one more date, and I kissed him one more time. He smelled like eucalyptus. He was also a good kisser.

But I decided not to have a fling with Julian. I'm not fling material. Never was. And that was the last time he and I went out.

———————

In November, as the last of the fall foliage peaked and slipped off the trees, I treated myself to the Boston Museum of Art exhibit *Monet in Normandy*. Dressed in new blue jeans (I was fitting into size six again), suede boots, and a soft, V-neck pink sweater that Maggie sent me from one of the New York boutiques, I graced the Boston sidewalks as if they were fashion runways. My hair grew long and fell in natural ringlets. I felt free. Alive. *Bellissima*.

Because it was a Friday night, Monet aficionados filled the exhibition galleries. However, this was not the most ideal way to look at the paintings, since, like David, I preferred to view the works from various angles and distance points around the gallery. In the second gallery, I backed up, only to turn around and spot the tall figure, in his black leather jacket and Gap blue jeans, trying to get a good look at one of the cathedral paintings.

I beamed.

Of course he was here—where else would he be? And I was pretty sure that I had wanted to find him.

At first, I watched him with delight. Watched him for a good five minutes, maybe more.

Then, as patrons sauntered from one painting to the next, I sidled next to him and looked ahead. Totally absorbed, as always, he never even noticed me.

"Don't you just *adore* Monet?"

H E WHISKED HIS HEAD AND HIS SIENNA EYES went ablaze for a split second upon seeing me, only to return to the painting. He said nothing.

Staring ahead, I leaned toward him and spoke again, very softly. "He's good at painting clouds, don't you think? It's hard to make clouds look real. Yep, that's what Monet is. A good cloud painter."

He feigned frustration and pretended to ignore me.

"How hard do you think it would be to do a paint-by-numbers of *Water Lilies*?"

He put his head down, as if disgusted, but I could tell he was trying hard to keep from cracking up.

"Would you please shut up? You're bothering the paintings," he said, gesturing in their direction.

"Do you think he called them 'happy water lilies' when he painted them?"

He covered his mouth and laughed. I pumped my fist in victory for breaking him.

Finally, he turned to scan me up and down. "You look real good," he said.

I was still beaming. "So do you."

We moved to the next painting.

"Well, you're speaking to me; that's a good sign," I said.

"Shhhhhh," he said. "It's *Monet*, dammit."

I gasped. "How dare you curse in front of Monet!"

We giggled as surrounding patrons glared at us.

We moved to the next painting. David backed up, then moved to the left, then went on his knees. My cheeks were actually starting to hurt from smiling so much.

He stood next to me again, and again I spoke after a beat of silence, the two of us still staring straight ahead.

"I was wondering if you're doing anything next Saturday night."

"Committing suicide," he replied.

"How about Friday night?"

Again we giggled.

Something occurred to me at that moment. "You know which Woody Allen movie that's from, don't you," I remarked.

He nodded. "*Play It Again, Sam.*"

At that point, we turned to one another, and our eyes locked in their own embrace. We'd embraced each other in this look before—it was a look among friends, a look of love, of familiarity, of comfort. And it was our own.

"Can we finish this exhibit and then get into the banter?" he asked.

I conceded. We finished the exhibit together, falling into our rhythm as if a day of separation had never passed. Afterwards, we ordered espresso and a piece of cake at the museum café.

"Happy anniversary," he said.

My heart leapt into my throat. "You remembered."

"I thought about calling you that week. Chickened out, I guess."

"I don't blame you."

"Congratulations on the novel, too. I saw it at the Coop."

"Thanks."

"I'm sorry I didn't go to your reading, either. I really, really wanted to, but—"

I held up my hand to cut him off. "It's OK. I have a copy for you, though."

"Thanks," he said. "I already bought one."

Of course he had.

"Congrats on *your* book, too. The chapter, I mean. I thought it was great."

This time he beamed.

"You read it?" He sounded like a child looking for approval from a parent.

"Every word."

One would have thought the sparks between us could've shorted out the lights.

"How are you?" he asked.

"I'm doing really well."

"You look it—you look like you've found some peace."

"I have."

"I'm so glad to hear that."

"How are *you*?" I asked.

"I'm doing pretty well."

"Are you seeing anyone?"

"No," he replied. "Are you?"

"No."

I think we were both secretly relieved to hear this. I knew I was.

"Were you seeing someone?" he asked.

"No."

"I saw you at Perch one day with Granola Guy."

"What were you doing in Amherst?" I asked.

"What were you doing with Granola Guy?"

"I'm not allowed to just hang out with guys?"

"You didn't look like you were hanging out."

"No?"

"You looked like you were flirting with each other."

"Where were you—hiding in the bathroom or something?"

"I passed by the window. You were sitting at the corner table."

"That's impressive—could you see his Birkenstocks from the window?"

"You didn't even see me."

"Well then, that proves it. I mean, if I didn't even see you, I must have been so engrossed in him. In fact, maybe that wasn't really us. Maybe we were off fucking each other and those were just our holograms."

"It's possible—there was a glare on the window."

"How do you know it was me at all?"

David cocked an eyebrow and gave me a look of *I know.*

"Did you fuck him?" he asked.

"I thought about it, actually."

"But you didn't."

"No."

"Why not?"

I entertained the notion of a fling with Julian one last time.

"He wears a pooka-shell necklace. I can't fuck a guy who wears a pooka-shell necklace. And he listens to Neil Diamond. That's a deal breaker right there."

He laughed, but I could tell he was relieved, his jealousy subsided. I looked pensively at my cake. "Seriously though, I really did spend most of my time with just me."

We stopped talking and people-watched for a bit before we resumed conversation.

"Not even a one-night stand for you?" I asked.

"Nada."

I raised my eyebrows, as if to say, *Wow*.

"I did date someone for a couple of months, though."

I froze, my fork in midair.

"And?"

"And we mutually decided to move on."

We continued to talk for another hour, catching up. But mostly we gazed at each other. He was Devin and David rolled into one. He was charming and serious, witty and wise, alluring and evocative. And I was…ordinary.

———

We left just as the museum café closed. Together we walked out into the cold Boston night air.

"Catching the T?" he asked.

"God, I missed you, Dev."

He pulled me to him and kissed me hard, and we then locked into an embrace. He picked me up and spun me around and kissed every part of my face. I could feel the steam from his breath on my cheeks.

CHAPTER
FORTY-TWO

W E TOOK THE T AND WALKED BACK TO HIS place, where we stood in the foyer, embracing and kissing each other.

"I'm so sorry I hurt you by leaving," I said in between kisses. "It was worth it, though. I swear it was."

"No more, Andi. I never wanna be apart from you ever again. And it's not because I wanna rescue you or need your approval or anything like that. I am in love with you, plain and simple. And I always will be."

"I love you too. And I don't need to be rescued. I know where I am now. I know *who* I am. I'm still Sam's wife—and I always will be. I hope you can live with that. He's always going to be a part of me. But I've finally envisioned a new life—in fact, I'm *living* a new life, and it's a life I want to share with you."

Jubilant, he picked me up, spun me around, and kissed me again.

"Is this it? Are you sure this is it?" he asked.

"This is it, Dev. This is where I wanna be. Here. I don't know about marriage, and I don't know about the house and where we'll live and stuff. But I'm OK with not knowing right now, if you are. I've learned that the unknowable can be a cool thing sometimes. It definitely lets you know you're alive."

As long as *here* was also *now*, then *here* was where I wanted to be. It was where I *chose* to be.

He nodded his head. "I couldn't agree with you more." And then he added with a wink, "Sweetheart."

———

Life with Sam was fabulous. Life with Sam was fabulous because Sam was fabulous.

Life with and as Andi Vanzant was ordinary. So was life with Dev.

ABOUT THE AUTHOR

Photo Credit: Larry H. Leitner, 2010

Elisa Lorello was born and raised on Long Island, the youngest of seven children. She earned her bachelor's and master's degrees from the University of Massachusetts-Dartmouth and eventually launched a career in rhetoric and composition studies. She has been teaching first-year writing to university students since 2000. Elisa currently resides in North Carolina, where she splits her time between teaching and writing. In addition to *Ordinary World*, she is also the author of the novel *Faking It*.